The Itchy Foot

Millie Curtis

Avid Readers Publishing Group
Lakewood, California

The Itchy Foot

Avid Readers Publishing Group

http://www.avidreaderspg.com

ISBN-13: 978-1-61286-363-4

Printed in the United States

In memory of a wonderful neighbor, Auline.

Acknowledgements

Many thanks to Amy Nishimoto, Elizabeth Blye, and Catherine Owens. This book would not be in print without their help.

Dedication

For Buz. A long and pleasurable journey.

Chapter 1

Jess Edwards stared up at the dark ceiling as he lay on the narrow bed next to his wife, Fannie. He was wide awake before the sun gave any indication of rising in the eastern sky. He reached down and fumbled at the pile of clothes that lay on the floor next to the bed. His intention was to dress without waking Fannie, but that was not likely unless she was in a state of deep sleep where she was lost to the world.

Jess rose to sit on the side of the bed while he slipped on his work shirt then stood to pull on underwear, pants, work socks and cowboy boots, the boots that always caused a stir in the town of Berryville. Tiptoeing across their one-room cabin, he meant to put over a pot of coffee before he went out to visit the outhouse.

Jess was a big man with dark eyes, black hair and dusky complexion. He had grown up in New York, the son of a minister. In his own words, he always had an itchy foot. He had worked on a ranch in Oklahoma, mined for gold in Colorado with his partner, Caleb Dunn, left there and returned to Oklahoma to the hard work of a ranch hand.

His ex-partner, Caleb, is the reason Jess is now in Virginia. Caleb is the foreman for the Lockwood estate. He was in desperate need of a seasoned cattle man so he sent word to his friend offering a job. What did Jess have to lose? Perhaps Virginia wouldn't be as hot, dry and dusty as Oklahoma.

Jess met Fannie when she came to visit Lockwood with her friend Adelaide. Addie was now married to Alex Lockwood, the owner. Jess and Fannie married after a whirlwind courtship.

Fannie was different from the many women he had met. She loved life and spoke her mind. She grew up in Washington, D.C., the oldest in a large Irish family. At eighteen, she was on her own working as a waitress and cleaning woman. Fannie and Addie met in Washington when they roomed at the same boarding house.

Jess smiled as he looked over at his wife in the dimness of the room. Red strands of silky hair looked dark as they straggled across her face.

He was startled when she said, "Is it morning? I feel like I just went to bed."

Jess walked around the bed to her side, smoothed back her hair and kissed her cheek. "It's early. Go back to sleep. I tried to be quiet."

Fannie groaned before she rolled over. She sat up with bent knees, and wiped the sleep from her expressive green eyes. "All right, Jess. Out with it."

"Out with what?"

Fannie patted the side of the bed for him to sit, which he did. "Don't play innocent with me. What's on your mind that you couldn't sleep?"

He hesitated, cleared his throat, and said, "How would you like to go to California?"

2

"For what?"

Jess shrugged his wide shoulders and shook his head. "I don't know. I've a yen to go."

She laughed aloud and poked him in the arm. "A yen? Wake up, Jess. You're dreaming."

"No. I've given this some thought. We have money in the bank. That should cover the cost of train fare."

"Jess, California is three thousand miles away."

"Wouldn't you like to dip your pretty toes in the Pacific Ocean? See all the sights between here and there?"

Fanny laughed again. "My toes are not pretty."

Jess yanked a foot from under the covers and put it in his lap. "See? One-two-three-four-five and they are as pretty as all the rest of you."

Fannie couldn't suppress a smile. She pulled her foot back under the warm sheet. "Although it is pleasant to hear, flattery doesn't work. I know you're serious. I like it here at Lockwood."

"So do I. We can always come back."

Fannie looked into his dark eyes and sighed. "In other words, if you don't go, you'll always wonder if you should have."

"Something like that," he agreed.

Fannie was leery. "Money in the bank may pay for train fare but we have to have money to live on. Just because the Great War is over and the country is beginning to prosper doesn't mean we are going to be a part of it. I like security."

3

"We'll make our fortune. Trust me, Fannie. Say you'll go."

Was there a choice?

She gave a deep sigh before she said, "Yes, Jess. My place is with you, and I want you to be happy."

He pulled her into his arms. "Fannie, my love, we are going to have one grand adventure."

Good or bad, Fannie knew he was right.

Chapter 2

With a jaunty step, Jess zipped up the back porch steps to the big white stucco house known as Lockwood and rapped on the back door. The maid opened it.

"Morning, Jess. You're here early."

"Good morning to you, Peg. Is Alex around?"

The maid and housekeeper was in her early forties. Her husband was dead, her two children grown, so when the position came open at Lockwood it was a perfect fit for her. She had her own room and spending money, not that she spent much of it. Peg was a frugal woman.

Jess stood and waited.

"The Lockwoods are having breakfast in the dining room."

"I figured they might be. How about doing me a good turn and let them know I'm here."

"They most likely heard you come in stomping them big boots on the steps."

"Peg, you're going to bring a tear to my eye making fun of my fancy boots like that."

She rolled her eyes. "I'll announce your arrival."

Jess widened his eyes. "Where did you learn those haughty words?"

Peg looked up at him and offered a sly smile. "I learned them just for you." She left to inform the diners.

"Show him in and bring another cup for coffee," Jess heard Alex say.

"Don't get up, Alex," said Jess as he entered the room. "Good morning, Addie."

Jess took a chair opposite Addie and next to Alex who was seated at the head of the mahogany dining table.

"You're here early. It must be something important," surmised Addie.

"It is and I want you both to hear what I have to say."

Alex poured Jess a cup of coffee from the ceramic pot on the table.

"Thanks," acknowledged Jess and took a sip before he blurted out, "Fannie and I are going to California."

Addie's mouth fell open and Alex looked stunned. The large room grew quiet.

Alex, recovering the voice control he had used as the lawyer he once had been, asked, "When did you decide this?"

Jess put down his mug of coffee. "It's been on my mind for a while. Fannie's up to it."

"I don't believe that!" exclaimed Addie. "Fannie likes it here. In a few years you can build your own house on land Alex will give to you."

"Adelaide," cautioned Alex. "It seems Jess has made a decision."

Addie simmered down but mumbled, "Not a good one."

As if he didn't hear the remark, Jess continued with the purpose for his visit. "We won't be leaving until the first part of June. That will give you time to hire a hand to take my place."

Alex gave a doubtful look. "That won't be easy. We will be coming into the busy time on the farm."

Jess nodded. "I realize that. I also think there will be men looking for jobs now they are out of the military."

Alex shook his head until he caught the fallen look on Jess's face. "You might be right. Thank you for informing me of your plans and for giving me some time to find a replacement. It won't be easy to get someone of your character and skills."

Jess was redeemed.

Addie had remained quiet after her outburst and the gentle admonition from Alex.

Jess finished his coffee and rose to leave. "I'd better get to work. I'll tell Caleb that I talked with you."

He wrinkled his brow at Addie. "You're not mad at me are you?"

"No, I'm not mad. Disappointed."

Alex left the table and walked to the door with Jess.

Addie watched them go. She waited until she saw Jess head for the barn before she left her chair and met Alex as he was coming back into the dining room.

"That announcement shattered this morning's promise of a new day," he remarked.

"I'd like to know where he got that big idea!" Addie threw a shawl over her shoulders. "I'm going to the cabin to talk with Fannie."

"Perhaps that isn't wise."

"Why not? She's my friend, Alex. Maybe she needs a friend to talk to. I can't believe Jess."

Alex smiled at his determined wife. It was of no use to try to dissuade Addie when her mind was fixed.

**

"Come on in, Addie," called Fannie.

"How did you know it was me?" asked Addie as she came into the room.

Fannie was kneading bread. "Let me put it this way. I knew Jess was going up to talk with Alex, which meant you would hightail it over here to ask me if my brain was twisted."

"Are you a mind reader?"

"No. I possess what my mother called common sense. I saved out a little bread dough. Have a chair and I'll fry up some to eat with a cup of coffee."

Addie pulled out a chair while Fannie placed the larger hunk of the dough in a greased enamel pan, turned it once and put a clean dish towel over the top to let the dough rise.

She went to the sink, pumped out water and washed her hands after she took the bread board off the table. "What do you want to hear?"

"Did you say you wanted to go to California?"

"I said I would go. I didn't say I wanted to."

"That's what I thought. Maybe you can change his mind."

Fannie put a skillet with grease over the wood stove. She turned to Addie. "Jess wants to go. I don't want to be the reason he doesn't."

Addie sighed a big sigh. "I can understand that. But Fannie, California is the other end of the country. There are a lot of things that can go wrong."

With the bread dough she had set aside, Fannie tore into small pieces and slid them into the hot grease. "You know Adelaide, you're a great one to talk. Weren't you the one who took off for Colorado, and the same one who went to Washington to work for the Red Cross?"

"I was eighteen when I went to Colorado. I wanted to see more of the country than Virginia. The Red Cross needed workers for the war effort."

"And, you wanted some excitement in your life. It is 1919, Addie, and I'm almost twenty-two. As I thought about going I decided maybe Jess is right. He's twenty-five. If we don't go now, maybe we never will. As he says, we can always come back."

Fannie placed the hot fried bread on the table with butter and a saucer of sugar before she filled mugs with coffee and took a chair opposite her friend.

Addie put butter on her hot fried bread dough and dipped it into the sugar. "I suppose you've got a point. What if you have a baby?"

Fannie shrugged. "I hope not. My big worry is money. We have saved up some in the bank that Jess says will cover train fare, and I have a little

9

I earned before we got married. That's my hidden emergency money. It isn't a whole lot."

Addie gobbled down two pieces of fried bread before she drank any coffee. "These are great, Fannie."

"My mother called them kigleys. She used to make them for us kids. I'll miss our talks, Addie."

"Our talks, and our Sunday dinners, and our games of cards, and going over to see Lottie, and going to Berryville to shop…"

Fannie held up her hand. "You're going to make me cry and I haven't even left."

"Maybe I'm being selfish, Fannie. It could be I'm jealous. Every so often I get the urge to see what's on the other side of the hill, but Alex isn't one to pick up and go without a planned destination or a solid reason."

"That's not all bad. I'd feel a lot better if I knew what lies ahead. California is a big state. I don't know what Jess thinks he's going to do out there."

Feeling more relaxed, Addie smiled. "He's resourceful. He'll take care of you."

"Or I'll take care of him," answered Fannie with a wry smile.

Chapter 3

Caleb was in the barn when Jess arrived.

"I thought you'd still be having breakfast," said Jess.

Caleb was throwing a pitchfork of straw into a stall. "Lottie woke me up early. She said this new baby coming is an active one."

"Three babies in three years. Won't leave much free time, I figure," said Jess as he grabbed another fork and dug into the pile of straw.

"What's on your mind, Jess?" asked lean and lanky Caleb as he threw another forkful. "I don't think its babies or my free time."

"You sound like Fannie. She about said the same thing. Fannie and I are going to California."

Caleb never looked up nor stopped the rhythm of the pitchfork. "I figured it was about time."

Jess threw a fork of straw at his friend. "You know me too well. When I came to help I told you I didn't know for how long."

Caleb put his fork down and shook off the straw. "You were honest and I do appreciate that you've stayed as long as you have. What does Fannie think about this?"

"She said she'll go. I told her we could come back. She likes it here."

Caleb nodded. "I hate to see you go, but I know you've got it in your craw for something

11

different, so you might as well go and get it out of your system." He moved on to the next horse stall.

Jess snickered. "I knew you'd understand."

Caleb dug his pitchfork into the pile of straw. "What did Alex have to say? I'm sure he wasn't happy. We're just coming into the busy season."

Jess finished spreading the straw around in the stall before he went on to the next to help his friend. "He didn't wish me well, but he didn't throw me out. He was glad I gave him enough notice."

"And Addie? How did she take it?"

"You know Addie. She's not liking the idea of losing her friend. It can get lonely out here."

"Can't say as I've ever had that feeling," said Caleb as he hoisted a big load on his pitchfork. "I can't even find enough time to change my mind."

"Is that supposed to be funny?" said Jess.

"No. It's the truth." It was Caleb's turn to shower Jess with a forkful of straw.

Jess guffawed. "I'm going to miss you, partner, but not too much."

**

As soon as Addie left the cabin where Fannie and Jess lived, she hurried down the lane to tell Lottie the news. The small brick house sat on the estate far enough from the big house and close enough to keep an eye on happenings.

Addie knocked on the door.

"Come in," she heard Lottie call.

Addie opened the door and her ears were greeted to the wail of a child. Lottie was struggling to sit her daughter in a high chair she had pulled up to the table.

"What's the matter with Lizzie?" asked Addie.

"Nothing. She needs to eat and she wants to play. What brings you here?"

Lottie tied a dishtowel around Lizzie's waist to keep her in the chair. Then she handed her a cookie.

Addie watched. "Shouldn't she have eggs or oatmeal or something before she has a cookie?"

"Anything to quiet her down. I'm not up to handling her little tantrums. This other baby better come soon. I'm worn out."

It wasn't like Lottie Bell to be in an irritable mood. Addie figured it was due to the new Dunn about to arrive. Lottie had always been short and pleasingly plump. Now she was short and enormous.

Addie couldn't help but question, "You are planning on only one baby aren't you?"

Lottie stood up straight and looked at her. "Do I look that bad?"

"Of course not. But, I don't remember you being that big with Little Cal or Lizzie."

Lottie teared up. "I know how awful I look. Dresses don't hang right, I'm clumsy, my feet are swollen, my..."

"Hold on a minute," Addie interrupted. "I'm sorry if I made you feel bad."

"No. It's not you. It's me. I've been too sensitive lately. Even Caleb says I've been touchy and he never criticizes."

13

"Do you want me to take the little ones up to the house this afternoon so you can get some rest?"

"Thanks for asking, but they'll be fine once we get breakfast over. Look at me not even offering you a chair. Have a seat, Addie."

Addie pulled out a chair and sat at the table while Lottie sat and began to spoon oatmeal into Lizzie's mouth.

"Jess and Fannie are leaving and going to California."

This news did not phase Lottie. "Caleb said he knew Jess would be leaving. He wasn't sure when."

"Do you think Caleb could talk Jess out of going?"

"No. And Caleb wouldn't try. They used to be partners, best friends, Addie, just like we used to be."

"We still are."

"We're still friends, but not the tittering teenagers we once were. We've grown up. I'm married and on my third baby. You're married and the lady of the manor, so our loyalties have changed a bit. Fannie and Jess need to find their own way. Life is never an easy ride."

The philosophic Lottie finished feeding the toddler and washed Lizzie's sticky hands and face. The little one twisted and turned under the wet cloth.

"I'll lift her out of the chair," offered Addie. She went to Lizzie, untied the dishtowel, and lifted her into her arms then snuggled her neck and kissed her cheek. Lizzie giggled and squirmed as Addie set her on the floor to find Little Cal who was playing with blocks.

Lottie was cleaning the table.

Addie watched the two little ones play. "I'm glad you put Adelaide as her middle name, although it's going to take some time for her to learn to spell Elizabeth Adelaide."

Lottie made a prune face at her friend. "Addie, only you would think of that."

"Probably. I hope you feel better, Lottie. Talking to you always makes me feel better even if you aren't in the best mood."

"That's good. Sorry if I was a sourpuss when you came in. I've got to put that garden in and I haven't felt up to it."

"Maybe you don't need the garden this year. I hated the garden growing up. All that canning and the smell of the pickles and putting up tomatoes in the hottest part of summer makes me shudder to think about it."

Lottie smiled. "I remember those days at your place. Your mom and you were busy every minute. It is work, but I like to see the pantry full for winter."

"The difference between you and me is you enjoy it. That's why you were the star in Home Economics class."

Lottie laughed aloud. "I'm glad you came, Addie. You brightened my day. Don't worry about losing Fannie and Jess. They might show up on your doorstep unannounced one day."

15

Addie sighed. "Could be. If you feel like digging and sowing seeds, I'll take care of your little ones."

"Be careful what you offer." Lottie laughed again.

Chapter 4

A week later Fannie sat in the kitchen in the big house. "When did Addie say she'd be ready, Peg? She told me nine o'clock, and I've been waiting twenty minutes."

"She'll be coming down soon. She wants to look presentable in town. Wouldn't do to have talk about the lady of Lockwood looking frumpy."

"I'm sure there was plenty of talk when a girl from a tenant house married the town lawyer fourteen years her senior," said Fannie. "That's the trouble being married to a notable man in the community. Jess and I don't have to worry, although I'm sure there was plenty of talk when we arrived here."

"I 'spect so 'cause you and Jess are not from around here. Locals say that if you weren't born in Clarke County, you're a stranger no matter how long you live here."

Fannie figured the housekeeper was right. "What do you say, Peg?"

"I say I like people for who they are. Don't matter to me where they come from. It sounds funny, but folks thought Jess was a holdover from Buffalo Bill's Wild West Show that came to Winchester a few years ago."

"Why did they think that?"

"The way he dresses in that hat, black shirt and pants and those cowboy boots he wears."

"I think he looks nifty. Did you see that show, Peg?"

"My land, no. The tickets were too much and I didn't have any way to get up to Winchester."

Addie flew down the stairs. "Sorry to keep you waiting, Fannie. I couldn't get my hair pinned the way I wanted. Do I look all right?"

She was dressed in a crepe royal-blue two-piece suit with a white high-collared waist beneath the jacket. The brown straw hat she wore had a side turned up, held in place by a large gold pin shaped like a bell. "Peg polished my shoes. I can almost see my face in them."

"Do you never not look all right?" asked Fannie. "Jess hitched up the buggy for us."

"Good, that's easier to drive, and we'll have a roof over our heads. I think it looks like it might rain."

"There are some darker clouds west of us. I put an umbrella under the seat."

"Where did you get that dress?" asked an inquisitive Addie. "That color green looks good on you. It brings out the color of your eyes." Addie took her umbrella off a hook behind the door.

"I had the material. I cut out the pattern and I watched the little ones while Lottie sewed it for me with that fancy sewing machine she has."

"That was a gift from the man she worked for in Colorado. I think she could make money as a seamstress if she had the time." Addie opened her pocket book and checked to be sure her money was in it. "Lottie hasn't been feeling well. I hope this baby comes before you leave, Fannie."

"Isn't Dr. Hawthorne supposed to deliver the baby?"

"The new doctor, Dr. Burke, is supposed to. But I guess either one depending on when the baby comes. I just don't want it to be me," informed Addie.

"In other words, if the doctor isn't here you want me to stand by."

"Not stand by. You take charge. You had to help deliver a couple of your siblings. At least that's what you told me."

Fannie grimaced. "Doesn't mean I liked it. You delivered your little sister, you said."

"I had to. I hated the whole process. If Lottie needs help you'd better be here."

"That sounds like an order, Adelaide."

Addie smiled at her friend. "I guess it did. I'm sorry."

"I'm pretty good at birthing babies," chimed in Peg, who had stood taking in the conversation of the two young women.

Addie and Fannie both turned and looked at the housekeeper.

"Peg, you've made our day!" exclaimed Fannie.

"I'm glad I could be of help," said the little woman. "You two had better get going before the horse gets jittery."

"We're going to Coyner's Department Store in town. Is there anything you need?" asked Addie.

"No. Thank you for asking. When do you expect to return if Mr. Alex asks?"

"I left a note on his desk. We will return before supper."

"That's all I need to know," said the maid, and she went about her duties.

Addie took her place in the driver's seat. Fannie was not one who had grown up with horses. She was content to climb up beside Addie and let her handle the horse and buggy. Fannie was a city girl.

The town was as busy as it usually was on other Saturdays. Addie drove down Main Street and parked the buggy across the street from the department store. She took off the leather gloves she wore to handle the reins and put on a pair of white cotton with fancy embroidery. Then she smoothed her skirt.

Fannie shook her head. "You go through a lot of trouble just to come to town."

"Nettie works in Coyner's. She doesn't miss a thing. And that nosy Lavinia Talley is probably peeking out her window right now."

"Lavinia, the editor's wife. Shall I wave?"

"Good heavens, Fannie. Don't even think about it. I do have to live here."

Fannie laughed. "I'll climb down from the buggy as royally as I can. Jess wants me to buy a razor and a new shirt for him."

They departed the buggy and started across the street.

"What are you going to buy for yourself? Don't you need something for traveling?" asked Addie.

Fannie stepped around manure in the middle of the street. "I don't dare spend the money. I think we're going to need every penny for this foolhardy trip."

Addie stopped dead and looked at her friend. "If that's the way you feel about it, why don't you tell Jess?"

"I told you before, Addie. Jess has his heart set on California. I'm not going to be the one who holds him back."

"I know. Let's go in and get scrutinized."

Nettie was behind the dry goods counter and looked them both over from head to toe. "Hello, Adelaide," was her syrupy greeting. "I see you brought your friend from the city. You haven't been in for a while."

"Hello, Nettie. The farm keeps us all busy."

"I hear Lottie's going to have another baby."

"Yes, any day now."

"Miz' Talley says she shouldn't be having babies so close together."

"Miz' Talley should have had a few of her own so she couldn't be nosing into other people's business," said Fannie.

Addie shot her a wary look.

Nettie tried not to look startled. "What can I help you with?"

"I need a razor and new shirt for my husband," informed Fannie.

Nettie came from behind the counter and went to the men's area. "We have two types of razors and a brand new shipment of shirts." She looked at Fannie. "We don't have any black ones."

"What a shame. Do you have pink with purple stripes?"

Nettie's eyebrows flew up.

Addie turned her back to suppress a grin.

Fannie lifted up a cream-colored shirt. "How about this one, Addie? Do you think Jess would like this one for travel?"

"Travel?" Nettie pounced on the word.

"Yes. Jess and I are going to California."

Nettie's smile went from ear to ear. She had a big tidbit to tell Lavinia. "What are you going to do out there?"

Before Nettie could ask more questions and Fannie could give off-the-wall answers, Addie asked for help with some bloomers. She also bought a pretty apron to give to Fannie as a gift when she and Jess left.

More shoppers came into the store as the two young women were paying for their purchases. Nettie zipped the sales slip and money up to Mr. Coyner's office on the balcony off the flight of stairs. He placed the change back into the small wood canister attached to a cable, then zipped it back to Nettie.

They picked up their packages and left the store.

"Fannie, you know Nettie is going to peddle that news."

"I hope so. Maybe someone who wants a job at the farm will come on out." She looked up at the sky. "Looks like we're going to get a spring rain."

"Hurry, let's go across the street and have lunch. I'll buy."

They picked up the pace as they crossed Main Street. "I'm not destitute yet, Addie. I can buy a sandwich."

"You said you needed every penny."

"I did, didn't I. Then you can buy lunch and I'll make you some kigleys before I'm off to the unknown."

"I wish you wouldn't say it like that. It sounds as though I'll never see you again."

Fannie looked over at her friend. "All right. Let's not let it ruin our lunch. And speaking of ruining lunch, look who's waddling down the street."

Addie shot a side glance. "Oh good heavens, Lavinia. Let's duck in before she spots us."

They weren't lucky enough. As they sat in a corner near the large window that faced the main street, in bounced the round little biddy hen and went straight to where they sat.

"I thought that was you, Adelaide."

"Good afternoon, Mrs. Talley. You've met my friend, Fannie Edwards."

Lavinia glanced at Fannie. "Oh, yes. The Irish girl from Washington."

Fannie offered a nod and fleeting grimace.

Lavinia turned her attention right back to Adelaide. "How are things on the farm? I understand Lottie Bell is expecting another baby."

"Any day now," she answered.

"You would think she would have more sense. Sometimes I just don't understand you young people. How is Peg working out as your housekeeper? Her husband didn't leave her with anything. It was fortunate you took her in."

"Alex and Addie take in all the strays. We'll tell Lottie and Peg you asked about them," said Fannie.

Lavinia gave her a disgusted look.

The waiter had to move around Lavinia as he brought the sandwiches they had ordered and a pot of tea.

"I'll be on my way. I have to stop in Coyner's on my way home. It was good to see you, Adelaide." Lavinia brushed Fannie with her skirt as she turned and toddled out of the restaurant.

"Miz' Talley's a frequent visitor," said the waiter.

"And, I'll bet she never spends a dime," remarked Fannie.

The waiter just smiled.

**

The minute they arrived back at Lockwood and Addie drove the buggy around to the back of the big house, both women knew something was awry. They saw Peg running towards Lottie's house and Jess passing her as he ran up the path.

"It's Lottie!" he shouted in their direction. "The baby's coming and something's wrong! I'm going to call the doctor."

"Fannie and I will go to Lottie's." Addie shouted back. She didn't wait as she cracked the whip over the head of the horse and he took off with the buggy at full speed.

Fannie held on with both hands as they barely skimmed the ground.

Caleb was in the house when they arrived. Little Cal and Lizzie looked bewildered. Their father was upset and their mama was in bed crying.

Addie and Fannie had never seen the usually calm Caleb so distressed. "Lottie's in the bedroom. I don't know what's happening. I was in the barn when I heard her holler."

"Take the children outside," ordered Addie.

Both Addie and Fannie rushed to where Lottie lay in agony. Bright blood greeted their eyes on the white sheets of the bed.

"My God!" gasped Fannie and made the Sign of the Cross. "We're here Lottie. The doctor will be here soon."

Lottie covered her mouth to stifle a scream when another sharp pain hit and more blood oozed onto the bed clothes.

Peg came into the bedroom carrying a bundle of rags. She whispered, "We've got to get that baby out. It isn't right her bleeding like that."

Fannie heard Jess enter Lottie's kitchen when he ran back from the big house. She went to meet him. "Lottie's bleeding. There's no sign of the baby."

Jess looked at her in alarm. "I've seen it happen with cattle a couple times. I think the afterbirth is pulling away too soon. That baby needs to come out!"

"Is the doctor coming?"

"Yes, but it'll take him too long to get here. We've got to do something or both the baby and Lottie could die! Scrub your hands and arms."

"Jess, I don't know what to do!"

"I'll guide you through it as best I can."

Peg came into the room.

"Boil up a darning needle," Jess ordered.

Fannie threw on one of Lottie's aprons and scrubbed as best she knew how before she went back into the room and whispered to Addie. "Jess says he knows the problem. We're going to try to get the baby."

Jess looked at an astounded Addie and said, "We'll need scissors and twine. Peg's got a needle boiling. Bring that in now."

For once Addie didn't question. She left the room removing her jacket and rolling up the sleeves of her blouse as she went.

Jess's voice was low and controlled. "Fannie, you've got to find how the baby's lying. You may have to push the afterbirth aside. When Addie brings the needle, poke the bag of waters and be careful you don't puncture the baby's head."

Fannie's mouth fell open and her hands shook. "I can't do it, Jess."

He took her by the shoulders and whispered, "Your hands are smaller than mine. They might both die if you don't try!"

Another sharp pain hit Lottie and she let out a loud cry as the sheets reddened with more blood.

Addie with a towel wrapped around her waist to cover her skirt brought the clean needle.

Jess guided Fannie as well as he knew how. "Slide your hand easy and see if you can feel if the baby is head first. Then Addie will hand you the needle and you prick the membrane."

Fannie's hands were slim. She eased one hand to where she could feel the back of the baby's head."

"It feels head first."

"That's good," said Jess. "Addie hand her the needle. Go ahead, Fannie."

Another pain shot through Lottie and she screamed.

Peg came running into the room with the scissors and twine.

In a gush out came a flood of grayish water mixed with blood and a baby's head. Another pain and Fannie was holding an infant followed by the afterbirth.

"Hurry and cut that cord!" hollered Jess.

Peg tied twine around the cord attached to the baby and in her haste cut the cord before Addie could finish tying the other end attached to the afterbirth. The cord slipped away, blood spurted like a garden hose. It was everywhere before Addie could stem the flow.

Jess swiped the baby's mouth with his finger to clean it out and tapped the blue-looking baby to make it cry.

Addie brought a warm blanket and wrapped up the baby boy.

Peg swept her hand down Lottie's torso to where she could feel the hard lump of the womb and began rubbing to stop any more bleeding.

Lottie had passed out.

Fannie put the afterbirth in a large rag and left the room.

Caleb espied Fannie covered in blood and left Little Cal and Lizzie on the lawn. "What's happening, Fannie? Is Lottie all right?"

"I don't know. I hope the doctor gets here. The baby is all right, I think, but don't go in yet, Caleb. It looks like a war zone."

"I've got to go in." He rushed past Fannie. When he opened the door to the bedroom he fainted dead away.

Jess picked up Caleb and took him to the well where he doused him with cold water. Fannie had taken off the once white apron and threw it in a bucket of cold water. She washed her hands and face before going to check on the children still playing on the lawn.

Dr. Burke arrived amidst the hubbub. He went straight to Lottie, took out his stethoscope and listened. Then he took her blood pressure with his leather cuff and turned to the worried faces of the two women left in the room.

"I'm going to give her stimulant medicine with a needle," he explained as he filled a syringe. A few minutes passed before Lottie's eyelids flickered and then slowly opened a slit.

"I'll ask you ladies to leave the room while I check further. Is the baby all right?"

"He's breathing. We've wrapped him in a warm blanket and put him near the stove," informed Addie.

The good doctor smiled. "I'll check the infant after I'm through in here, and then you can explain what went on. This place looks like a battlefield."

Caleb had pulled himself together. He and Jess came into the kitchen. "I hear I have a boy."

"You can't go in with Lottie. The doctor's in there, but your son is bundled up over here by the stove," Addie said.

Caleb went to the wicker basket, pulled the blanket back and shook his head in wonderment. "He's a big one. He's also a mess. Looks like he's covered in cottage cheese."

"We didn't dare clean him up until the doctor says we can," Peg told him.

"I think we can all use a cup of coffee," suggested Jess.

Peg was quick. "I'll make it. I don't want any of that strong cowboy coffee you make. Fannie says it can grow hair on a bald head."

Fannie came into the kitchen with the children and caught the last sentence.

Jess looked at her. "Fannie Edwards, did you criticize my coffee?"

"I only repeated what I heard Caleb say."

"Now don't go getting me in trouble," said Caleb. "I've been through enough today." He was sitting in a kitchen chair and the two little ones had crawled up onto his lap. "You two have a new baby brother," he told them. They were oblivious.

Dr. Burke came into the room. "Mrs. Dunn is asleep. The bleeding has ebbed, but it's going to take time before she regains her strength. I'll see to the baby now."

Addie led him to the basket where the baby lay quietly. The doctor checked him over, and the new baby Dunn gave a loud cry. "That's what I like to hear." He swaddled the infant when he was done. "Do I smell coffee?"

"A fresh pot," announced Peg. "Would you like to have a cup with us?"

"I would," answered Dr. Burke. "While we're all together, perhaps you can fill me in on what went on before I arrived."

They all started talking at once until Addie held up her hand. "I'll tell."

They squeezed around the table while Peg poured the coffee and Addie began the tale. When she was finished, the doctor was silent as he put the facts together. "We have a medical term for that condition. The afterbirth breaks away from the wall of the womb too soon and puts the life of both the baby and the mother in jeopardy. Abruptio placenta. Thank the good Lord it doesn't happen often."

"You were right, Jess," said Fannie with pride in her voice.

"I've seen it happen with cattle," he explained.

Dr. Burke smiled. "Quick thinking. You are all to be congratulated."

Fannie smiled. "I wonder how long it will take for Lavinia Talley to get wind of this. You might make the *Courier*, Jess."

"She won't hear it from me," answered Dr. Burke. "But, I wouldn't be surprised to see it headlined one of these days." He finished his cup of coffee, left orders and medicine and rose to leave. "I'll check in on Mrs. Dunn one more time. Will there be someone to stay with her?"

"Yes," the three women answered in unison.

"Good. I'll be back in three days. If there are any problems call me right away."

Everyone nodded.

After Dr. Burke left, it was decided Peg would take the first watch after the women cleaned up the room. She was the most experienced.

Caleb and Jess were happy to leave for the barn.

Alex had been gone the whole day at a cattle auction. Peg had left a roast with vegetables in the oven so Addie served their dinner and related the story in great detail to Alex.

He listened to every word and shook his head in disbelief. "I'm glad I wasn't here," was all he said.

In the cabin, Fannie had supper ready when Jess came in for the evening. "I didn't have time to put a big meal together," she apologized. "I cooked up peas, meat and gravy to put over potatoes. Will that be enough?"

"It sounds fine." He took his seat at the table while Fannie poured glasses of milk. She set the warm food on the table before she took her seat.

Fannie always said a short blessing before they ate. Jess waited to fill his plate.

He patted her hand. "You did a great job today, wife of mine. I'm proud of you."

She smiled at him. "I have never been so frightened in all my life."

"Neither have I," he admitted.

Her eyes widened. "You? You acted so calm and collected."

"I had to. Caleb was of no use. I wasn't even sure if my suspicions were right, but I figured one way or the other the baby was going to die if we didn't try to do something. And, maybe we would have lost Lottie also."

"I want to forget that whole mess."

He laughed. "Mess is right. It must have taken you three women hours to clean up that room."

"We left all the bedclothes soaking in a tub of cold water. They may never come clean. Poor Lottie, I don't know when she's going to be strong enough to take care of her little ones again."

"That isn't going to cause a problem with us leaving, is it?"

The question caused Fannie to snap her head in his direction. She shrugged her shoulders. "I don't know. I'm not going to leave if she needs my help."

Jess was busy eating. "Let Addie and Peg take care of it. I want to be out of here by the beginning of the month."

Fannie let her fork fall on the table. "Jess Edwards that sounds callous and selfish! Caleb

Dunn is your best friend. He wouldn't walk out on you!"

He grinned at her. "Got your dander up didn't I? I know it sounds selfish. Caleb told me he didn't want his problems to hold us back from going."

"That sounds like a man. He has no understanding of what it takes to care for three little ones and keep the house going. As long as their clothes are clean, the food's on the table, and the bed is welcoming, men are happy." Her face matched the color of her hair.

"I didn't expect you to be so upset. Are you saying that we will have to stay?"

"I'm saying California isn't going anyplace. It will be there no matter when we get there. We will leave when the time is right!"

Jess wasn't going to argue because he knew he'd be on the losing end. "All right, Fannie."

She simmered down. "Do you want a piece of pie?"

"It's not going to end up in my face, is it?"

Fannie laughed, rose from her chair, put her arms around her husband's shoulders and kissed his cheek. "I love you, Jess."

That night when Fannie said her prayers she gave thanks for the new baby, asked for Lottie to recover, and asked for forgiveness if she had been too sharp with Jess. She put the trip to California in the Lord's hands. Could it be she and Jess were not meant to leave Lockwood Farm?

Jess lay awake long after Fannie had drifted off to sleep. He had agreed to let her decide when they were going. Was that a mistake? Should he have put his foot down like any normal husband and demanded they would either leave by the first of the month or he would go by himself? No, he had done the right thing. He knew Fannie well enough that she would probably hand him his hat and tell him to have a good time. If he wasn't married he could take off anytime he wanted. Had he married too soon? They had only known each other a few months. Then he chastised himself for even letting those thoughts creep into his tired mind. He looked over at his level-headed wife and could only make out the outline of her face. He smiled to himself in the dark of the room. He loved Fannie and could not imagine life without her. He had wrestled with his conscience enough and settled into the fact that he was a lucky man. The warmth of her body and measured breathing lulled him to sleep.

Chapter 5

Addie made breakfast the next morning.

Alex sat at the dining room table where he had spread out some papers. "I bought cattle yesterday. You'll have to take care of these sales papers," he said as Addie came into the room.

"I'll take care of them after I go down to see how Lottie is doing."

"We can't let the paperwork get behind."

Addie looked straight at him. "I believe I can handle that in my own good time!"

He was startled by her reply. "I didn't mean to make it sound like an order. We're coming into the busy time and I haven't found a replacement for Jess."

"That's no excuse. Peg has been at Lottie's since the baby came. She'll be exhausted."

"Can't Fannie relieve her?"

This remark annoyed Addie. "Alex, eat those eggs and go to the barn before I say something I shouldn't. I will go to Lottie's, then take care of your precious papers."

He didn't say another word as he finished his breakfast.

Addie cleared away and washed the soiled dishes.

When she arrived at Lottie's, she found Fannie there feeding Little Cal and Lizzie.

"How is Lottie?" she asked.

Fannie looked over at her. "Completely worn out and pale as a ghost."

"I came to relieve Peg."

Fannie washed the faces of the little ones and removed Lizzie from her high chair. "Peg said she found a bottle and has given the baby some boiled goat's milk. She's not sure Lottie is up to nursing."

Peg came out of the bedroom when she heard their voices. "Good morning, Miss Addie. I'm sorry I didn't get up there to make breakfast."

"It's not the first breakfast I've ever cooked. You are to go to the house and rest. No housework today. How is Lottie doing?"

"She's awful weak. It's going to be some time before she's back to taking care of things."

"Do you think Alex should hire someone to come and stay?"

"I've got hot water on the stove," interrupted Fannie. "Let's have a cup of tea and make some decisions."

It was decided that finding someone to come and stay was the best solution if Alex was willing to cover the cost.

"Do you think Alex will agree?" Fannie asked.

"I don't know," answered Addie. "He's probably peeved with me at the moment. I don't think men understand these kinds of situations."

"They don't," agreed the other two women.

Fannie was to spend the day at Lottie's. "I'll have to be home to make supper for Jess. He can come with Caleb for lunch."

Satisfied they had come up with a plan, Addie went to take care of the office work and Peg went to take a well-deserved rest.

In the barn, Alex was telling Caleb and Jess about the cattle purchase he had made. "This place must have been in an uproar yesterday. I made a casual remark to Addie this morning and she got huffy. Why? I don't know. Sometimes I don't understand women."

Caleb and Jess nodded in agreement.

**

Alex and Addie were having supper. "Addie, I don't think we can afford to pay another worker."

"Peg, Fannie, and I can handle what needs to be done for a week at least, but Lottie needs more time than that. It will take me away from bookwork, Peg away from running the house, and Fannie away from making preparations to leave."

He looked up with a half-smile. "Maybe Fannie can take over and that will give me Jess a while longer."

"I would love to keep Fannie here, but you know he wants to be on his way. He was fair in giving you a month to find another man."

Then Alex smiled. "You're right. I pay Jess better than most. Perhaps I can find someone at less pay and use part of that money for a caretaker at Lottie's. How long do you think this will be?"

"Dr. Burke is due in a couple of days. He should have an idea."

"Then we'll wait until he comes."

Addie let out a small sigh. "Thank you, Alex."

"Are you angry with me?" he asked.

"Why should I be angry with you?"

"You were irritated with me this morning for some reason."

"Yes, I was and I'll not try to explain." She blew him a kiss. "You are my love."

He shook his head and smiled. "Adelaide, you do confuse me at times."

In the cabin, Fannie was washing dishes. "Jess, Addie is going to ask Alex if he will hire someone to take care of Lottie and her house until she is back on her feet."

He was sitting in his stuffed chair. "That's a great idea. That would take the pressure off everybody and we can go on with our plans."

Fannie wiped her hands on a dish towel and came to where Jess sat. "I was thinking that instead of hiring a woman to come in, I could take over and Alex could pay me. That would give us more money to take to California."

She could tell by the look on his face that he wasn't pleased. "Don't even think about it. I told you we have enough money to get there."

"I know, but I worry about having money to fall back on if something goes wrong. It would make for a more comfortable trip."

"No, Fannie. Alex can hire someone. We are going to leave as planned and that's final. You can do what you can for Lottie before we leave."

Fannie knew it was useless to try to change her husband's mind. Still, she would feel better if they started out with more money.

Chapter 6

Three days later Dr. Hawthorne arrived. He explained Dr. Burke was off on a house call the other side of the river. Both Fannie and Addie were at Lottie's.

"Dr. Burke told me about the heroic efforts to save the baby and the mother. I'm not sure a good outcome would happen again," he said in a low voice.

They kept their voices confidential because they didn't want Lottie to hear. It wouldn't do to upset her.

"We have some questions for you when you're done," informed Addie. "May we fix some tea or coffee for you?"

"Tea would be perfect."

After he examined Lottie and the baby he came to sit at the table. "Before I give you instructions, I want to hear your questions."

Fannie let Addie take charge. "Our biggest concern is how long Lottie will be laid up."

"That's difficult to pinpoint. However, if she improves daily, I would expect three months."

The women drew in their breath.

"It will take time for her system to build up the blood she's lost. Even then, she won't be ready to assume all the household duties and care of the children or she'll be dragging around for a year."

"Do you think it is safe to say six months with help?"

He shook his head. "That's a fair estimate."

Fannie cut in. "We have been feeding the baby boiled goat's milk. Should we add water to it?"

"I would say the goat's milk is the best choice because Lottie is not going to have the strength to nurse this one. How has the baby been handling it?"

The women looked at each other and shrugged their shoulders. "Good, I guess," said Addie. "He hasn't been throwing up. He sleeps most of the time."

"That won't last long," said Dr. Hawthorne. "He's a big baby and he'll be getting hungry. If he isn't throwing up or crying with cramps, I'd say he's fine with what you've been doing."

"Dr. Hawthorne, do you know anyone we can hire to come and take over until Lottie is well?"

"It's going to take a younger woman to handle this. Right off hand I can't think of anyone. I'll ask my wife when I get home. She can ask around if you'd like."

"I would appreciate that. My housekeeper, Fannie, and I can take care of things for a while. The sooner we find a replacement, the better."

"I have your phone number, I'll ask Grace to give you a call. Now, I am leaving medicine for Lottie. This is to build up her blood, this one is for pain, and this one is to boost her spirits."

"I could use some of that," quipped Fannie.

The doctor smiled. "There are times when we all could. The directions are on the bottles. I don't want Lottie lying in bed all the time. She is to get up three or four times a day, walk around the room. By next week she can take her meals at the table."

Dr. Hawthorne assured them their actions had averted a tragedy. As long as Lottie gained a little each day they could breathe easy and allow life to return to normal.

Chapter 7

The next week Grace Hawthorne called Addie. "Good afternoon, Adelaide. Thaddeus told me you are looking for a young woman to help with Lottie."

"Yes, Mrs. Hawthorne."

"He also said Alex is looking for another hired man."

"That's true," answered Addie.

"I checked with the minister at church. He told me his minister friend knows of a young couple who are needing work. The young man is originally from the other end of the county, but his wife is not from here. They returned to live with his parents down in White Post."

"Why isn't he working?" was Addie's immediate question.

"Reverend Adams said, according to information he has received, the young man broke his leg while he worked for the railroad and they let him go. However, he is healed from the injury. I am thinking that perhaps the wife could help with Lottie."

Addie hesitated then said, "I guess it won't hurt to interview them."

"Adelaide, if you can give me a time, I'll call Reverend Adams and he can contact his minister friend to set it up. I believe any time would do."

Addie checked the calendar. "This Wednesday at one o'clock in the afternoon will work for both Alex and myself."

"If for some reason this time isn't good, I will call you. Keep in mind, Adelaide, I have not met this young couple, but Reverend Adams says his friend speaks highly of them."

"Thank you, Mrs. Hawthorne."

"You're welcome. I hope it works out for everyone. Meanwhile, I'll keep inquiring. Goodbye, Adelaide."

"Goodbye." Addie sat the ear piece back on the hook as she sat at her desk. She mulled the information over in her mind doubtful this would be the answer to their needs. It was too easy.

On the other hand, it was going into three weeks of the three women rotating, sometimes two of them, helping with the laundry, meals, and watching Little Cal and Lizzie. Lottie was still as weak as a rag. Fannie was preparing to leave the next week and Peg was wearing thin trying to keep up the big house also.

Addie gave Alex the news as they ate supper in the cavernous dining room.

"I'd prefer they were people Grace and Reverend Adams knew." He sighed. "At least it's a start. I haven't found a satisfactory man to take the place of Jess."

Addie poured them each a hot cup of tea. "I am resolved to the fact that Jess and Fannie are not going to stay forever, although I wish they would. They are already delayed and it isn't fair to them."

"I know," her husband agreed. "How do you think Lottie is doing?"

"Her recovery is slow."

"I believe you told me Dr. Hawthorne said it would be at least three months before she builds up her stamina."

"He did, Alex. And six months before she could resume all her duties."

"I've talked with three men, none of whom I would ever hire. Grace Hawthorne didn't have any other suggestions when she called?"

Addie shook her head. "She told me she would keep inquiring."

Alex frowned. "That's half-encouraging. Why can't Lottie's mother come out and stay?"

Addie set her cup on a saucer. "We've been over this before, Alex. Mrs. Foster isn't up to it. She'd probably last a day at the most."

"How about Ella who used to work for us?"

"Alex, you know she helps your brother, Clay and Rebecca. Besides, Ella and Charlie are expecting a baby."

"Wishful thinking on my part."

Addie bristled. "What does that mean? You wish we were the ones expecting? I know you would like to have a child."

"No, Addie. Our baby will come when the time is right. We'll talk with this couple and maybe they'll be an answer to our needs."

Addie brightened. "I wonder what they look like." She mused.

Alex looked at her with a puzzled expression.

"People, I imagine," was his answer.

Chapter 8

Wednesday after lunch, Alex and Addie were going over some papers when they heard a buggy come to the back of the house.

Addie looked out the window. "Well, I'll be darned."

"What is it?" asked Alex. He jumped up from his chair and went to look out the window. A young black couple was in the buggy.

"Well, I am surprised. I wonder who is the minister friend of Reverend Adams."

Peg answered the knock at the back door. She asked the young couple to wait in the hallway while she went to the office door with raised eyebrows. "There are two people here that say they have an appointment with Mr. Alexander Lockwood."

Alex chuckled. "I guess that would be me. Show them in."

The timid pair appeared at the office door.

"Good afternoon." Alex greeted them. "I am Alexander Lockwood and this is Mrs. Lockwood."

The young couple nodded their heads.

"What are your names?"

"I am Nathaniel and this is my wife, Crystal."

"How old are you, Nathaniel?" asked Alex.

"We are both eighteen."

Addie's hopes diminished.

"Come in and have a seat," encouraged Alex. "I have questions."

There were two straight chairs in the office, but the couple chose to squeeze together on a small bench.

Alex began, "Our minister friend advised us that you are looking for work, Nathaniel."

He nodded. "Yes, sir. I go by Nate, that's what my family calls me." He was of average height and of muscular build with a ready smile.

"Very good, Nate. My needs are for a strong man who knows farm work. I raise a special breed of cattle that take careful handling. I am looking for someone with experience. I expected you to be a bit older."

"I worked on a farm since I was twelve. Last year I left for a job with the railroad because the pay was better, until I broke my leg. They hired somebody else."

"That's too bad."

"It won't hold me back none," Nate was quick to report. "I'm good as new, sir."

"What were your duties on the farm?"

"Duties?" Nate looked at him as though Alex didn't know much about farm work.

"I guess everything it takes: feeding, mucking, helping calves to be born, handling the bulls, bringing in crops, plowing and planting. I know a lot about horses. Mr. Anderson taught me."

"James Anderson?"

"Yes, sir. He's the best when it comes to horses."

Alex smiled. Indeed that was true.

"Tell me how you broke your leg."

From the look on his face they could see Nate was embarrassed. "Sir, I could say I broke it swinging the sledgehammer but that wouldn't be the truth. I saw a big red apple in a tree, and when I climbed up to get it I fell when the limb broke."

Alex fought back a smile. "That's unfortunate."

"It was bad for my leg and to lose my job, but the tree was on a farm where I met Crystal." They looked at each other with a quiet smile.

Addie had only been listening up to this point. "Crystal have you ever worked?"

"Yes, ma'am. In the summers. The farm had a stand that sold the products raised there. Of course, besides the gardens, I always helped my mother in the house."

"Only the summers?"

"Yes. ma'am, for the stand. That's when the vegetables and fruits come in. The rest of the time I was in school."

This revelation caused Addie and Alex to exchange glances.

Addie continued, "I have a friend here on the estate who has recently had a baby. We need someone to care for her, her house, and her two children."

Crystal's smile was as pretty as Nate's. "I can do that. I may not look it but I'm strong."

Crystal was short and slim.

"I'll tell you what I'll do," said Alex as he rose from his chair. "Nate, I'll take you to the barn where you can meet my foreman. If he agrees then I will offer you the job on a trial basis. If he isn't satisfied after a month or two, I will have to look for someone else."

Addie rose also. "Crystal, I'll take you to meet Mrs. Dunn."

The four of them left the house by way of the back porch. Alex and Nate headed to the barn while Addie and Crystal took the path to where Lottie and Caleb lived.

**

It was settled. Nate and Crystal were hired. They would return and live in the cabin once Jess and Fannie left.

Alex was satisfied that Nate had some experience. He was pleased that the young man appeared strong and honest. Best of all, Jess's salary would cover both Crystal and Nate's work. Two for the price of one?

Addie liked that they were both neat and clean and that Crystal had schooling. But, what Addie liked best was the fact she would be relieved of any child care and household duties.

Alex was the boss and held the purse strings. He had been fair. Both Nate and Caleb knew Nate's employment depended on how well he performed.

How could Caleb or Lottie object if they wanted to? Caleb needed a hired man, and Lottie was still so weak and washed out she was happy to have someone feeding her family and taking care of the house.

Jess was elated. He and Fannie could leave within the week. Fannie was resolved to that fact.

Chapter 9

The next day after she finished some book work, Addie went to see Fannie.

She was ironing. "Come on in, Addie."

"Getting ready to leave?" Addie asked as she entered.

"A lot of good it will do to iron these clothes," complained Fannie. "They'll get wrinkled in the suitcases."

"They'll be ironed wrinkles," Addie said with a forced smile. "When are you leaving?"

"Tomorrow. Jess has the train tickets."

Addie drew in her breath. "So soon? That isn't even enough time to get everyone together to say goodbye."

"It's better that way," replied Fannie. "What do you think of the couple Alex has hired?"

"They're young and seem ready to take on the chores."

"Where are they going to live?"

Addie was caught with a question she didn't want to answer. "They'll live here in the cabin," came her soft reply.

Fannie swallowed the lump in her throat. "So this will be our last night here. I love this place."

Neither one of them spoke before they burst into tears. Addie went to Fannie and put her arms around her. "Oh please, Fannie. Talk to Jess and tell him you don't want to go."

51

"I'm sorry, Addie." She picked up the heavy iron, moved from Addie's arms, and placed it on the stove. "I don't know what came over me."

Addie stood back, wiped her eyes and blew her nose. "I do. We have both tried to be strong and not show our true feelings. You don't want to leave and I don't want you to go, but it isn't our choice, is it. I know you need to go with Jess. My only hope is that you will return."

Fannie wiped her eyes with her apron. "Let's have a cup of tea."

After Addie left, Fannie went out to sit on a fallen log that sat by the small stream behind the cabin. It was a lovely day. Tiny white wild flowers contrasted with the violets to give a pretty pattern to the green grass.

What would California be like? Would they get there safely? What is it Jess is searching for? Why are we leaving? Questions, questions. Fannie took in the view of the sky, the wooded hills, the open fields and the Blue Ridge Mountains. She would keep the image in her mind and heart.

Fannie rose from the log. It was time to go say goodbye to Lottie where parting wouldn't be as painful. She could smile at the mental picture of the infant she had helped bring into this world. Could this be the reason she was sent here in the first place? At least she would leave Lockwood knowing she had made a worthwhile contribution.

Chapter 10

The next day Jess and Fannie sat in the big dining room at Lockwood with Alex and Addie. Peg entered with a large platter of eggs and ham, which she placed on the buffet and followed up with bowls of grits and fried apples. Then she placed a basket of warm biscuits and honey on the table.

She looked at Jess. "I didn't want you to go away hungry."

Jess smiled at her. "You make a tasteful meal, Peg, even if you do poke fun at my boots."

"I can always tell when you come up the steps. I think I'm going to miss that sound." She didn't say another word and went back into the kitchen.

The room grew quiet.

"Let's fill our plates," suggested Alex. "Peg has prepared plenty. We'll be leaving in about thirty minutes. You don't want to miss the train, Jess."

"For sure we don't, do we Fannie?"

"No, I guess not. Are you riding in with us, Addie?"

Addie shook her head. "I'll say goodbye here. I don't want to look like a crybaby at the station."

"I thought you two said goodbye yesterday," said Jess.

"We cried together. That isn't the same," Addie answered.

"It isn't like we'll never come back, Addie."

"Isn't it, Jess? You don't know what lies between here and California."

"Enough of this," ordered Alex. "You are not to discourage our friends, Adelaide."

"I'm sorry," she apologized. "I do wish you both the best, and we will be looking forward to your letters telling of your travels".

Fannie gave a genuine answer, "Thank you, Addie. I woke up this morning feeling much better about this trip."

Jess grinned and patted her hand. "That's the spirit!"

Fannie and Addie exchanged wry smiles.

Addie stood on the massive front porch between two tall columns. She waved as the Franklin automobile carrying Alex, Jess and Fannie made its way down the long winding drive. Her feelings were a mixture of regret to see them leave and a yearning to go with them.

Peg came out on the porch. "Have they gone?"

"Yes."

"It's going to be quiet around here. It's just spirit-lifting with them around."

"Yes, it is, Peg. We both have plenty to keep us busy so maybe we won't notice their absence so much."

Peg nodded. "Maybe."

They both knew that wasn't true.

The *Norfolk and Western* was being loaded with freight when Alex pulled into the station off

Main Street in Berryville. Across the tracks, Fannie saw lots of activity at the Clarke Milling Company. She always used their *Queen of Hearts* flour, and Jess loved the bread she baked. How long will it be before she can knead another batch of dough? Fannie tried to put the thought out of her mind as Jess was so eager to get started. She didn't want to dampen his enthusiasm.

Alex shook hands with Jess and kissed Fannie on the cheek. "There will always be a spot for both of you at Lockwood."

The conductor took their suitcases and set them aside to store them in the baggage car. He offered Fannie a hand as she and Jess came up the metal steps where they entered the third passenger car and sat in the second row. They settled into their seats and waited until the conductor signaled the engineer to pull out.

"We'll have to change trains once we get to Maryland. They have a great station there in Hagerstown where we can eat lunch," said Jess.

"Peg sent some apples, jerky, cheese and crackers. Do you want that for lunch?"

Jess smiled. "Good for Peg. Guess we'd better hold onto them. We change to the *Baltimore and Ohio* to get to Chicago. That's a long trip and we may get hungry."

"They must have a dining car on that train."

"Probably. We might not eat in the dining cars too much. That can get expensive."

Her expression was a frown. "Jess Edwards, you assured me that we had enough money to get to California."

"I believe I said for train tickets," he corrected. "I didn't say anything about eating in the dining cars. Some trains only allow passengers in the lounge cars or Pullmans to use the dining cars. We're traveling coach class."

This revelation irked Fannie. She kept her voice low as she leaned into him. "I have been concerned about money since before we left. We could have saved up more money if we had stayed longer."

"Well, Fannie, my love. We would have dived right into the busy season on the farm and I didn't want to get tied up in it. We'll do fine as long as we are frugal."

Fannie fell silent and turned away to look out the window. She wished she hadn't because they were passing through Gaylord. Up on a hill was the stately white stucco house of Lockwood. Fannie closed her eyes until the train rode out of its view.

It wouldn't do to feel peeved and spoil the better mood she'd forced upon herself. Fannie decided to push her peevish feeling away and enjoy the countryside from the window of the train, which could use a good washing. "How long before we get to Hagerstown?" she asked Jess.

"I figure under two hours. It probably depends on how many stops the train makes." He looked over at her and took her hand. "I'm sorry if I misled you."

"I should have asked more questions. I want your promise that you will be completely honest from now on. No more weasel-wording."

"Is that what you call it?"

"Cunning is what I should call your attempt to get me to agree to come."

"I promise no more twisting words." He crossed his heart. "Are you peeved with me?"

"No. Now that we have the unpleasantness out of the way let's enjoy the ride."

He leaned over and kissed her cheek. "I do love you, Fannie. Who knows? Maybe we can take all our meals in the dining car."

She looked at him. "I wouldn't bet on it."

The conductor came through the railcar asking for tickets. He looked to be in his thirties with a big nose set in a round face and hair the color of acorns poking out under the black cap he wore. "You're a big one," he said to Jess. "Ought to get up and stretch your legs every so often. These seats are built for short guys like me." Then he chuckled.

He punched the tickets Jess handed to him and touched his cap to Fannie. "Pleasure to have a handsome woman on board."

"I'll bet you say that to all the women who ride your train," replied Fannie.

"No, ma'am, only the pretty ones. Staying in Hagerstown?"

"No," Jess said. "We change trains there. We're on our way to California."

The conductor let out a low whistle. "That's a far piece."

"Have you ever been there?"

"No, ma'am. I'm happy to stay right where I am. I've been working for the railroad 'bout ten years. I get enough riding; I don't need to go three thousand miles."

"That's what I tried to tell my husband, but he says he has an itchy foot."

The conductor snickered. "Could be that itch will get scratched before you get there."

Fannie raised her eyebrows. "One can only hope."

The conductor moved on to the next seat.

Jess leaned in toward her. "What kind of a conversation was that?"

"Him saying I was handsome?"

"No, you telling him I have an itchy foot."

"Well that's what you told me."

"You don't have to announce it to the world."

She patted his hand. "Sorry. He did kind of say we might not make it all the way."

"He needs to keep his mind on punching tickets," said a disgruntled Jess.

Chapter 11

They rode through West Virginia, crossed the Potomac River into Maryland until they stopped in Hagerstown where both Jess and Fannie admired the two and a half story brick station with classical appointments.

"You were right, Jess. It is a lovely station. It's not as big as Union Station in Washington, but it is impressive."

They waited on the platform for the baggage to be unloaded. Jess spied their suitcases right away and hurried to pick them up before an attendant could beat him to it.

"Is that what you call being frugal, Jess?"

He looked at her. "What do you mean?"

"A slick way to avoid a tip."

Jess snickered. "That dime may buy you a cup of coffee in the dining car."

"I should hope so!" she exclaimed. "Ten cents for a cup of coffee?" She slipped her hand around his arm as he carried the two suitcases.

Jess had Fannie sit on a bench where he set down the cases and went to the ticket booth to be sure the time of the arrival of the *B&O*.

On his return to where she sat, the heels of his cowboy boots resounded as he clattered across the marble floor. Fannie smiled when he neared.

"Why the big smile?" he asked.

"You looked so good walking toward me, I was glad to be your girl."

He chuckled and brushed her cheek with his finger. "You will always be my girl. We've got a half hour to wait. Do you want a cup of tea?"

"No thanks. Let's sit here and watch the people."

"Watch the people?"

"Yes. Haven't you ever people-watched and tried to guess where people were going or what they do for a living? See if they're young or old, happy or sad? For instance, look at that young woman over there with the two kids. Maybe she's going to meet her husband, or maybe her husband died and she's going back to her parents, or maybe she doesn't even have a husband."

"Fannie, my love, if that's the way a woman's mind works, no wonder men get confused."

"I think she's waiting for her husband."

Jess looked in the young woman's direction. "Well, I hope so. She's having a devil of a time trying to keep those two under control."

The words were no sooner out of his mouth when both youngsters broke free and went running in the direction of a tall man who scooped them both up in his arms. He carried them to the young woman, set them down, and the four walked out of the station together.

"I was right," said Fannie with a broad grin.

"Maybe he was her brother."

"Brothers don't look at sisters like he looked at her."

60

"Why didn't he give her a big kiss?"

"Because they are in public. It might not set a good example for their children."

"That wouldn't bother me. If I were in his shoes and met you in the station, I'd grab you up and plant a big kiss right on those luscious lips."

Fannie smiled and shook her head. "No doubt you would. Whatever he is, the woman looked a whole lot less frazzled once he appeared."

"True," remarked Jess. "I'm going to close my eyes and get a rest before the train gets here. You can people-watch." He pulled his cowboy hat down over his eyes and slouched on the bench.

"I wonder what they think about us?" said Fannie.

"Probably that you're one lucky gal to snag this good-looking cowboy," he mumbled.

"Or the other way around," she answered. "You're not a cowboy, anyway; you just dress like one. You're from New York."

"I was trained to be a cowboy in Oklahoma, and once you're a cowboy in Oklahoma, you're a cowboy anyplace."

The train arrived on schedule. Jess picked up their suitcases and they hurried to find good seats. They walked past Pullman cars to get to the less expensive class.

"I wonder what it would be like to travel in a Pullman." Fannie remarked as they walked past one.

"Most likely more comfortable than what we'll be. If we make our fortune in California we can travel back in one."

"I hope we make enough money to travel back."

The conductor was waiting by the iron steps that led up to the railcar. He put a step stool down for the ladies because the first step was a high one. "Good afternoon folks. Looks like a clear day for us. Never know what the weather's going to be in Chicago."

"Is there a dining car on this train?" Jess inquired.

"Best one headin' west." He chuckled. "It's two cars up from this one. You'll only have to pass through one car to get there. Leave your cases here, I'll store them in the back of the car. Save you time when we unload."

"Thanks," Jess said and ushered Fannie to the second seat on the left side. We won't get the sun beating through the window on this side."

"Will the view be as good?" Fannie asked.

"Should be. Once we pass through eastern Ohio the land tends to flatten out. Not much of a view in my estimation. Chicago's a bustling place. You'll get to see Lake Michigan."

"How do you know about Chicago?"

"I worked a few days in the stockyards."

The remark surprised Fannie. "Jess, you never told me that." What else hasn't he told her?

The conductor came by to punch their tickets. "You were wise to sit on this side, less sun. O' course you can open the window if the people around you don't complain. Plannin' on stayin' in Chicago?"

"No, we're on our way to California," replied Jess.

"Plenty of sun out there," he replied and moved on.

"Do all conductors look alike?" asked Fannie. "He could pass as a brother to the one we left on the last train."

"They probably come in all sizes except tall like me. There's not much head room. The most they do on a train is punch tickets, ride, sleep, and wave to the engineer, I'd guess."

The train whistle sounded and they were off in a lurch of the railcar. They could feel as each car was yanked into line as the *Baltimore & Ohio* headed out of Hagerstown.

Fannie felt a twinge of excitement. As long as Jess was by her side, and if nothing went wrong, she might even enjoy this experience.

Neither she nor Jess tried to make conversation because the train was too noisy. Fannie's seat was next to the window where she watched as the countryside passed by. She was getting used to the train stops, not that she looked forward to them. The train would blow its whistle, slow down, wait as passengers came and went, then start up with a jerk each time.

The aroma from the dining car wafted back to where they sat. The cooking started early in the afternoon. They planned to eat at six o'clock because there was a long night until breakfast. Those with more expensive seats ate earlier. Colored waiters in white jackets and black trousers carried covered trays through the aisle to the Pullman section. As they passed the food smell lingered increasing the hunger of the coach class passengers.

"I'm getting hungry," said Jess. "Let's hope the dining car isn't full before we get a chance to get there."

"The conductor said there is only one car ahead of us."

"That's in this direction. I don't know how many cars are ahead of us."

"I've got the food Peg sent."

"We'll hold on to it. Are you hungry?"

"Starved. Maybe you can trip one of those waiters as he goes by. What time is it?"

Jess pulled out his pocket watch. "Five-thirty."

"Let's go."

They left their car, crossed into the next and found a line of people waiting to enter the dining car. They stood in line and watched as a waiter opened the door and allowed only a number of waiting passengers for which there were seats.

They stood in the narrow aisle rocking back and forth as the train rushed along the rails. Jess leaned over and whispered to Fannie, "Good thing we decided to come early."

She whispered back, "I'm glad you have a sense of humor. I get hungrier by the minute."

Finally after forty-five minutes, they entered the dining car. Jess and Fannie were fortunate to find a table for two. It was a squeeze for Jess.

The waiter brought menus and Fannie's eyes popped wide when she saw the prices. She looked up at Jess. "I can see why you suggested we may not eat in the dining car often. Coffee is ten cents a cup!"

"They have us cornered. Where else could we eat?"

Fannie continued to read the menu. "The meatloaf comes with mashed potatoes, gravy, and a vegetable. The meal is seventy cents but it should fill me up."

Jess nodded. "Good idea. I'll have the creamed chicken."

The waiter came by and took their orders. He poured glasses of water so Fannie decided she would pass up the cup of coffee. Water was free.

Once the waiter left, Fannie looked out the window and remarked it was getting dusk. "What time will we be in Chicago?" she asked.

"Late evening tomorrow. The next train won't leave Chicago until the next morning."

Fannie's look was one of surprise. "Where are we supposed to sleep?"

"They do have hotels in Chicago."

"No. I mean tonight."

"In our seats. Maybe they pass out pillows."

She looked at him in disbelief. "If I have to sleep sitting up tonight, we will sleep in a hotel in Chicago!"

Jess was quick with an answer, "Hotel it is, and I've tickets for a sleeper on the next train because we'll be almost three days before we get to the land of opportunity."

"Keep your dream alive, Jess. I pray it doesn't turn out to be a nightmare."

Chapter 12

When the train reached the Chicago station early the next evening, Fannie was ready to depart. The night on the train had been cramped and cold. If she slept at all, she couldn't recall any peaceful moments.

The Chicago station was huge. Jess guided her through the maze of people to the exit.

"Addie told me to be sure and look at the clock tower outside the station."

"What fascination did she have for a clock tower?"

"I don't know. She was eighteen and impressionable. The only elevated clock I've seen in Berryville is on the Bank of Clarke County. It's not what I would call a tower."

Jess chuckled. "Well then, we'd better find this tower so you can report to her."

"I wonder how things are going at Lockwood. I wish we could have waited a few more weeks."

Jess stopped walking and looked at her. "Fannie, I have explained why we couldn't stay. I don't want to hear any more regrets."

Fannie knew enough to button her lips but she didn't apologize. "I hope you find a good hotel."

When they came out of the station there was the lighted clock tower standing as a sentinel crow watching over the comings and goings of train travelers.

"Oh, my! I can see why Addie was in awe. It is lovely isn't it, Jess?"

He stood beside her. "It makes me smile. Would you be disappointed if I told you I've seen it before?"

"No. I recall you said you worked in the stock yards. They don't drive cattle hundreds of miles anymore, so it's unlikely you rode your horse. It didn't take a lot of thought that you most likely rode a train."

Jess chuckled. "It didn't cost me a penny. The cattle and I rode together."

"That must have been a cozy, smelly ride."

They turned from the tower and resumed walking. Jess carried the two suitcases so she put her hand through his arm as they navigated the streets heavy with taxis, city buses and rattling cars.

They stopped on a curb before entering State Street.

"Do you know where we're going?"

"A few blocks. It's good to stretch our legs," Jess answered.

A short distance later they stopped in front of a seven story building. "This is it," said Jess.

Fannie read the big sign. "The Palmer House! Jess, I've heard of this place. It's probably the most expensive one in this city. We can't afford to stay here."

"It is our big splurge. One night. We didn't have a honeymoon."

Fannie glimpsed at the expensive retail shops on the ground level.

"We don't fit in here. Look at the way people are dressed."

"Fannie, our money is as good as theirs."

"Maybe you should take off that big cowboy hat."

"No. I learned in Texas that the Stetson doesn't come off. They'll think I'm a big rancher."

Fannie gave a deflated sigh. "In this plain cotton dress and straw hat they're not going to think I'm a well-to-do rancher's wife. I hope they don't kick us out."

The doorman opened the door and Fannie almost swooned at the opulent lobby with Greek mythology murals pained on the high ceiling. Tall lighted candelabras lent a homey glow along with electric lamps with globe-shaped porcelain shades trimmed with glass fringe. The place smelled of money.

Jess guided her to a tapestry covered chair while he went to the desk.

Fannie sat straight as an arrow. If anyone was looking at her, she didn't want to know.

Jess arrived with a bellhop who picked up the suitcases. "Please follow me," said the young man.

"We're on the seventh floor," whispered Jess. He offered his arm and Fannie rose without saying a word.

They waited in front of ornate doors etched in gold. The car stopped with a smooth ping and they stepped on.

"Seventh floor," ordered the bellhop.

"It's a lovely evening out there," said Jess to break the silence.

"Yes, sir. It is," answered the suitcase carrier.

"I wouldn't know," chimed in the young operator. "There isn't any sign of weather going up and down inside this box."

Fannie could see by the look on the bellhop's face that he was uncomfortable with his co-worker's glib remark.

Jess chuckled. "Do you get tired of riding up and down?"

"I can't say as there is much excitement in it. I do meet some genial people along with a couple of grouches."

The elevator passed the fourth floor.

"Johnny, please remember we are trans-porting guests," cautioned the bellhop.

The operator's face reddened. "Sorry if I over spoke."

"No, son. You were honest. I asked and you answered," said Jess.

"You fellows with the big hats are easy to talk to. It's the men in the three-piece suits that cause me to clam up."

Fannie giggled. "Johnny, don't ever change."

He gave a wide smile. "Seventh floor."

They stepped from the elevator and Jess handed Johnny a quarter. "Thanks for the ride."

"Thank you, sir!"

The bellhop put the key in the lock. Fannie and Jess entered without saying a word while the bellhop set down the large cases.

Jess handed him a tip, also.

"Thank you, sir. If you need anything there is a phone on the desk."

Once the door closed, Fannie threw herself onto the high bed. "Oh, Jess: silk sheets, brocade drapes, desk, telephone. I think I'm in heaven."

He stood watching her. "We're seven stories up. I guess that makes us a lot closer."

She hopped off the bed and ran to the window. "My goodness. Look at all the activity down there. It looks like an army of ants hurrying to do whatever ants do."

He came to her side and put his strong arms around her. "Are you happy now?"

"You are good to me, Jess. I know this won't last but we are in paradise for one night."

"I love you, Fannie Edwards," he whispered in her ear.

She turned in his arms and kissed him fondly. "Jess promise me that we'll never fall out of love."

"Love takes a lot of twists and turns," he said, "However, I promise to love you forever."

Fannie chuckled. "That sounds poetic."

"I am a man of many talents."

"We'll see how talented you are to get us back to Lockwood."

He kissed her cheek. "Come on. Let's explore the bathroom. Maybe the tub is big enough for both of us."

Chapter 13

The next morning Fannie put on a yellow dress patterned with white daisies. She thought it looked more stylish that the plain cotton she'd worn yesterday. She tied a white ribbon around the only hat she had brought.

"You look right nice," said an admiring Jess. "We'll be walking quite a bit. Are your shoes comfortable?"

"It's not like I have a big choice." There was a two inch heel on her brown leather shoes with a strap across the instep.

Their suitcases were packed so that they could leave them at the desk to pick up when they were to meet the train.

"Be sure and bring that food Peg sent," said Jess. "We'll find a spot near the Lake and eat it for lunch."

"A good idea," replied Fannie. "It is a couple of days old. Cheese and crackers age well. The apples might be a bit pithy, but the jerky lasts for years."

Jess chuckled. "Better than buying lunch."

They had breakfast at a small restaurant near the hotel. The price was reasonable and they had a full meal of eggs, sausage, fried potatoes and hot biscuits.

Fannie liked the feel of the city. Growing up in Washington, D.C. she was accustomed to the crowds of people, sounds of the trolleys and buses, and the many tall buildings that held offices and stores of all descriptions. A bustling city was familiar to her causing her to appreciate it once in a while, but she preferred the sounds and solitude of the country.

They shopped in Marshall Fields and F.W. Woolworth. Then they walked up and down Michigan Avenue while gawking at the expensive store displays of china, silver and jewelry. In Marshall Fields, Jess had admired a handgun.

"Whatever would you want with one of those?" asked Fannie.

"You never know when a rat will pop up."

"Two-legged or four-legged?" questioned Fannie.

Jess was serious. "There's a part of this city that isn't safe. The hoodlums now have Tommy guns. The more I read the headlines the more I'll be glad to leave Chicago."

"We're in the safe part, aren't we?"

"As far as I know," he replied. "According to the papers it reads like gangs are running rampant in the South End. I used to carry a pistol."

"Did you ever use it?"

"Only for target practice. I stayed out of the bars and never looked at another man's gal. Caleb and I used to bet on each other with our marksman ship."

"Who won?"

"We ended up pretty even."

"I think that might be fun," mused Fannie.

"Target shooting? I know quite a few women who know how to shoot."

"Will you teach me, Jess?"

"Maybe one day. Right now I'm ready for Peg's two-day-old lunch."

They had reached a park on the shore of Lake Michigan where Jess wiped off a bench with his bandanna before Fannie sat.

Fannie opened the canvas bag she carried and took out the cheese and crackers. "Peg sliced the cheese but you'll have to put it between the crackers."

As they nibbled on their lunch they looked out at the dark blue waters of Lake Michigan as it lapped at the shore. "The lake looks like it goes on forever," remarked Fannie.

"It does at that. But, it's a lake. Wait until we get to the ocean. The surf explodes."

Fannie had never been to an ocean. Jess made it sound exciting. "Have you been to California, Jess?"

She needed an answer. He cleared his throat. "As a matter of fact, I have. It was a couple of years ago."

Fannie continued eating her cracker and looking at the lake. "So, this won't be your first trip out there. Just what is it you're looking for?"

"I don't know. We had to take some cattle out to a man who had a big spread. Another pal and I traveled around. The place looked prosperous, like somebody could hit it big."

"Like your gold mining stint in Colorado?"

"That was a mistake," he answered.

"What makes you think this trip isn't?"

"I've got good feelings about it."

"Jess, I will tell you right now. I will give you two months to find whatever it is you're hoping to find. If it doesn't appear in that time, I'm heading back to Lockwood."

He gave her words some thought. "Your place is with me."

"You know it was not my idea to leave Virginia. I believe I am being honest and fair. I can't say the same for you."

He shrugged his shoulders. "Because I didn't tell you before we left that I have already seen California?"

"It would have helped if I'd known."

"Would you still have come?"

"I don't know, Jess."

They sat in silence looking out at the lake.

"Will you leave without me, Fannie?"

In a quiet voice she answered, "If I have to."

Jess didn't answer right away and Fannie was afraid of what he would say.

After a few moments he spoke, "It's settled then. Two months. We'll look at how things are going and make plans from there."

Fannie was so relieved she jumped up from the bench and threw her arms around him touching her forehead to his. With a catch in her voice she said, "Thank God, Jess."

"Did you think I would let you go without me?"

"I wasn't sure."

He kissed her gently. "You know that cabin won't be ours again since Nate and Crystal moved into it."

Fannie moved back to where she had sat and took his strong hand in hers. With a wistful sigh she answered, "I know. Jess, maybe we can go back and build our own. I loved that little place. Addie said Alex would let you have some land."

"Let me buy some land."

"He's going to give Caleb fifty acres."

"Fannie, my love, fifty acres if Caleb works for five years and stays on as his foreman."

That was true, thought Fannie. "All right. Let's look at it this way. You make enough money in California so we can go back and buy the land."

Jess stood up and helped her to her feet.

"That's called putting the cart before the horse. Right now we need to board that train."

By the time they reached the *Los Angeles Limited*, direct from Chicago to LA, Fannie's feet hurt. She had seen what she knew was only a small part of Chicago. It was enough. Three more days on this train and they would be in California.

Fannie used the bathroom in the train station before she boarded the *Union Pacific*.

One time Fannie had to use the smelly toilet on the train that was used by men, women, and children alike. It was a challenge. Because of the wobbling of the train on the rails some well-aimed targets were missed. She had to hike up her skirt, wash off the lid, and try to secure her feet in a dry spot on either side of the stool. She vowed she would only use the toilet when the train pulled into a station.

Fannie settled into the seat next to Jess, took off her shoes and rubbed her sore feet. "You did say this train has sleeping berths, didn't you?"

Jess pulled out his ticket stub. "It says right here. We have berths nine and ten."

"And it does have a dining car?"

"The car behind us."

"After spending so much money at the Palmer Hotel, do we have money to eat?"

Jess smiled at her. "Did you enjoy the hotel?"

"It was fabulous."

"Good. Hold onto the memory because we are going to pinch our pennies for the rest of the trip."

Fannie shook her head. "You should have worked a couple more weeks."

"Fannie…"

"All right. I'll try to not mention it again."

"The dining car is open," announced the conductor.

"Oh, good," said Fannie. "I'm starved. Maybe we can afford a biscuit."

"That isn't funny," replied Jess.

Chapter 14

It was close to six o'clock when they went into the dining car. Fannie ordered ham, beans and turnip greens which came with a slice of bread. Jess ordered the same.

"That should hold us until morning," he said.

Fannie nodded her agreement. "I still have the jerky Peg gave us. Have you seen where we will be sleeping?"

"The sleeper is the car ahead of us."

"Let's turn in early," suggested Fannie. "We've had a long day. I hope I'm able to sleep and the rumbling of the train doesn't keep me awake."

"We should be pulling into Cheyenne, Wyoming in a few hours."

Fannie groaned. "Which means that I will stay awake and use the necessary room at that station before we retire."

Jess laughed. "A wise idea. You will be so tired you'll drift off to sleep rumble or no rumble."

In Cheyenne, a waifish looking young woman was approaching the dimly lit station along with Fannie.

"Good evening," said Fannie. "It does feel good to leave the train and stretch."

"Yes, ma'am. It does," the young woman replied.

"Are you going to California?" Fannie asked.

"No. ma'am. I'm going as far as Ogden, Utah. My aunt runs a place there and wants me to come and work."

They went into the area reserved for women. "What will you be doing?" asked Fannie.

"I'm not sure. Aunt Emma wrote to Ma and said she's right busy. She's also got work for girl friends of mine if they wanted to come. According to what she wrote, since they started mining coal the place has brought in a lot of people."

"Is anyone with you?"

""No. I came by myself."

That piqued Fannie's interest. "How old are you?"

"I'm sixteen, ma'am. From Kentucky."

Fannie knew what it was like to be sixteen and working, but she had not ventured from home.

"Your parents approved of you coming out by yourself?"

The girl snickered. "Ma said it sounded good. I can send some money home and she needs it."

"What about your father?"

"Pa died last year and there's four other kids. I'm the oldest."

Fannie smiled at her and thought the teen might be attractive with different clothes, a little more weight, and her brown straggling hair under control. "I came from a large family also. Will you go to school out there?"

"I don't know. I guess it depends on Aunt Emma. I only met her once when I was about five. She is Pa's sister."

They used the toilets, washed their hands and prepared to go back across the dusty street to the train.

"Good luck to you," Fannie said as they headed for different train cars.

"Thank you, ma'am. It was right nice to talk to you."

Jess waited outside the railcar and gave Fannie a hand up onto the metal steps. "Who was that girl you were talking to?"

"She's from Kentucky. Sixteen. I didn't get her name. She said she's going as far as Ogden where her aunt has a job for her."

"That's a rough place. I heard even Al Capone, the crime boss of Chicago, said it's too wild for him."

Fannie stopped short in the aisle causing Jess to bump into her. "Jess, do you think she's headed for trouble?"

"How should I know? Grab your satchel and let's go to the sleeper. I'm tired."

They wound through the narrow aisle of the sleeping car and found berths nine and ten. Jess opted to take the upper. Fannie opened the heavy curtain sheltering the space and crawled onto the lower berth. There was a small window with a curtain and about enough room to slip off her shoes. It would be no easy chore to change into her nightgown. Fannie decided to sleep in her street clothes and used her nightgown to cover the pillow. Who knows whether the pillow cover had been changed or whose head slept on it last. There was a folded blanket if she got cold. Fannie wondered how Jess was going to manage his large frame in the above pinched area. That wasn't her problem. Before she fell asleep she said a prayer for the young girl from Kentucky that all would be well with her. After Jess told her about the town of Ogden's reputation, Fannie felt ill at ease.

Chapter 15

The brick Ogden Union Station in Utah was separated from the tracks by an underground walkway. The station held a central clock tower, thirty-three hotel rooms, a restaurant, and a barber shop.

While Fannie and Jess stood there looking, a voice said, "Hello, miss. I didn't think I'd see you again. I'm off to find my aunt's place."

Fannie turned to see the young Kentuckian smiling at her. "Oh, hello. I'm sorry I didn't ask your name last evening."

"It's Ota, ma'am. Ota Lee Henry."

"I'm Mrs. Fannie Edwards and this is Mr. Edwards. Do you know the way to your aunt's business?"

"I figure it can't be far. I've got her address from the letter she wrote to Ma. I'll ask somebody."

"Let me go ask that fellow in the baggage area," offered Jess. "What's your aunt's name?"

"Emma Henry."

Jess walked over to the man who looked up from his work. "Excuse me, sir. There is a young lady over there who has just arrived. She is looking for her aunt, Emma Henry."

The man furrowed his forehead. "Her aunt, huh?"

"That's what she said."

"Fat Emma's place is about a block down." He pointed with his finger.

Jess's eyebrows flew up. "Fat Emma's? I take it it's not a hotel or café."

"You take it right. It's not food they serve in that place. You ain't from around here?"

"No."

"Didn't think so. Don't let this handsome station fool you. I've got a decent job so I stay, but this town is filled up with miners, gamblers, drunks, thieves, and prostitutes ever since they struck coal. If it ain't legal you'll find it here."

"Thanks," said Jess. He walked away wondering how he was he going to tell Fannie what he just heard?

"I'm going to treat Ota to a sandwich," Fannie announced when Jess returned to where they stood.

He kept his voice low. "I need to talk to you."

"Can't it wait?"

"No, Fannie."

"Ota, you go ahead into the restaurant and decide what kind of a sandwich you want. I'll be right in," ordered Fannie.

Off went the teen without question.

"Just what is it that can't wait?" asked a disgruntled Fannie.

"Emma Henry runs a brothel. According to the gentleman unloading the baggage, this whole place is a hotbed of corruption."

"Jess, that can't be. Her mother wouldn't send her out here if that's true. Let's take her to her aunt."

"What good will that do? Our train leaves in another twenty-five minutes."

"I am not going to send her to a house of ill repute, Jess."

He laughed. "That's a nice way of saying it. She's sixteen, Fannie. Lots of girls are married by then."

"Marriage is different. We're taking her. I want to see this Aunt Emma and the place she runs. Maybe you misunderstood. Ota can eat her sandwich on the way."

Jess knew better than to argue when Fannie's mind was set, and he didn't want to miss the train. "I don't see what good that's going to do."

"If this Emma isn't legitimate, I have some extra money that I saved for an emergency. I'll buy the girl a ticket back to Kentucky."

Jess gave her a wry look. "Now who isn't being completely honest?"

"You never asked me if I had any money. It's fifty dollars that I saved before we were married."

Ota was waiting. "They've got a ham and cheese sandwich."

"Good," said Fannie. "Go ahead and order it, but you'll have to eat it on the way while we take you to your aunt's house."

A smile popped onto the young woman's thin face. "That's right kind of you."

It was hot and dusty as they walked down the dirt street. They passed saloons with ogling men and dandies loafing on the front porches. Fannie was glad to have Jess at her side.

He lifted his tall hat and wiped his sweaty forehead with a bandanna. "Damn, it's hot. You've had better ideas, Fannie."

She shot a grimace in his direction.

Emma Henry's faded white clapboard house was a block away from the train depot. The small yard was fenced by a short wood picket fence in need of paint. There was an attempt to spruce the area up by planting a rose bush in a pot by the four steps that led up to the covered porch. From the bleak look of the whole town, it appeared not much vegetation grew in the poor soil of Oden, Utah.

They walked up the steps and Jess rang the bell that hung next to the door.

A short, very fat woman with mousey blond hair opened the door. She looked at the three standing before her. "I don't rent rooms," was her greeting.

"No ma'am. We've brought Ota," informed Jess.

"Ota?" asked Emma with a confused expression.

"Your niece, Ota Lee Henry," said a disgusted Fannie.

"Aunt Emma?" came a timid voice from behind Fannie.

Emma's expression changed to recognition. "Oh, sure. Harley's girl. Did you bring anybody else?"

Fannie took charge. "Ota says you have a job for her."

"You bet I do. I'm busy as all get out."

"What job do you have for her?" asked Fannie.

Emma gave her a nasty look. "Doing what all the rest of my girls do. Who are you anyway? One of those do-gooders who don't mind her own business?" Emma turned to Ota, who looked as frightened as a cornered rabbit. With a motion of her head, Emma said, "Get on in here girl!"

Jess watched as Fannie's face flushed and her fists clenched. "Don't move, Ota!" Fannie looked Emma in the eye. "I know what kind of a place you run here, and I am not about to let this young girl be taken advantage of."

Emma thrust out her jaw. "She's my kin. Her ma can use the money. We Henrys stick together. I'll call the sheriff if you don't get off my porch!"

"We'll get off it all right and Ota with us."

"That girl stays here!" said a red-faced Emma, whose breath was beginning to come in puffs.

Jess knew it was time to leave before Fannie's patience was no more. "Come on, Fannie. We need to get back."

Fannie never said a word. She turned on her heel, grabbed Ota's arm and pulled her along down the street.

The girl was speechless.

Jess hurried to catch up. "If Emma decides to call the sheriff you can get arrested for abduction. What do you plan to do now?"

Fannie talked through clenched teeth. "I don't know, but I couldn't leave her there. I'm going to buy her a ticket to come with us. It'll give me time to think."

Jess gave a deep sigh. "I hope you know what you're doing."

"So do I."

Chapter 16

The next morning Jess, Fannie and Ota sat in the dining car. Fannie hadn't slept well worrying most of the night as to what to do with the young woman she had rescued. She thought she had enough money to buy her a ticket back to Kentucky.

Jess was not overly pleased with Fannie's decision to bring the girl with them, but he understood. That didn't mean he slept any better. His money was running low and Fannie's emergency supply would only go so far. The money spent on Ota might be better spent on themselves.

"Order whatever you want," Fannie said. "Do they call you Ota at home?"

"Pretty much they call me Lee-Lee."

Lee-Lee. What kind of a name is that, thought Fannie. "I'll call you your given name."

Ota shrugged.

The waiter came and took their order of three omelets and coffee. Jess breathed an inner sigh of relief that Ota hadn't ordered an expensive meal.

What a switch, he thought. Fannie had been the one concerned about money at the start. Now she was spending her money on this girl from Kentucky they didn't even know. Ota didn't appear to realize how fortunate she was to have escaped Aunt Emma's.

Fannie looked at her and smiled. "Ota, do you want me to buy you a ticket back to your home?"

At these words the young teen came alive. "Oh, no, ma'am. I can't go home, not after I didn't stay at Aunt Emma's. Ma said she was counting on that money I'd send home. She'd whip me good."

"Do you know how you were going to earn your money at Aunt Emma's?" asked Fannie.

"I suppose cleaning and cooking around her house."

Fannie was point blank and used words she thought the teen would understand. "Your Aunt Emma doesn't earn her money honestly. She hires women whose job it is to please men. Pleasing all kinds of men in all kinds of ways."

Ota's eyes grew big and her hand flew up to cover her mouth. She sat for a few minutes before she spoke. "Do you think my ma knew what Aunt Emma wanted me for?"

These words caused Fannie to swallow a lump in her throat.

"That's a question we can't answer," said Jess as he realized Fannie couldn't reply without breaking down in tears.

The waiter came by and refilled their coffee cups, which helped Fannie to recover.

After they finished breakfast, Ota went to her coach and Jess and Fannie went to the lounge car.

"Jess, what are we going to do?"

"I tried to make you see what you were getting us into. We can't save every unfortunate we're going to meet. This is wild territory out here, Fannie. Young people have to grow up fast."

"That may be so, Jess Edwards, but they don't have to grow up in a bawdy house!"

He laughed aloud. "Our next stop is Salt Lake City. It's filled with Mormons and they take a lot of wives. Maybe she'll meet one of the old codgers who'll be glad to take her in."

Fannie shot a look of disdain in his direction. "This is no joking matter. Maybe I can get word to her mother and Ota will be able to go home without worrying about what's going to happen when she gets there."

"How do you propose to do that? I'm going to take a nap." Jess pulled his hat over his eyes and leaned back in the lounge seat.

"I'll have to think of something."

Chapter 17

When they reached Salt Lake City in the early evening, Fannie thought the Union depot was a gem in the wild. The station was sandstone with a slate roof. Inside she admired the French terrazzo floors, stained glass windows, and murals of Mormon pioneers. There were many rooms off each side: separate waiting rooms for men and women, emergency hospital room, lunch room, baggage rooms, and offices.

Fannie felt grungy because she had slept in the clothes she wore, the same clothes she had worn walking the gritty, hot streets of Cheyenne and Ogden.

Ota came to meet her in the station before Jess went to the men's area. "We have an hour," he said.

Fannie and Ota went to the women's area, "I have a clean waist in my satchel that I'm going to change into. Let's comb our hair and get washed up. These train rides always feel grimy. Do you have anything clean to put on?"

"No, Miss Fannie."

"If I had another clean blouse, I'd let you wear it, but I only have one. At least you can wash up and I'll pull your hair into a braid if you'd like me to."

"You can try, Miss Fannie, but I ain't got no ribbon to tie it with."

"I do," said Fannie. "I hope to send a note to your mother about Emma's place and ease your path to return home."

Ota shook her head. "I don't want to go back home."

"Of course you do. If you don't want to go back to Kentucky, how are you going to take care of yourself?"

"I know a good bit about how to clean and cook and take care of little kids."

When Fannie was sixteen she knew the same things, but she hadn't ventured away from home. "There's a lot you need to know about living on your own. However, I'll look for a lady that needs your help and can pay you."

"What lady is that?"

"I don't know yet. We'll have to find one."

"Why can't I stay with you and Mr. Jess?"

Ota asked too many questions. "Because Jess and I don't have much money, and we don't know where we're going."

"You said you were going to California."

"Yes. That is our intention. We don't know where or what we'll find, so it isn't likely we can take you with us."

"But you don't know where you're going to find a lady for me to work for. Maybe there's one in California."

The teen could be exasperating. "Ota, get over here and let me braid your hair!"

When they went back to meet Jess, he smiled at them both. "Hello, ladies. You do look refreshed and pleasing. Do you want to take a walk outside? We'll be back on the train soon."

Salt Lake City didn't look much different than the flat, dry country they'd already passed through. But, it was a bigger city with storied buildings, not as tall as in the bigger cities. There were people and cars on the streets. The one thing Fannie had heard about Salt Lake City was the Mormon Tabernacle and she wanted to see it.

Jess pulled out his pocket watch. "We've enough time to look at it from the outside if you want."

There was no trouble locating the massive stone and wood edifice on Temple Square. It was said the temple held four thousand people and had the grandest organ in the country. They stood and gazed at the monumental structure with towers and spires reaching to the sky.

Salt Lake City was a bustle of movement. They even advertised a local baseball team called the *Salt Lake City Bees*. This city caused the most enthusiasm Fannie had felt since they left Chicago.

Chapter 18

The train reached Las Vegas in the early morning hours. It would be a longer layover. Fannie hurried into the station to use the women's area. She looked for Ota but she wasn't around. No doubt she was still asleep. Fannie thought the sleeping berths on the train, although more expensive, weren't much better than sitting up all night.

Jess was asleep when she left the train and still asleep when she returned. Could he sleep through a war? With the jolting and rumbling of the train, the conductor announcing the coming and going, and people moving about, it had been impossible for her to sleep.

She pulled back the curtain, reached up and poked Jess with her finger. He stirred a bit. Fannie stood on her berth and said quietly in his ear, "Wake up. I'm hungry."

"Where are we? What time is it?"

"Shh, there are people asleep, Jess. It's almost six in the morning and we're in Las Vegas."

Jess groaned, pulled on his boots, grabbed his hat, and Fannie accompanied him to the station where he could freshen up.

When he returned to where she waited, he asked, "Do you want to wait to eat in the dining car or should we find a café?"

"We'll find a café. I think the locals can use the money. The conductor said people have been leaving here since the war. It might even become a ghost town."

"This is our last stop before California. Shall we splurge on a big meal?"

"Let's," replied Fannie. "I still have thirty dollars left."

"It's good you brought it, Fannie. Although you did spend some of that hard-earned cash on Ota."

They walked out of the station onto the unpaved streets of Las Vegas, Nevada.

"I haven't seen Ota this morning, Jess. Do you think she's still asleep?"

"Most likely. We can eat breakfast with just the two of us. You can check on her after we finish."

Seven in the morning and it was already hot. "I hope California isn't this hot," Fannie complained. "Here it is an early June morning and I know the afternoon is going to be sweltering."

"Fannie, California is going to be paradise."

"So you try to convince me. I miss Virginia, I miss Lockwood, and I miss Addie. I can't help wonder if Lottie is doing better, and if Nate and Crystal are working out. I also miss that cabin, which will never be ours again."

"Fannie, my love, you have to look forward." He stopped in front of a small restaurant. "Here's a place called the *White Spot Cafe*. Looks like they're open for breakfast. Some food will improve your outlook."

"Don't be too sure."

Chapter 19

Addie sat in the office area of the big house. She wished Fannie would phone her, but she knew they probably hadn't reached California yet. Had it only been a week since Fannie and Jess left on that foolhardy trip? Perhaps it wasn't right to begrudge Jess dragging her friend across the country, but Addie couldn't help feeling that way. She had news to tell Fannie. The most important was that Lottie wasn't much better. If only Fannie were here. Addie knew it was selfish on her part, but she didn't care. She missed her friend.

Alex came into the office where Addie sat looking out the window. "Have you filled out the lineage charts for the new cattle?" he asked.

"No, I haven't started. Do you think Jess and Fannie are all right?"

He shrugged his shoulders. "Why shouldn't they be?"

"I don't know. I wish Fannie would call."

"Give her time, Adelaide. You have to get used to them being gone. It's possible they won't come back here."

"What makes you say that?"

"If Jess finds whatever it is he's looking for they may stay right where they are. Or he might get the urge to travel on to another spot. Fannie loved living here. I keep my hopes up they will return. Are you pleased with Nate's work?"

"Caleb says he's learning, but he doesn't have the experience of Jess."

"I know Crystal is doing what she can for Lottie. It doesn't seem right that Lottie isn't better."

"The doctor said it would take time. It's only been a few weeks since the baby was born," he reminded her.

Addie heaved a deep sigh. "I know. I still wish Fannie was here. I'll get started on those charts for you."

"Thanks," he said and kissed her cheek. "Perhaps by October we could take a few days away from Lockwood."

Addie offered a doubtful smile. Alex wasn't one to leave the farm for any length of time.

Alex left by the back door in the direction of the barn.

Addie had worked for an hour when she saw Crystal hurrying up the path to the back porch.

Addie met her at the door. "Good morning, Crystal."

Crystal's dark eyes were big as saucers. "Miz' Addie, Miz' Lottie's awful sick. She's been throwin' up and she can't get out of bed by herself."

"Hurry on back to the children and I'll call the doctor."

The two doctors in town now had a receptionist, who acted as a barrier between the doctor and the caller. Addie told her the problem as Crystal had relayed it to her. The all-important receptionist said she would tell Dr. Burke.

"Tell him to come," Addie ordered and hung up the phone. She hollered to Peg that she would be at Lottie's.

Forty-five minutes later Dr. Burke was driving up the lane to Lockwood and continued down the pock-marked lane to Lottie's house, where Addie hurried out to meet him.

"Good morning, Dr. Burke. I'm glad you came. Crystal says Lottie has been throwing up and having the runs all night. She's too exhausted to get out of bed and she feels like she has a fever."

"I came as soon as I could."

Crystal was in the yard watching the two children at play. She was holding the baby. "Miz' Lottie's awful hot and not talking right," she called in the doctor's direction.

"You ladies wait here and I'll go on in," said the physician as he went onto the porch and entered the front door.

Addie made her own decision. "Crystal, you stay with the children. I'll take the baby and put over a kettle of water."

Twenty minutes later Dr. Burke, with a concerned look on his face, came into the kitchen where Addie sat feeding the baby a bottle of goat's milk. He sat down opposite her at the table. "How is the infant doing?"

"He eats well and seems to be gaining weight. What is going on with Lottie?"

He cleared his throat. "I think Lottie either has dysentery or possibly typhoid fever. I saw a lot of this during the war. I don't think it's typhoid fever, but she does have a rash. It could be from the fever."

Addie's eyes opened wide. "Oh, dear God!"

"Is anyone else sick?"

"No."

"Has she been in contact with anyone other than here on the farm?"

Addie had to think. She put the baby on her shoulder and patted his back until she heard a loud burp. "Not that I know of," she answered as she lay him in the cradle, which was still in the kitchen. Addie saw her hands shake as she lay him down. "Wait. Suzi Johnson rode out with her son when he came to look at a calf. I don't know if she went to see Lottie."

Addie went to the door and called, "Crystal, did Mrs. Johnson come in to see Lottie?"

"Yes, ma'am. She brought Miz' Lottie some chicken soup."

"Did she hold the baby?" Dr. Burke asked.

Addie called out to Crystal. "Did she hold the baby, Crystal?"

"No, ma'am."

"I'll need to take Lottie to the Hawthorne House for a few days," said the good doctor. "She needs to be quarantined and under constant care. If she doesn't show signs of improvement she may have to go to the hospital in Winchester."

"Are the rest of us in danger?"

"I'm not sure. I'll know in a two or three days. If no one else is ill it seems to be contained in

Lottie. I'll leave instructions for cleaning the house. Most important is to boil all water used for drinking and cooking. Everyone is to wash their hands before handling any food."

"Do you think it was the food Mrs. Johnson brought?"

"That is a possibility. I'll pay a visit to her after we get Lottie cared for."

Addie was a strong young woman but the enormity of this caused tears to surface. "It's very serious, isn't it?" she whispered.

"I wish she had recovered her strength from the birth before this hit," was his response.

"I'll go find Caleb. He needs to know," said Addie.

"Of course he does. With Caleb's help, I can get Lottie into the back seat of my car and drive her to town. I'll write instructions while you get him."

Addie ran from Lottie's house in the direction of the barn. Troubled thoughts clouded her mind as she sped along the path. What if Lottie dies? If only Fannie were here. "Damn you, Jess Edwards!" Addie shouted as she ran.

Chapter 20

Fannie felt something was wrong. She didn't know what. But, when she went back to the train there was no sign of Ota.

"Where do you think she is, Jess? The train is going to leave in ten minutes."

"Fannie. You have to realize she is sixteen and not your concern. She'll be back in time to leave unless she's found something else to keep her here."

"That's what bothersome. She hasn't seen much of anything outside of that little place where she grew up in Kentucky. She could easily be led astray."

He linked his arm through Fannie's. "Come on. Ota has a ticket that will take her to California. If she wants to go, she'll get there. We need to get aboard."

Fannie looked about before she went up the iron steps. "I hope something hasn't happened to her."

Jess guided his wife up the steps and through the aisle. She took her seat by a window and craned her neck to see the station platform. There was no sign of Ota Lee Henry.

Chapter 21

The next morning, Fannie and Jess were in the dining car.

"Did you get any sleep?" he asked. "You look a little bleary-eyed."

"Thank you. That makes me feel good."

"Sorry. You have got to stop worrying about Ota Lee."

"It's not only Ota, Jess. I feel something else is wrong."

"What could that be? One more stop in San Bernardino and we'll be on the last leg of this trip before we pull into Los Angeles. We've had a smooth ride so far."

"I don't know what it is, it's like something isn't right. I can't explain it. It's an uneasy feeling I have."

The waiter brought them coffee and took their orders for breakfast. Fannie ordered toast only. She didn't have an appetite.

"Maybe I just have the jitters about what we're going to find once we get to Los Angeles."

He smiled at her over his cup of coffee. "That could explain your unsettled feeling."

**

The train crossed the state line into California where Fannie looked out the window. The scenery didn't look any different. It was flat country with sparse vegetation and mountains in the distance. But, Fannie had seen pictures of the long state and hoped the scenery would change as they traveled farther north. Hills and trees would be nice.

It was early evening when they reached their final stop. Los Angeles was a large city with over 300,000 people. Fannie knew because she read a sign that said so. The minute they stepped off the train they saw trolleys, cabs, delivery trucks, automobiles and people, people, people.

"Here we are, Fannie, my love. Our future awaits," said a glowing Jess.

Fannie looked about on the train platform as Jess retrieved their suitcases. It was sunny, warm with a pleasant breeze. Los Angeles had a far different feel than Washington, D.C.

"I'm going into the women's area, Jess."

"Go ahead. I'll inquire about a hotel for the night."

Fannie washed her face and hands and was repositioning her straw hat when her mouth went agape. In the mirror she saw Ota Lee Henry coming through the door followed was a tall, stout young woman with rosy cheeks, a creamy complexion. She wore her blonde hair in braids wound around her head.

"Ota!" exclaimed Fannie as she turned around. "Where have you been? I was worried about you."

"That's right nice of you, Miz' Fannie. This is Greta Olson. We met in Las Vegas when we had that long stop. Greta this is Mrs. Fannie Edwards. She's the one I told you about who saved me from my Aunt Emma."

"It's nice to meet you, Greta."

The shy Greta blushed as she gave a slight curtsy and answered in a soft voice, "Thank you, ma'am."

Even though Fannie was glad to see Ota, she was chagrined that the teen had not made any attempt to contact her after the train left Las Vegas. "Why didn't you let me know you were back on the train? It would have saved me some anxious hours."

"I didn't think about that. I guess I should have, but Greta had a hamper of food so we didn't need to go into the dining car or back to where you and Mr. Jess rode."

"What are your plans now?"

"Greta's cousin wrote that she needs helpers to wash dishes, clean her eating place, help cook food, and those kind of chores."

"Do you know your cousin, Greta?"

Greta looked young like Ota, but she was a good head taller and pounds heavier.

"Yes, ma'am. She and her husband lived with us until she came out here last year."

Her answer satisfied Fannie. "That's good to hear."

"Don't worry about me, Miz' Fannie," Ota said as if reading Fannie's thoughts. "I learnt what to look for since we went to Aunt Emma's."

Fannie still had questions. "Where are you going to stay? This is a big city?"

Greta's got five dollars for a hotel room. Tomorrow we'll go to her cousin's place."

Fannie reached into her purse and took out a five dollar bill. "Here, Ota. Now you each have five dollars."

Both of the teens held wide smiles. "Miz' Fannie, you might need that money. Where are you going to stay?"

"I guess that's up to Jess. I am so glad I have seen you, Ota. I wish you both well."

"You too, Miz' Fannie."

Fannie left the women's area excited to tell Jess what had just occurred.

"I told you she'd make it here if she wanted to."

"I was annoyed she didn't try to find us on the train."

"She's sixteen, Fannie. Teenagers don't always think. You did the right thing by saving her from Fat Emma."

"That's an awful name, Jess."

"She's an awful woman," he replied.

The hotel was five blocks from the train station. Fannie and Jess had walked in the balmy evening, which had been a welcome change from the train seats they had occupied for a week.

There was no elevator so Jess carried their suitcases up three flights of stairs. Fannie felt like she was back in the boarding house in Washington.

The room held only a bed and dresser but it had its own bathroom with hot and cold running water. The tin tub wasn't any bigger than a round laundry tub. Fannie was grateful to take a bath and rinse out a few articles of clothing she had worn for three days.

Jess opened a window because the room felt a bit stuffy. All that accomplished was bringing in the sounds of street noise. So, he closed the window and they put up with the closeness of the air. The two worn out travelers were too tired to care and slept through the night.

Chapter 22

Jess found a small café where they sat eating breakfast.

Fannie liked the feel of clean clothes. She wore a long sleeved white blouse with a high collar and a royal blue cotton skirt. Jess was in his usual comfortable cowboy attire.

"What are we going to do today?" she asked.

"I talked with a few people at the hotel. They said jobs were good in Hollywood because the place is growing and there are needs for carpenters, painters, groundkeepers."

Fannie interrupted him. "I haven't seen many grounds to keep up."

"This is the heart of the city. The Hollywood area is not as populated but it's growing every day, so they say. There's a trolley that goes out."

"That's encouraging," remarked Fannie.

Jess reached over and patted her hand. "It'll be good, sweetheart. You'll see."

"I'd like to call Addie. She said I could reverse the charges. How are we doing for money?"

"I'm down to seventeen dollars. That should get us a room for a week and some grub."

"And trolley fare?"

"And trolley fare. If the jobs are as plentiful as they say, I'll have a job tomorrow."

"And if they aren't?"

Jess pulled his hand back and sent an annoyed look. "It's not like you to be down, Fannie. What is it?"

Her intense eyes looked directly at him. "I don't know, Jess. I wish I did."

He sat back in his chair in silence.

Fannie took another sip of coffee.

After a pause he suggested, "Although I'd rather you didn't, call Addie. Then we can get on with the rest of our day."

Fannie thought it over. "No, Jess. I'll try to be better company. Maybe I'm homesick. I've never felt homesick before. I'll call Addie once we are settled and I can pay for the phone call myself."

His expression brightened. "I like that idea. How much of your reserve money do you have left?"

She may as well be honest. "Twenty-five dollars. I gave five to Ota."

He chuckled and shook his head. "And you were the one worried about money."

The owner of the café directed them to the trolley stop. He wasn't sure what time it ran because, according to him, "no set schedule". They walked a few blocks, sat on a short wood bench and waited for over an hour. Fannie was glad she wore the long sleeves because the sun was hot and her fair skin burned easily. She wished she had an umbrella. Perhaps the rim of her hat would shade her face enough.

Fannie saw palm trees swaying in the slight breeze. Here in California the sky seemed bluer, the sun nearer and the air drier. It was pleasant sitting next to Jess. He took her hand while they sat, neither saying a word, drinking in their new surroundings. Perhaps everything will work out.

The trolley stopped with the sign *Hollywood* above the front window. The green trolley with yellow lettering was without windows, open to the air. The fare of two dollars caused her to flinch. Trolley fare, the same amount they had paid for their hotel room? That meant Jess was down to fifteen dollars. Fannie thought their money wouldn't last long at this rate.

The ride from Los Angeles lasted over an hour winding its way through the brushy country on the single trolley track. The trolley car was full of passengers: men of all ages and dress, a few couples, a group of four young women wearing more makeup than was proper.

The four sat giggling and laughing and having a gay old time. The one next to Jess looked at him. "I'll bet it was hard for you to squeeze into that seat. They don't make trolley seats for big good looking men like you."

Jess gave a quiet embarrassed smile.

"We're coming out to be in the moving pictures. Are you?"

"No, I'll be working out here," he said.

Fannie looked over at the young woman who, under all that makeup, appeared to be in her late teens.

The glib young woman looked at Fannie. "With that red hair and green eyes you must be Irish."

Fannie was annoyed by her boldness but she offered a stiff smile.

The girl's attention went back to jess. "You look like a cowboy with that hat and those boots. Do you know how to ride horses?"

Jess nodded.

With a coy smile, she said, "I do like cowboys."

That was enough open flirting for Fannie. Her eyes flashed and bore into Miss Flirty Girl. "So do I!"

The three companions laughed aloud. Fannie heard one of them say, "Behave yourself, Darla, or you may get yourself in trouble."

Darla's apology was half-hearted. "I didn't mean nothin'." She settled back and giggled with her giddy friends.

The trolley stopped on Hollywood Boulevard. There were hills in the distance, signs of construction in every direction, and a sizable town.

"We'll see if there's a local paper. Places for rent may be advertised," Jess suggested.

There were electric and telephone lines along the streets, which gave Fannie an inward smile. She could call Addie.

As they walked along the sidewalk there were signs in store windows advertising places to rent. Most of them were three dollars a night or by the month.

"Here's one with a stove, ice box and use of laundry tubs," said Jess. "Seven dollars a week, just outside of town. Shall we try that?"

Just outside of town was over a mile and up an incline. By the time they reached the older

109

Spanish style, adobe house with red tile roof Fannie was hot, sweaty, and her feet hurt.

Jess rang the bell, which was opened by a little lady unmistakably of Spanish descent.

"Hola," said Jess causing Fannie's head to jerk in his direction.

He pointed to the copy of the rental ad he had taken from the store window. The little woman nodded and motioned with a finger for them to follow. They followed her under a trellis, heavy with ivy, to the back of the small house.

The diminutive Spanish woman, dressed in an ankle length black skirt and unshaped black top, opened a heavy wood door with a large key.

The room was cooler inside. A colorful tiled floor with sporadic designs reminded Fannie of pictures she'd seen of Mayan drawings. There were no windows, but there were thick, cubic, translucent panes of glass where light filtered in. This time of day the ray of sun shone on a small crucifix affixed to the adobe wall. Open vents at the tops of the walls allowed circulation. The one room was small but comfortable with a wood table, two straight chairs, and a worn sofa of navy blue velvet. No place to sleep but on the floor crossed Fannie's mind.

The stove was kerosene with two burners and the ice box held ice on one side and not much room for food on the other. Fannie wondered how long ice lasted in this heated climate. There was a small sink but no inside water pump.

Then came the surprise. The woman opened a small door that opened into a bedroom with an ornate large wood bed painted black with fine lines of gold trim and a dresser to match. The sheets and pillowcases were spotlessly white. Atop the bed there was no spread but a woven blanket of red, blue and cream colored yarns was folded at the foot.

Fannie looked at Jess, smiled and nodded her head.

The ad said room. Jess swept his hand to encompass both rooms. "All? Todas?" he asked in Spanish

"Si," the woman responded as she held out her hand palm out. "Siete."

Jess handed the woman seven one dollar bills.

She handed him the key and left her new renters standing in the bedroom wondering if they were as lucky as they thought they were. Seven dollars a week instead of twenty-one.

"I didn't know you could speak Spanish, Jess."

"I can't. A few words to get by."

"Doesn't she speak English?"

"If she does she isn't going to let us know yet."

"That doesn't make sense to me," said Fannie.

"Maybe she wants to feel us out; see if she can trust us."

Fannie shrugged. "I guess. I'm glad we didn't stay in the busy part even if we have a long walk to get places. It's a far cry from the Palmer House in Chicago."

"But not too far from the cabin in Virginia."

"At least we had water pumped into the kitchen in that cabin," she reminded him.

Jess kissed her. "I'll go look for a job tomorrow. Next week we can find a place with indoor plumbing."

"We'll take our time," Fannie replied. "It's good we bought that bread and peanut butter before we came out here. That will have to be supper and breakfast."

"Yeah," Jess agreed. "And we still have Peg's jerky."

Fannie slipped off her shoes. I'm going to rest. I'll empty the suitcases later."

"I'll go outside and look around."

Outside Jess found the well on a patio beside the house and the outhouse on the other side. The wooden structure leaned a bit on a slight incline. However, it looked solid.

The patio held a couple of benches with a pergola covered with vines. There was a pleasant balmy breeze that caused the swaying of stringed dried onions and red peppers hanging on a wood brace.

Jess sat on one of the benches. Had he done the right thing to bring Fannie three thousand miles where he had come on a whim? She was fair when she said she would give him two months. So far all had gone smoothly. Once he brings in some money, Fannie will feel better about this adventure, he was sure. That meant he had better get a job tomorrow.

Chapter 23

Jess left early the next morning. Fannie woke up later and stretched herself awake before she slid out of bed and felt the cool tile of the floor under her bare feet. Jess had told her the well was to the right and the outhouse to the left. She slid her feet into her walking shoes, left them untied, and threw a shawl over her long cotton nightgown. Who would see her but the old woman? They had passed only a few shacks on the way here, none near enough for anyone to see her traipse about. She wished she had lighter shoes but knew her crocheted slippers would bring in the sandy soil and probably irritate her feet in the process.

Never having been on a true vacation, Fannie thought this must be like being on one. But people on vacation probably had a good supply of money, which was not the case of Jess and Fannie Edwards. Another thought popped into her mind. Maybe this will be like a vacation to Jess and he'll be ready to return home before long. At least long enough to satisfy that itchy foot he said he's always had.

All that thinking aside, Fannie knew she needed to call Addie today. The nagging feeling of the past couple of days had persisted. Talking to Addie may be exactly what would push that feeling away.

The loaf of bread and jar of peanut butter had been opened, which meant Jess had made a couple of sandwiches. Pieces of the jerky were gone also. He left a pail of water by the sink and there were pottery pieces and utensils to use. She poured a mug of water and slaked her dry throat.

Fannie was still full from tortillas and a mixture of beans and rice left at their door last evening. They had heard the bell outside ring and found the food when they opened the door. The quiet landlady was nowhere to be seen. The remembrance of the kind gesture brought a smile to Fannie's face.

She put on the plain cotton dress Lottie had sewed together on that fancy sewing machine she had been given. The dress was wrinkled but clean. Perhaps Jess wouldn't approve of her walking into the busy part of the place by herself. However, she would risk his disapproval because she had to talk to Addie.

Fannie was pleased to find she had packed a small umbrella. The rim was narrow yet wide enough to keep the sun off her already sun-tinged face. She pinned on her straw hat and covered her hands with white cotton gloves. The California sun did not agree with her complexion.

Fannie locked the door and dropped the key into the tote bag she carried. She left to walk down to the busy town. An annex of Los Angeles, it was becoming big enough to be a city of its own.

She knew the way they had walked the day before and remembered a hotel that advertised a pay telephone.

The road from town was no wider than a lane big enough for a wagon or a car. This part of California was strange with none of the trees she was familiar with like the tall black cherry, elms, and sycamores. There were plenty of neat rows of orange, grapefruit and lemon groves. Pine trees and shorter trees she couldn't name dotted the hills behind. Cactus and sagebrush grew in the dry soil. Fannie admired the wild clematis and morning glories that wound their tentacles up the fences along the road. These did remind her of home in Virginia.

Close to town she passed a lady selling melons, dates and avocados. She had never eaten an avocado and dates were expensive in Mr. White's general store in Berryville. Would it be worth some of her reserve money to buy these on her way back to the adobe house?

There had to be people with money in Hollywood because there were some big mansions in the town and in the hills surrounding it. On Hollywood Boulevard she stopped at a black wrought-iron fence to admire a lovely two-story Victorian. The center of the mansion reminded her of a silo with rounded metal roof, while long wings of the house extended from each side. The rounded section was much prettier than a silo and had windows. There was a lady rocking in a rocker on a covered balcony and a fancy black car was parked in the circular driveway. What would it be like to live in a house like that, she wondered.

Fannie turned from the sight and continued walking. The house reminded her of some she had seen in Washington. As she felt tears welling up, she picked up the pace and hurried to the hotel that had a pay telephone.

The pay telephone was a phone set in a tight closet-like area. She would make the call, the operator would tell her the cost, and she would pay the hotel owner. He said a call to the East was usually a dollar a minute. Fannie would have to talk fast.

The telephone sat on a narrow shelf. A stool allowed her to sit after she closed the narrow door, careful not to catch the skirt of her dress as she closed it. Fannie picked up the receiver and held it to her ear and gave the operator Addie's number in Virginia.

Ring, ring, ring. "Hello."

"Addie?"

"Oh, dear God, Fannie! Where are you?"

"In California, a place called Hollywood outside Los Angeles."

"Isn't that where they make movies?"

"I guess. Addie, I can't talk long. We have found a place to stay. I'll write and give you the address. How are things at home?"

The hurried, worried voice of Addie caught Fannie by surprise. "Lottie's sick. The doctor isn't sure but it may be typhoid fever. She's at the Hawthorne House under quarantine. We had to soak her bedding and clothing in a solution of carbolic acid. We burned some of it, and I had Alex burn down their outhouse and put up another one."

Fannie sucked in a deep breath. "I knew something wasn't right. Is anyone else sick?"

116

"No, but Crystal is worried that she might get it. I wouldn't be surprised if she and Nate didn't just pack up and leave."

"It's not like you to be so upset, Addie. I wish I was there to help."

"But you aren't and I blame Jess for that!"

"It isn't his fault, Addie. I agreed to come out here."

Addie's voice softened. "I know. I do miss you, Fannie. Do you like it out there?"

"I haven't been here long enough to know. It's different, everything is strange. Look, I can't talk long because it's expensive. I'll write and you can tell me how things are going. Poor Lottie. What about the baby?"

"I brought him here to the house. Peg and I are taking care of him."

"I don't even know the baby's name, Addie. Lottie and Caleb hadn't named him before we left."

Addie chuckled. "Francis Edwards Dunn. They named him for you and Jess."

It was Fannie's turn to chuckle. "I'll tell Jess. Addie, it is so good to hear your voice. I will say a prayer for Lottie and Caleb. He must be in turmoil."

"Caleb keeps going, but I know he is terribly worried. Dr. Burke wasn't overly optimistic when he drove away. I should hear from him tomorrow. God keep you, Fannie."

"Goodbye, dear friend."

Fannie had to sit on the stool for a minute to be sure her legs would support her. The news from Addie had drained her strength.

Once outside in the sunshine, the world seemed brighter. Fannie opened her umbrella to begin the long walk back. What will Jess think of the news she had heard?

Fannie stopped at a store and bought a small jar of dried beef and a package of powdered milk. There was no ice in the icebox so it was useless to buy anything that needed refrigeration. They would have chipped beef sandwiches for supper. And she would buy a melon on the way home, maybe even some dates. Her money was dwindling.

Jess had better come home with a job!

Chapter 24

Jess had been disappointed at the news of Lottie's illness. It overshadowed his good news of finding a job as a carpenter. "There isn't anything we can do, Fannie. Even if we were there, she would still be sick," he'd said.

Fannie knew that was true, but did he not realize their presence would be a comfort to those on the farm? Why are a man's feelings so different from a woman's? Or is it relief not to be in the middle of the upset? It seemed Fannie's mind was always working with questions.

She was alone in the house pondering that question when there was a knock at the door. Jess had gone to work. She opened the heavy door expecting to see the old woman and gasped at the vision of a bronze-complectioned, handsome man looking at her. He was dressed in black with a wide silver belt and silver band around the black hat he wore. The silver spurs on his boots glistened in the sunlight as did his pearly white teeth when he smiled. His jewelry was a silver necklace, peeking out from his open shirt collar, a silver cuff bracelet and turquoise ring.

He touched his wide-brimmed hat. With an accent in his speech, he said, "Hello. I'm sorry to bother you. My name is Gabriel Flores. I heard my mother had rented this part of the house. I thought it wise to meet the renters."

Fannie, who was never at a loss for words, was awestruck. When she recovered, her first words were, "You speak English." She could feel the rising heat of her embarrassment and hoped it didn't show on her pink sun-tinged face.

He laughed. "I also speak Spanish."

"My husband isn't home. Would you care for a drink of water?"

"I would. We can sit out here on the patio."

Fannie wasn't one to feel nervous, but she did. She poured two mugs of water and willed her hands not to shake as she carried them to where he sat.

Fannie took a seat on the opposite bench.

He took a good drink before he said, "I own a ranch about ten miles (pointing with his finger) that way. I have asked my mother to come live there but she refuses, so I have to make the trip to check on her. This has always been her home."

"You must have placed the ad for the apartment," surmised Fannie.

He nodded. "I did. She neither reads nor writes. But, don't let her fool you. She understands English quite well and can speak some. However, she prefers her native language."

Fannie chuckled, feeling more relaxed. "My husband speaks a little Spanish. I'm Fannie Edwards from Virginia. Actually, I grew up in Washington."

"The Capitol, not the state?"

"That's right," she answered.

He removed his hat and ran his fingers through thick wavy black hair. "What are you doing way out here?"

"Jess, that's my husband, had a yen to come out."

He smiled. "A yen?"

"That's what he called it. He likes to see different places." Egads, was she sounding like those ditsy teenagers?

"I'm sure you find this much different from Virginia, Mrs. Edwards."

"A whole new world."

"When can I meet your husband?"

"I'm not sure when he will be home. He started work as a carpenter today."

"That's his occupation?"

"My husband is a man of many talents."

He smiled that wide pleasant smile. "You are proud of him."

Fannie had never thought of that before, but she liked the sound of it. "I am."

"Are you satisfied with this apartment? There is much competition for rentals in town. I wish my mother would give up this idea of making her own money. The rent is priced to make up for the inconvenience of being so far from town."

Any tension Fannie felt was gone. "Perhaps you should set the rent higher. If your mother doesn't have a renter, she would have to come and live with you."

"I have thought of that. I have also thought it would not be a nice way to treat my mother. She has friends in the area who help watch out for her, and she can walk to the little chapel."

"I haven't seen a chapel," said Fannie.

"It's over the hill. A priest comes out on Sunday."

Gabriel finished his mug of water and handed the empty cup to her. "Thank you for the drink," he said as he replaced his hat. "I'll be on my way."

With a slight bow, he said, "Mrs. Edwards, it was my pleasure to meet you. It appears I will not have to worry about the renters my mother has chosen."

"I wish you could have met Jess."

"So do I. One day you will both come out to the ranch for dinner."

Fannie shook her head. "If you live ten miles away that isn't likely."

"I'll send one of the hands out to give you a ride."

The thought appealed to Fannie. "Your mother will come also."

"If you can get her to come. I'll send a note."

He whistled through his teeth and a sleek black horse appeared with as much silver on his bridle as its owner wore. This man who had thoroughly rattled the usual collected Fannie, swung into the tooled leather saddle and waved as he galloped away.

Fannie stood with her mouth agape. Wait until Jess hears about this!

Chapter 25

The next morning Jess was having a cup of coffee on the patio before heading for work. Fannie joined him.

"I've been thinking about what you told me. Are you sure the man who came yesterday is the old woman's son?"

"Of course. Who else could he be?"

"I don't know, but it doesn't seem to fit."

"What doesn't seem to fit, Jess? He came out to check on his mother and her new renters. Why else would he come if he isn't her son?"

"How do you know he checked in on her?"

"I don't. I took his word for it. He's a nice man, Jess. Why are you doubting?"

He shrugged a shoulder. "I don't know. But, we have a landlady who keeps to herself and only answers questions in one word. You said the man speaks excellent English. Maybe it isn't good for you and the old woman to be out here by yourselves."

She sat the coffee mug on the bench beside her. "Don't make me uneasy. I've never heard you talk this way."

"We've only lived at Lockwood. There were always friends around. Living here is foreign to us until we get to know the place. There are people drifting in from all over."

Fannie was miffed. "Don't forget, Jess. It was your big idea to come here. I grew up in a big city so I am used to a lot of different people. I know how to be cautious."

He nodded. "I guess it would help if we were closer to town."

"Gabriel said his mother has always lived here so I don't believe there is anything to be concerned about. You ought to get a horse."

"Gabriel?" He chuckled.

"That's what he asked me to call him."

"And, he calls you Fannie, I suppose."

"I didn't exchange that curtesy. You sound jealous."

Jess winked at her. "Maybe he'll give me a horse from that ranch of his, if there is one." Jess stood from the bench. "I'd better be on my way. Fannie, my love, I get paid today."

"Finally, some good news!" She threw her arms around his neck and kissed him soundly. "Don't worry about me, Jess. I feel comfortable out here. Mrs. Flores is out in her garden every day. Maybe I'll go out to help her and find out if she has a son named Gabriel."

He laughed aloud. "That should be fun."

"Her son says she understands English. How do you say son in Spanish, Jess?"

He shook his head. "I wish I knew. Good luck. You can fill me in when I get home."

Fannie smiled as she watched her big strong Jess walk down the long narrow road that led to town.

124

She had been sitting in her cotton nightgown. The sun was up and it was going to be hot. Fannie took the empty coffee mugs into the house.

She slipped a plain, gray, one-piece dress over her head. The material was lighter than her green and she didn't want to wear a waist and skirt to dig in dirt. The dress was simple, no buttons, snaps, or hooks. Over the dress she put the flowered apron Addie bought at Coyner's store and given to her as a going away present. She could hear Addie's words as though she were standing next to her. "You'll need a pretty apron, Fannie."

She missed her good friend, but didn't want to get maudlin. Instead, she stuck a cloth into a pocket of the apron, placed the straw hat on her head and went to see if the old woman was out in her garden. On the way, Fannie picked up a small trowel that lay on the patio and put that into the other pocket of her apron.

The neat garden was to the right of the adobe house. The old woman was out there dressed head to toe in her usual black garb and large straw hat that shaded her body from the sun. The old woman looked up when Fannie appeared then went back to her work without a word or sign of acknowledgement.

Fannie was determined. She went to the woman, tapped her on the shoulder and showed her the trowel. "I came to help you."

Still silent, the woman got to her feet and left the garden.

What had Fannie done? She stood there with a puzzled look on her face. Well, Fannie came to help in the garden so she took her little excuse for a spade and started digging.

A few minutes later the old woman came back. She carried a huge straw hat with a brim that must have been a foot wide. She also carried a pair of worn leather slippers that looked like moccasins. The woman walked to Fannie, held them out and motioned for her to put them on.

Maria Flores stood to watch as Fannie untied her leather shoes, rolled down her cotton stockings and placed them inside her shoes. She put on the moccasins and replaced her straw hat with the one Maria had brought. The old woman nodded and returned to where she had been working before Fannie arrived.

The hat fell on her forehead and covered her ears, but it definitely shaded her from the unrelenting sun.

Still silent, the woman motioned Fannie to follow her to where some vines were growing along the ground. The old woman was good at gesturing. Fannie understood she was to straighten out wines that had become entangled so she set to work.

Her mind wandered as she busied herself with the vines. Lottie loved her garden at Lockwood and she had taught Fannie, the city girl, much about caring for one. How was Lottie? How was Caleb? And the children? How was Addie? Fannie shook her head to get rid of the troublesome thoughts running through her mind.

She stood from her crouched position and stretched. The vines looked much better. She spied a weed and bent to pluck it when something jumped out from under a leaf and caused her to jump and shriek.

The old woman looked over, saw what had startled Fannie and laughed aloud. She came, picked up the horny toad in her hand and said, "No hurt."

Fannie was not about to touch the ugly little monster. "It surprised me," she said. "Is Gabriel your son?"

The wrinkled face smiled at her. "Gabriel?" Then she nodded.

"I like him," Fannie said. "He told me you understand much English."

The woman shrugged and waved her hand back and forth.

"Maybe I can learn much Spanish."

The old woman laughed again and shook her head.

"I can try."

They went back to work. The melons were growing. There were rows of onions, okra, cucumbers, beans, potatoes, and a bed of strawberries.

The old woman picked up two baskets, gave one to Fannie and they picked what was ripe of the berries.

By two o'clock it was too hot to stay in the garden. The old woman gave Fannie one of the baskets of berries, a few onions and a couple of cucumbers.

Fannie shook her head. "No, these are yours. I just wanted to help."

"Take," the woman insisted. "Tomorrow you help too."

127

Oh, oh, thought Fannie. What have I got myself into?

Chapter 26

Dr. Burke called Addie on the second day of Lottie's quarantine in a room at the Hawthorne House.

"I have taken a sample up to the hospital in Winchester. The laboratory should be able to discern if Lottie's condition is typhoid. Until I get the results, I will keep her here."

"How is she doing? What shall I tell her husband?"

"The fever has reduced, so that is good news. We are giving her only tea and she has been able to keep some crackers down. Her intestinal complaints remain. I am hoping for a turn around, but I am not optimistic."

"I assume no one can visit her until you get results from Winchester."

"That's the way it is. Is there any other sickness at the farm?"

"No. We have brought the baby here to the house. Crystal, Peg and I have followed your instructions."

"Good. It is better to be on the safe than sorry side. Remind everyone that hand washing is very important. I am taking a trip out to Mrs. Johnson's place today."

Addie felt better when she hung up the receiver of the phone. She knew Dr. Burke was being cautious regarding Lottie's condition. That was all right with her. She would go find Caleb and tell him the fever was less and tests were being done. She wouldn't tell him the rest.

Caleb was throwing hay to the cattle in the pen near the barn. "Hey, Addie."

"Hi, Caleb. I just got off the phone with Dr. Burke. He said Lottie's fever is down."

Caleb continued to throw the hay from a pitchfork. "What else did he say? That she's going to be back home and back to her old self in a week?"

"Caleb it's not like you to be sarcastic."

He leaned the pitchfork against the fence and pushed his hat back with his gloved hand. "I'm worried, Addie. I know how sick she is. We went through that bout when she had pneumonia in Colorado. She was lucky to survive that."

There was a breeze and Addie brushed her honey-brown hair back from her face. "I haven't forgotten."

"And, now I've got three young ones. How am I going to take care of them if she doesn't get better?"

"Don't think that way, Caleb."

"I have to. Having her gone, not being able to see her tears my heart apart. I try not to let my feelings get in the way, but it hurts, Addie, it hurts a lot."

What could she say? She felt the same way. "Is Crystal doing well at taking care of the children and keeping the house?"

He nodded. Then he sighed and cleared his throat. "She's still worried she might get what Lottie has. And, Nate is doing what I ask, but he isn't Jess. Jess knew what to do without me having to tell him. Have you heard from Fannie?"

Thankfully they were off the subject of Lottie. "Fannie called me two days ago. They are in California and have found a place to stay. She couldn't talk long because long distance calling is expensive."

He picked up the fork and resumed feeding. "I expect."

"Are you angry with Jess for leaving?" Addie had to ask.

"No. I wish he hadn't gone, but I know Jess, and he had to satisfy his urge to try and find something different. That's just the way he is."

"I was angry with him," Addie admitted. "Part of that was being selfish, I guess. Do you think they'll come back?"

He shook his head, "I truly don't know."

Addie turned to go.

"Addie, thanks for coming down to tell me. I didn't mean to sound so down."

She smiled at him. "I would be disappointed if you weren't."

Chapter 27

Fannie sat at the wood table in the adobe with pencil and paper before her. It was time she wrote to Addie. She was supposed to put a return address in the body of the letter. How could she do that when she didn't know what it was? It hadn't been in the ad for the rental. The ad had only given directions how to get here. If Mrs. Flores didn't read or write there was no need to ask her.

Fannie decided to write the letter. When Jess came home, he could either tell her the address or take the letter into the post office and ask.

Fannie poured a cup of tea from the ice box. With Jess's pay, he had sent the ice truck with a chunk for the ice box.

The delivery man had unwrapped the block of ice from burlap and carried it in with ice tongs, dripping drops of water across the tile floor. "Ain't been out here for a year," he'd said. "Lady who used to stay here moved or died. I ain't sure which." He'd placed the block in the side of the ice box and chipped off a few pieces so it fit. Then he handed her an ice pick, "You might need this," he said and went out the door.

Fannie used the pick to chip some pieces into her tea. She took the tea mug along with the pencil and paper to the patio to write her letter. It was more pleasant to sit outside in the balmy breeze than in the house.

Dear Addie,

I am sitting on a small patio underneath a trellis of ivy here on the 15th of June.

First, I must tell you how distressing it was to hear of Lottie's illness. I am here by myself when I could be there helping in some way, if only to sit and discuss the sorry state of affairs at the Dunn house.

The trip out here was long and hot most of the time. It seemed once we left Chicago all the scenery was flat and dusty. There were always mountains in the distance.

After Chicago, where we stayed at the exclusive Palmer House, our stops were in: Cheyenne, Ogden, Salt Lake City, Las Vegas, San Bernardino, and finally Los Angeles. You know the states where those places are.

We found a two room rental in the back of an adobe house, over a mile from Hollywood, and the landlady is an old Spanish woman who neither reads nor writes. She does understand some English. It it not easy to communicate with her, but she is a master at gesturing.

Her son stopped by the other day to check on her and check out the renters. Jess wasn't here. He has a job in town as a carpenter. Addie, this place is growing at a fast pace. It is also more expensive living here.

Anyway, to get back to the son, he is probably around the age of Alex. I thought my knees were going to give way when I answered the knock at the door and saw him standing there. He is a handsome man with a commanding presence. He owns a ranch about ten miles from here and has invited Jess and me to dinner. We don't have the invitation yet, but he seemed sincere.

Jess laughed when I told him about the visit. He doubts if the man owns a ranch, and he doubted if he was the old woman's son, One day I helped her in the garden and she affirmed that he is. His name is Gabriel Flores.

Jess did make me a bit uneasy before I knew he was the son. Living so far from town there is no one around except Mrs. Flores and me. She has lived here all her life and is still alive so I guess I have nothing to worry about.

The sun is not kind to my skin. I cover up as many exposed areas as I can. I don't know if it ever rains out here. I haven't seen any sign of even one drop.

The old woman tends her garden every day. Vegetables, fruits and flowers grow in abundance. Water is scarce, however, and we carry water to the garden. I have been here over a week and have yet to take a bath in a tub. We have no indoor plumbing. Jess says he can fix up an outdoor shower. I'm not sure how he thinks he's going to do it. I am not going to take a shower in cold water out of the well.

I must stop because Jess will be coming home soon. It's almost too hot to cook. He fixed up a stone outdoor fireplace where I can cook vegetables and some meat. The inside of this adobe stays pleasant so I don't want to fire up the kerosene stove to heat the room up. The kerosene two-burner is a surprise as there are no other conveniences.

I am in good spirits and rather like discovering new things. Certainly, I will keep you informed as life unfolds.

Meanwhile, I pray fervently for our Lottie.

Gabriel says there is a small chapel that his mother attends. Perhaps I will go along with her one day.

Addie, know that I miss Lockwood and all the people there. Please give them my best regards. I am in hopes that Jess will miss it also. At this time, I see no signs of disappointment on his part.

Your friend,
Fannie

Fannie placed the letter in the envelope and addressed it to Addie at Lockwood Farm, Berryville, Virginia. She wished she could travel right back with it.

Chapter 28

On Sunday morning a cart pulled by a pony drove up to the adobe house. Jess and Fannie were having coffee on the patio. They watched the old woman come to the cart and walk beside it as the driver guided the pony to the garden.

The driver appeared to be a younger version of the landlady. She jumped off the seat and helped Mrs. Flores load the yields of the carefully tended garden.

"I wonder where she's going with that," mused Fannie.

"She's probably got people to give it to," suggested Jess.

"I wonder where they are. I haven't seen anyone coming or going."

When the cart was loaded, the younger woman helped the old woman up onto the seat then resumed her place as driver.

Jess and Fannie watched the cart as it went back to the road and turned in the opposite direction of the town. They kept it in their view until the cart wobbled out of sight over the high hill.

"I haven't been over that hill, Jess. Maybe we should take a walk and see what's over there."

"That's not a walk, Fannie; that's a hike."

"Let's take a hike. The morning is still comfortable. We'll be back before the sun gets too warm."

He grimaced. "I take a hike every day to and from town."

Fannie ignored him. "The chapel must be over there. I'd like to see it," she persisted.

Jess groaned. "All right. You may have to carry me back."

She laughed. "I'll roll you down the hill."

Fannie changed from the leather slippers she found comfortable into her cotton stockings and walking shoes and the loose-fitting gray dress. As an afterthought, she placed a religious medal around her neck.

Once outside she put on the big straw hat the old woman had given her and felt prepared to keep the sun at bay.

"We'd better carry water and take the rest of Peg's jerky," said Jess. "I hate to see that go."

"Do you miss Lockwood, Jess?"

He shook his head. "Not yet."

They walked leisurely along the narrow hard-packed road. There was a slight breeze as there usually was. Jess said it was from the ocean, which Fannie had yet to see.

The climb up the high hill was taxing, but their reward was at the top where they saw a valley below. They espied the small chapel with a cross on top in the center of a village. Scattered about were adobe houses that looked more like huts.

Fannie sucked in her breath. "I didn't expect this."

"What do you think, Mrs. Edwards? Shall we venture down?"

"I don't know, Jess. Don't you think it strange that we haven't seen these people coming and going on the road? What if they don't want us to come in uninvited?"

"The old woman's down there. She isn't going to let anything happen to her renters. Besides, I don't think they'd have a chapel if they are unfriendly. You're Catholic, Fannie. Maybe that will give us some positive points."

"I haven't been to church since I moved out of the city. There is no Catholic church in Berryville. I would love to see inside the chapel."

"So would I."

The going was easier on the downhill side. When they reached the bottom there were many carts and varieties of goods laid out on colorful blankets on the sandy ground. Children were running and playing and stopped to watch them. Adults looked up as Jess and Fannie walked by but gave no indication they saw them.

The women were dressed like their landlady; the men in loose white collarless shirts and baggy trousers. And, similar to the old woman they did not let their emotions show on their faces.

Did these people think the pair were intruders?

Fannie and Jess both smiled as they walked toward the chapel and the people went back to tending their wares.

When they reached the chapel, a priest was sitting outside on a bench under a tree, reading a book. He looked up at the pair as they neared.

"Hello," he greeted them, took off his glasses and set his book aside. He wore a cassock and wide straw hat. "We seldom get visitors. Welcome."

The Spanish padre like Gabriel Flores spoke very good English.

"We weren't sure we should come. I'm Jess Edwards and this is my wife, Fannie. We are renting over the other side of the hill. My wife had heard about the chapel and wanted to see it."

"Of course you are welcome. I come from town every Sunday to serve Mass." He was a head shorter and wider than Jess when he stood up from the bench. "You must be staying with Maria Flores."

Jess nodded.

"Her son, Gabriel, would rather she didn't rent, but she refuses to live with him and feels independent with some extra dollars. These are good people who are reluctant to give up the old ways."

"I have met Gabriel," informed Fannie. "I never expected to see this settlement. We've been here almost two weeks. Do the people not leave?"

"Once a month a few of the younger men go into town, do some trading and bring back the profits and supplies that are needed. On Sundays the people here bring what they have from their homes and trade among themselves: baskets, pottery, food, clothing, and such." He waved his hand to encompass the village. "Whatever they need is here."

"Without much money how do you keep the chapel going?" asked Jess.

"The people take care of it. Men can do repairs and the women keep it spotless. There is no plumbing or stove so there is no need for firewood or pipes to break or rust out. It is a place of worship. They even make the hosts and wine for communion."

Jess smiled at the man. "It sounds as though you have your own heaven here on earth."

"Close to it," answered the padre. "I do have to spend the week in the town, which is growing much too fast. This simple way of life here may not last. With what they call progress, the young people will get a taste of an easier life, or the evils that come with it; some slick land buyer will offer more money than these people ever heard of, and slowly it will dissolve."

"That's sad to think about," said Fannie.

"For now it is a restful place. We have a big meal after the trading is done and you are welcome to attend." He patted his round middle. "You can see they feed me well. Come, I'll take you inside."

They entered through one of the double wood doors that sat in an alcove under an arched entryway. There were six benches on either side of a central aisle and a high ceiling. As they looked toward the front they saw a kneeling rail and a plain altar.

The outside walls each held two stained glass windows depicting various saints. Behind and above the altar was a Rose window. Along the walls were Stations of the Cross. To the left of the altar was a small statue of Mary, holding the infant, Jesus. To the right a statue of Joseph.

"I see you wear Mary's medal," the priest said to Fannie.

"Yes, I am Catholic but I haven't been to church in almost a year."

"Because you chose not to go?"

"Oh, no. The church was too far away."

The Spanish padre offered a big smile. "Now you have one near. Can I expect to see you?"

"I would like that," said a sincere Fannie. "Before I leave, I would like to say a prayer for a dear friend who is sick."

"That's what our chapel is for," answered the priest as he and Jess turned to leave, and Fannie went to offer a prayer for dear Lottie.

The priest turned to Jess as they walked away. "And you, Mr. Edwards. Will you be coming with your wife?"

Jess chuckled and shook his head. "Not likely. Perhaps we can arrange for Fannie to come with Mrs. Flores."

"We shall miss seeing you. You will come to one of our celebrations?"

Jess couldn't help but grin. Was this priest trying to pull the heathen in? "That's a possibility."

Chapter 29

Finally a letter from Addie arrived. Jess carried it home from the post office in town. With a big smile he handed it to Fannie. "Fannie, my love, I bring you news from Virginia. That should put a smile on your pretty face."

Fannie grabbed the envelope from his outstretched hand. "Have you read the letter?"

"Of course I haven't. The honor is yours."

"I'm almost afraid to."

Jess was tired and hot from his long day at work and walk from town. "Let's read it out on the patio. I'll sit and listen."

"Go ahead out. I'll bring you a glass of water."

Jess wet his bandanna in the bowl by the sink and washed his face and hands while Fannie chipped off ice and put it in a tall pottery cup before she poured water into it.

Jess had been given two folding wood chairs with rattan seats by the people whose house he was helping to build. They said they didn't need them as they were buying new ones. It took two trips to carry them home, but he and Fannie knew they were a luxury they couldn't afford. They used the chairs on the patio.

Fannie opened the envelope with a mixture of delight and dread.

June 30, 1919

Dear Jess and Fannie,

I cannot express how happy we all were to receive your letter. It is good to know that you are settled.

The house you described must be quaint and comfortable. You also describe the weather as being sunny most of the time, so the lack of an indoor water pump is likely not a big drawback, although the lack of a tub for bathing must be a nuisance. Has Jess fixed up a shower for you?

As for Lottie, she is home. Dr. Burke said her condition was due to food poisoning not the typhoid we feared. I believe we could have saved ourselves a lot of work scouring everything in sight. Alex told me I was going too far burning down the outhouse, but I insisted. Lottie thinks the new one looks much better. I guess it was like a welcome home present.

When Dr. Burke made a trip to the Johnson place, he could see that drainage from their outhouse had seeped into the chicken pen.

It was a kind gesture of Mrs. Johnson to bring Lottie food, but the food was chicken soup.

I have seen the Johnson place. Those people are not the cleanest and that house still has a dirt floor. If I had been Lottie, I wouldn't have eaten anything she brought. But, you know Lottie. She didn't want to make the woman feel bad so she had some of the soup. It was enough to make her sick.

Dr. Burke also said that in Lottie's weakened condition the food poisoning was more severe. He honestly didn't expect her to pull through. She is still a skeleton of what she used to be. I want the old Lottie back and I will give her a wagon load of cookies if that is the answer.

We have kept the baby here at the big house. He is six weeks old and growing well. Peg or I take him down so Lottie can hold him. It is sad to see her cry when we leave. But, Crystal has stayed and it is too much for her to take care of Lottie, the two little ones and the house.

Enough of that. Now, what about this Gabriel? Have you received an invitation for dinner? Does he really own a ranch? You must write again to tell us of your adventures. I do envy that part of your trip, although I'm not sure I have forgiven Jess for dragging you out there, especially when I could have had your help with this trouble with Lottie.

Both Peg and Alex send their best thoughts. Peg says she misses the sound of those boots Jess wears coming up the back steps

I hope you are both doing well and we all look forward to your next letter.

Your forever friend,
Addie

"I knew Addie was miffed at me," said Jess. "You'd think she would be over it by now."

Fannie folded the letter and put it back in the envelope. "She's been worried about Lottie."

"As I said before, our being there wouldn't have prevented Lottie from getting sick. What about Gabriel? You had to tell Addie about him?"

Fannie shrugged her shoulder. "Why not? His visit was one of the most surprising things that has happened since we arrived."

"He hasn't invited us to dinner, yet, has he?" He scoffed, "Dinner on that big ranch of his."

"I can only repeat what he said. If we get an invitation, I'll go by myself."

"Walk ten miles to have dinner in a house likely just like this one?"

Fannie shot a disgusted look. "You might be surprised, Jess Edwards."

He took the last drink of cold water from his tall cup. "I think I'll take a short nap."

While Jess took a nap, Fannie went to start a fire in the outdoor fireplace. She was gathering dry brush when she saw a man, dressed like the men from the village over the hill, walking toward the house. She knew the old woman was inside but the man didn't go to the front of the house. He walked toward where she was getting the dry twigs for her fire.

He touched his big straw hat. "Buenos tardes, Senora." He held an envelope in his outstretched hand.

Fannie was startled by his presence, but she smiled and dropped the brush she had collected before she took the missive.

He touched his hat again, turned and left.

Fannie couldn't wait to open whatever it was the man had handed to her.

When she did, she found an invitation from Senor Gabriel Flores requesting the presence of

Jess and Fannie Edwards for dinner on the next Saturday. He would send a man at two o'clock to drive them out.

"Whoopee!" said Fannie aloud and threw the invitation up into the air. She picked it up from the ground along with the kindling she had found and hurried back to tell Jess.

This day was turning out to be one of the happiest she'd spent in a while.

Fannie was still in high spirits when she woke Jess up from his nap. She waved the invitation under his nose. "Guess what, Mr. Edwards. We are requested to attend dinner at the home of Senor Gabriel Flores next Saturday."

Jess took the invitation from her and perused it with care. "Looks legitimate to me," he said and playfully pulled Fannie onto his lap. "Did I ever doubt?"

Fannie laughed and kissed his tanned cheek. While Fannie was doing her best to protect her skin from the sun, Jess was getting darker by the day.

"I'd love to sit here all evening, Jess, but I need to get supper ready. Mrs. Flores gave us some corn and I'm going to fry up green tomatoes."

"Sounds good to me," he replied. "I work up an appetite."

Fannie rose from his lap. "How is the house coming?"

"It's huge. I think it could house four or five families. I'm not sure when it will be finished."

"Do you like what you're doing, Jess?"

"It's not my favorite form of employment, but it brings in money. Once we save up enough then I'll be able to look around for something else."

For some reason those words dampened her elation. Fannie began shucking ears of corn. "Look around for you don't know what. We've been here a month."

"Are you getting restless, Fannie?"

She pursed her lips and wrinkled her nose. "I don't know. It seems all I do aside from helping in the garden is cooking, doing the laundry, go to bed, get up, and do the same thing the next day."

"You did cooking and laundry at the farm."

"And, I had tea with Addie, or went over to Lottie's, or talked with Peg, or went into Berryville, or I could even take the train into Washington."

"You've met some people in the village. You could learn some of their skills. You could make baskets or learn to do pottery."

"Jess, you don't understand. They speak Spanish. Celebrating Mass with them is one thing, trying to converse with them is another."

"Maybe we should move closer to town."

Fannie looked over at her husband. No, he didn't understand. Fannie missed Lockwood farm and the people who lived there.

Chapter 30

Three days later was church. Fannie didn't ask to ride in with the woman who gave Mrs. Flores a ride in the cart. Fannie preferred to walk. The walk was good physical exercise along with letting her mind wander.

This was Fannie's third week attending the chapel. Women sat on the benches, men stood in the back and children knelt or sat on the wood floor. The chapel was crowded.

Father Jose's usual arrival was about noon. He celebrated Mass and that was followed with a big meal put on by the villagers, and to which Fannie was invited. As she didn't contribute to the meal, she was reluctant to eat. So she had left to return home.

This Sunday Father Jose caught her before she left and spoke softly. "Fannie you have not eaten at the meals."

"No, Father. I didn't feel right eating without bringing anything. I don't have an oven or I would bake a cake or bread or something."

"Not eating the food they've prepared makes them feel bad. It sets you apart as though you feel you are above them."

She felt the color rise in her cheeks. "That isn't true. I would love to join in their meal."

"Then stay and eat with us. I realize their language is not yours, but they understand a smiling face. Come, I'll be at your side. Maria usually sits with a small group and there are a couple in that group that speak enough English that you will feel comfortable."

Fannie sighed. "If you think I should, then I'll try, but I'm not so sure it's going to be comfortable."

He chuckled. "We never know until we try. There are plenty of wild flowers, Fannie. Next week you can bring a bouquet to put on the table. You'll feel like you're contributing and they will be pleased."

It was a thought. She walked beside the priest to where Maria Flores was seated. The padre told them in Spanish that Fannie was going to stay for the meal and explained why she had not stayed before.

Fannie couldn't understand what he was saying but his body language and their nodding seemed to mean they understood.

The younger woman who owned the cart came to stand beside Fannie. "You are welcome."

Fannie smiled at her and said, "Thank you."

Fannie thought the woman was in her thirties, but she found it difficult to tell ages except for the older women who walked with a stoop or smiled with wrinkled faces. And the young teens were easy to spot with their spirited ways, but between twenty and forty was not easy to tell. Many had children or maybe they were grandchildren, and their hardworking husbands were tanned and leathery from the heat and the sun.

The priest left the group to lead everyone in grace before the meal. Then Fannie went with the younger woman Father Jose had introduced as Rosetta.

"You speak some English," Fannie remarked.

Rosetta nodded. "Little," she said. She pointed at Fannie. "Espanol?"

Fannie shook her head and pointed her thumb down.

Rosetta laughed aloud. Those around them turned to look. Rosetta pointed her finger at Fannie and apparently told them Fannie did not speak Spanish. Then she aped Fannie's move of thumb down.

They all roared. Fannie wasn't sure if this was a good sign or a bad one. She looked at Rosetta, smiled and shrugged her shoulder.

Rosetta patted Fannie's hand, returned her smile and they filled their plates.

They ate in the small group of women who chatted among themselves. This was the way it had been with Addie and Lottie, thought Fannie. Women sharing their thoughts, trials and happy times.

Rosetta insisted that Fannie ride home in the cart with Maria, the landlady who had only smiled and laughed when Fannie was startled by the horny toad. Fannie wished she would smile more, but Maria was a serious person, which caused Fannie to wonder even more. Had something happened in her life to take away her smile?

The ride home was quiet. It was a pleasure not to walk after the big meal she had eaten. As they came over the hill Fannie looked down at the brown flat land and saw the town in the distance. Perhaps Jess was right about moving closer to town. At least in town she could talk to people.

Jess was on the patio when she arrived. "I heard the cart."

Fannie sat in the chair beside him. "Rosetta, she's the one with the cart, wanted me to ride and I didn't want to refuse. Father Jose told me I'd made them feel bad not staying for meals after Mass. So, I stayed and stuffed myself."

"Maybe I should go with you. I could use a big meal."

"You're not going to get one here," she replied. "I've been thinking about what you said about moving closer to town."

Jess rose from his chair and stretched. "I'll check around for a place we can afford while I'm there. I wouldn't miss that walk to and from. Right now I wish we had some of that bread you used to make."

"I wish I had an oven. As I think about it, in this climate I'm not too sure I'd want to heat it up. Jess, we should ask Maria to go to Gabriel's next Saturday."

"I don't think my Spanish is that good."

"Then I'll ask her while she's in the garden. Gabriel said she understands more than she lets on."

"Give it a try. What are we having for supper?"

Fannie left her chair. "I still have chicken in the ice box. If you'll start the fire, I'll cook that up with whatever is left over. I'm not that hungry."

Chapter 31

Maria Flores was in her garden. Fannie helped in the morning and quit before the heat of the afternoon sun. Maria worked at one end of the garden while Fannie worked at the other.

I might as well ask her now, thought Fannie. She rested the handle of the hoe on her shoulder as she walked to where Maria was chopping at some thick stalks. "Mrs. Flores."

The woman didn't stop or look at Fannie.

"Mrs. Flores," Fannie repeated in a louder voice. When this didn't get her attention, she tapped the old woman on the shoulder.

The woman stopped and looked at her.

"Your son, Gabriel, wants us to come to dinner next Saturday. He will send someone at two o'clock."

The old woman went back to chopping.

Fannie tapped her on the shoulder again. "Do you understand?" She could tell by the look on Maria's face that she was irritated.

"Si," she replied.

"Will you go?"

Maria shook her head and almost spat out the name, "Gabriel."

"He wants you to come."

Maria waved Fannie away with her hand and went back to work.

This reaction puzzled Fannie. It was clearly with distaste that the mother said her son's name. What could be the reason?

Chapter 32

Fannie wore a white long-sleeved blouse with high collar and ruffled front. She dropped her navy blue skirt over her head, wiggled it down to her waist and buttoned the five buttons on the side. She opted to wear only her bloomers underneath. It would be cooler. It wouldn't be the first time she had gone without a slip or petticoat.

Jess was dressed in the shirt she had bought at Coyner's store. Working as a carpenter had kept him in good physical shape. With the cream-colored shirt and black pants complementing his tanned skin, he looked handsome to Fannie. "I think I'd marry you all over again," she teased and kissed his cheek. He grabbed her around the waist, pulled her close and gave her a passionate kiss.

She smiled up at him and twirled a lock of his hair between her fingers. "Yes, I definitely would."

Her husband was pleased before he released his hold on her. "Are you ready?"

She began dabbing on lavender toilet water Jess had bought for her in town. "I will be once I pin on my hat."

"I'll be on the patio. It's almost two. I expect whoever is coming for us will be here shortly. Any second thoughts about going out to that ranch for dinner?"

"No second thoughts. I'm bubbling with curiosity." Fannie pinned on her straw hat and took one last glance in the small hand mirror as she heard the clip-clop of horse's hooves.

Jess was waiting for her next to a two seat carriage with a covered top, which brought a smile to her face. A blessing, she would be shaded from the sun.

The driver was Spanish and spoke broken English.

"Senor Flores say you will come."

Jess nodded and took Fannie's hand as she climbed onto the back seat. Jess sat beside her.

Back to the hard-packed road the driver turned toward Hollywood, but they didn't go into town because he took a fork in the road that went either east or north. Fannie wasn't sure. They traveled up and down rolling hills and the driver took a couple more forks in the road.

Fannie and Jess had ridden quietly behind their silent driver watching as the countryside pass with its dry earth, scrubby bushes, wildflowers, and stunted trees. California was so much different than her beloved Virginia.

"Jess, which direction are we going?"

"The sun is moving to the west so I assume we are northeast of where we started."

"It seems longer than ten miles. We've been riding for almost two hours."

No sooner had she spoken those words when they went over a rise and before them was a valley with grazing land spotted with both sheep and cattle. Then they saw the ranch house.

The closer they got they could see it was one story of yellow stucco. The roof was red tile and the long wide low porch on the front was wood.

The minute the carriage stopped Gabriel Flores came off the porch to meet them.

"Mr. and Mrs. Edwards," he said. "Welcome! I am happy to see you."

Gabriel was as impressive in his manner and dress as he had been when Fannie first saw him. "Gabriel this is my husband, Jess."

Gabriel offered his hand. "Mr. Edwads, I am pleased to meet you. Your wife and I have already met."

Jess shook the bronzed outstretched hand. "So I understand. Thank you for the invitation. We are comfortable with first names, Jess and Fannie. I noticed some nice looking cattle on the way in."

This brought a pearly-toothed wide smile from Gabriel. "You are a man who knows cattle?"

Jess nodded. "I am."

"Come. It's too warm to stand here in the sun. We will sit on the verandah and have a drink before we eat."

They passed a small garden with snap-dragons, vinca, and geraniums on their way to the screened verandah on the side of the house. A gentle breeze was drifting in. This ranch house wasn't imposing like the mansions going up in Hollywood, but it was spread out, pleasant and comfortable. Jess and Fannie sat on a high-backed bench with a cushioned seat. Gabriel sat across from them in a large cushioned chair with a rounded back.

Without a word or signal from Gabriel a servant appeared with a tray of three glasses filled with a fruit-scented liquid. It wasn't lemonade. Fannie wasn't sure what it was and she was too polite to ask the host. The drink was refreshing.

Gabriel was telling about his ranch as they sipped, and Jess looked over and smiled at her. Was he glad they had come?

According to what she heard, this whole area had been in Gabriel's family for a couple hundred years. After all, California had once been held by the Spanish, he reminded them.

"That's true," Jess remarked. "How is it you managed to hold onto this ranch?"

Gabriel laughed. "I was lucky. I was educated in Jesuit schools where we studied much history of California. The land is rich in minerals. Los Angeles was growing by the day. I discovered sand and gravel pits on our land, leased them out. I kept the good grazing land and began this ranch."

Jess looked over at Fannie. "You see why I said this is a land of opportunity."

"Everyone is not so fortunate," Gabriel corrected him. "There are many poor people here. I am concerned our way of life will be threatened by those moving in. Especially over in the Hollywood area."

Fannie's head felt a bit fuzzy. Perhaps it was the heat or lack of food. "Is that the reason you would like to have your mother move here?"

"My mother is old and refuses to give up the old ways."

Fannie informed, "I asked her to come today, but she declined. I know she understood me."

His jovial manner disappeared. "It is a sad story between me and my mother."

Fannie was sorry she had opened the subject of Maria Flores because it had brought an uncomfortable silence to where they sat. What could have caused a rift between the two?

"You asked if I knew cattle, Gabriel. I worked on a ranch in Oklahoma, and we lived on a farm in Virginia where the owner is raising a new breed."

Gabriel finished his drink. "I would like to hear about them."

A young girl appeared. "Senor Flores, the food is ready."

"Gracias, Elana. Tell your mother we will be right there."

Jess had finished his drink but Fannie's was still half full. She would feel better after she ate.

The low-ceilinged dining room had a tiled floor with a heavy black wooden table and ornate chairs with red velvet upholstery. Pictures of bull fighting with the color and grandeur of bull fighters and Spanish architecture hung on the walls.

Then Fannie saw a small picture of the chapel over the hill from Maria's house. She pointed to it. "I have gone to Mass at the chapel three times," she informed Gabriel.

He smiled at her. "I have good memories of the chapel. Does my mother go with you?"

"Rosetta Alvarez gives her a ride. I did ride home with them last Sunday."

159

"It's good my mother attends," was all he said. "Will you say grace for us?"

Although her head still felt fuzzy, her mind was clear enough. Fannie blessed herself and offered, "Thank you, Father for the food we are about to receive from your bounty and thank you for the new friend we have made." She blessed herself again and Gabriel joined her in the Sign of the Cross.

"You are not a Catholic, Jess?"

"Not yet, anyway."

Gabriel roared with laughter. "I'm not so sure I'm a good one," he said.

Elana and her mother, a short, round woman, brought in the food. They started with chicken soup followed by tortillas, beans, rice and meat dish, roast lamb and beef, a salad of various greens and vegetables, and a fresh fruit mixture of oranges, bananas, pears and pineapple. They drank cold tea.

Fannie felt as though she had stuffed herself. Her head felt a little better not as fuzzy as it had been earlier.

Jess was having a great time talking with Gabriel about the house he was helping to build, how he hoped to find his future out here, the cattle Alex was raising, and his failure at gold mining in Colorado.

When Fannie heard him talking about finding a future out here, was that to mean Jess wanted to stay out here? That his true intention was not to return to Virginia? Fannie had said she would leave without him. But she knew that was an idle threat. Perhaps Jess did also. His words made her uneasy.

Gabriel seemed to be enjoying himself as much as Jess. "Would you like to take a ride around? I own hundreds of acres."

Jess was eager. Fannie felt like taking a nap.

"Why don't you two go ahead? I'll take a walk and stay close to the house."

"You won't think it impolite of me?" asked Gabriel.

"Of course not. Jess would love to see your place."

The two men headed to the barn where she saw them saddle two horses in a corral. That was unexpected. Fannie thought they would ride in a cart or wagon. If she had chosen to go, she would not be riding a horse.

Fannie watched them go. Her brawny Jess was as agile as the slimmer Gabriel. She went back to sit on the verandah where the breeze was soothing.

The young Elana came to where she sat. "Senora, do you want a drink of water? My mother told me to ask you."

"Yes, I would. You speak very good English, Elana."

"Senor Flores wants all of the help to learn the language. I go to school."

"That's good. Does your mother speak English?"

"No. She says Mexicans don't speak English."

Fannie laughed. "And this Irish lass doesn't speak Spanish. I think Senor Flores is right. You will need both languages." Fannie knew better than to pry, but her curiosity won. "Do you know Senor Gabriel's mother?"

Elana nodded. "The Senora used to come with Senora Doncia before she was married."

"That would be her daughter?"

"Yes," she replied and left to get the water.

This information piqued her curiosity even more. Fannie had not seen any sign of a daughter. She knew better than to ask further, but she would discuss the news with Jess. Perhaps Gabriel would allude to something as he and Jess explored the ranch.

Fannie sat in a rocker and drifted off. When she awoke, she found Elana had set the glass of water on a table next to her. She pulled out her pocket watch. It was four o'clock. Where were Jess and Gabriel? It would be after six when they got back to the adobe, and Jess needed rest before his work the next day.

Fannie drank half the glass of water, left the verandah and started toward the barn when she saw the two horsemen coming at a gallop. Were they racing each other? She stood and watched. Of course they were and Gabriel won by a head.

"No fair," she heard Jess call. "You have the fastest horse."

Gabriel guffawed. "He's carrying a lighter weight. Do you like that horse, Jess?"

Jess swung out of the saddle. "She's a beauty."

"Then take her with you," offered Gabriel.

"I couldn't do that. I can't afford her."

Gabriel shook his head. "She is a gift. In exchange, you stay at my mother's house and keep an eye on her, give her help if she needs it."

Fannie was at the corral and heard the conversation. She waited for Jess's reply. She had given him two months to find what he wanted and a month had already passed.

Jess declined. "It is kind of you to offer."

Gabriel hesitated. "Take the horse". He turned to Fannie, "What do you think?"

"The decision is up to my husband."

Gabriel laughed his good-hearted laugh. "You have a good wife, Jess. Hold onto her."

"I intend to."

Jess led the horse toward the corral. "I'll unsaddle her."

"No. I will feel ashamed if you turn down my gift."

Fannie knew the Spanish people were sensitive and she didn't want this beautiful day spoiled. "It isn't right to disappoint our host," she said.

Jess sighed. "All right. I'll take the horse and return her if we leave."

Gabriel patted him on the shoulder. "That makes me happy. And, Antonio will be happy he doesn't have to drive you back in the carriage."

"That means I have to ride on the horse?" Fannie asked.

Jess grinned. "You can have the saddle and I'll ride behind and hold the reins. I'll have my arms around you so you won't fall off."

Fannie was leery of being atop a horse. "As long as I can sit sideways."

Jess rested and watered the horse before they said goodbye to Gabriel and headed the long way back. Gabriel drew a map for a short cut to his mother's house.

When they were on their way Fannie asked, "Can you follow those directions? I don't want to get lost out here."

"Fannie, my love, I'm a regular Daniel Boone."

Chapter 33

It had taken them over three hours to get home last evening. Fannie's Daniel Boone had taken a wrong turn.

This morning she heard Jess whistling up a storm as he fed and watered the horse.

Fannie was glad for Jess, and she liked the horse. Gabriel named the horse Gres, Spanish for grey she'd been told. Fannie liked the sound of the word and called the horse Grace. She thought the words were close enough not to confuse the horse.

It was a pleasant Sunday morning. Fannie had a slight headache and thought perhaps she should skip church. The headache was a hangover from the drink she'd had at the ranch. Jess had chuckled when she told him about feeling fuzzy headed.

"Good thing you didn't drink the whole glass. It had tequila in it."

"You should have warned me."

"I tried to catch your eye, but you were sipping happily."

She explained, "What I drank was refreshing after the ride out."

Fannie took an aspirin before she put on her green dress. She was going to help at the meal after Mass so she tucked the apron Addie had given her into her tote bag.

The apron brought Addie into her thoughts. What was Addie doing? How is Lottie? Are Crystal and Nate taking care of the cabin? Are the daisies in bloom? Fannie shook her head to clear it of thoughts of Virginia.

She left the house and called to Jess who was installing a corral for the horse. "I'm off to church. Do you want to go? You'll get a big meal afterward."

He looked up from his task and called back, "Are you trying to bribe me, my love?"

"Just a thought. I think I'll learn to ride Grace, then I won't have to walk."

"I told you I'd teach you. Wait and ride with Rosetta. How is your head?"

"Probably feeling like my father's used to after a night on the town."

He laughed.

Fannie waved at him before she started out. He blew her a kiss.

Along the way Fannie picked some wild-flowers and delicate brush. She pulled a blue ribbon from her tote and tied the bundle so that it looked like a spray. She would lay it on the table as her offering for the meal.

Fannie was determined to find out the reason for the split between mother and son. It would have to be serious. Jess had told her to forget about it. It was up to Maria and Gabriel if they wanted to mend fences.

But it nagged at Fannie's mind. The thought occurred to her that Father Jose might know the answer. She would ask him when the time was right.

After Mass, Fannie put on her pretty apron and helped put dishes on the long table. The spray of wildflowers was at the head of the table.

The priest came to her side. "The people are pleased to have you join them."

"I wish I could understand them. Father Jose, Jess and I went to Gabriel Flores ranch yesterday for dinner. Maria refused to go with us. I know there are bad feelings between them. I wish I could help bring them together."

"Maria has not learned to forgive," was his answer. Fannie didn't push further.

Fannie filled her plate and went to sit with Rosetta and Maria's group. She still felt like an outsider, but she listened intently as they chatted away.

At one point Rosetta turned to her. "They ask if you have a man?"

"A man?" she asked. "Do they mean a husband?"

"Yes."

Fannie smiled and nodded and they went back to chatting among themselves.

"They ask do you have nino or nina."

Fannie was sure that meant children. She pointed to toddlers playing.

"Yes," said Rosetta.

Fannie shook her head.

The group of women looked at each other as though that was unheard of. This woman had a husband but no children.

Fannie smiled, spread her hands and shrugged her shoulders.

The women all laughed. Even Maria cracked a weak smile.

One of the younger women whispered to Rosetta and she relayed the message to Fannie, "Rosa will light a candle for you."

Fannie knew that was a kind gesture, although a child was far from her wants at this time. She smiled at the young woman called Rosa.

After the meal, Fannie rode home with Rosetta and Maria. It was always a quiet ride but Fannie was determined to talk about going to the ranch yesterday.

She talked to Rosetta so Maria could hear. "Jess and I went to Gabriel's ranch for dinner yesterday. The food was very good and Gabriel was happy to see us. He wished his mother had come."

Maria spat out some words and Rosetta repeated in English. "Maria says, Gabriel is no son of hers."

"Why is that?"

"It is for Maria to tell."

Fannie turned to Maria. "Why do you not forgive your son?"

Maria turned away and didn't answer.

When they arrived home, Fannie gave the spray of flowers to Maria. She took a long look and finally took them. "Gracias," she mumbled.

Jess was sitting on the patio. "I fixed up a small space for the horse, but I'll have to figure out some way to get feed to her. I was thinking I can use a bit of our savings to buy a cart. What do you think?"

Fannie plopped into the chair next to him and took off her hat. "I hate to use that money. Could it be Gabriel's gift is going to cost us money?"

"I've also been thinking about what Gabriel said about leasing his quarries. We can look around for some land and get a start."

"Land costs money we don't have," she replied.

"We can look around. That doesn't cost money."

"What if it turns out like your gold mine in Leadville? A gold mine with no gold."

He rose from his chair and kissed her cheek. "Fannie, my love, I am inspired. This could be the beginning of our fortune."

"You'd better find it quick. We're nearing August."

His hand was on the back door handle. "I'm going for a cup of water. Can I bring you one?"

"Yes and an aspirin along with it. If we ever go to Gabriel's again I will shun his offer of a refreshing drink."

Fannie didn't know it, but Jess had done a lot of thinking while she was gone. Gabriel Flores might just be the person to help him find land and loan him the money to buy it.

Chapter 34

Monday morning Fannie watched Jess saddle up Grace and swing into the saddle. She was going to have one more cup of coffee before she went to help Maria in the garden. Was Maria unhappy with her for asking about Gabriel? She would risk it.

Fannie drank her second cup of coffee, put on her apron and gloves, then picked up her spade. Maria was in the garden as usual.

Fannie walked to her. "Where do you want me to start?"

Maria pointed to the melon patch.

Gabriel said his mother spoke some English and understood much of the language, but apparently Maria saw no need to use any language. She was a master at gesturing.

"Mrs. Flores, I'm sorry I asked about Gabriel. It is none of my business."

Maria sighed deeply and stood up. "Doncia, my daughter. Gone."

"Gone?"

The woman shrugged. "With Gabriel's man."

Fannie stood for a time absorbing what Maria had said. "That's why you are angry at Gabriel? Because your daughter left?"

The old woman nodded and went back to her work.

Fannie persisted. "How is that Gabriel's fault?"

Fannie had pushed too far. "Gabriel not stop, Doncia! No more son." She spat the words as though they were hot coals in her mouth, and left the garden.

Fannie stood unsure of what she should do. At least she had the answer she had been searching for. Why would a mother disown her son because his sister ran away? Maybe it was because the man she ran away with worked for Gabriel. "I don't understand it," she said aloud and went to clean out the melons.

Fannie knew the men from the village would come the next day to take Maria's produce to town to sell it so she picked the ripe fruits and vegetable and piled them in a sheltered spot where Maria always put them. Then a thought struck her. Would the old woman be upset with her for picking the crops? It was for sure Fannie wasn't going to put them back.

When Jess came home Fannie told him about her conversation with Maria and that she had taken it upon herself to ready the produce for tomorrow.

"Don't overstep your position, Fannie. We are only renters."

"I know. I tried to make up for stirring up memories of her daughter. Why do you think Maria blames Gabriel?"

Jess shrugged. "I don't know. Maybe he helped her leave. What's for supper?"

171

"I can't believe it doesn't bother you. Gabriel is hurt that his mother has tossed him aside."

"Fannie, my love. You don't know that's true. The problem is between Gabriel and his mother."

She made a prune face. "All right. It's none of my business. We're having for supper what we usually have except the meat is chicken. If I had an oven I could bake something."

Jess was defensive. "Do you want me to buy you an oven?"

"No. I don't want to heat up the inside of the apartment. Besides, how would I use an oven on that two burner kerosene stove?"

"I'm going to take care of Grace."

Fannie kissed his cheek. "Sorry I'm being a sourpuss. Was it easier getting to work riding the horse?"

"It was sheer pleasure and my legs don't feel like they're going to fall off."

He turned before he left the room. "I have an idea. Why don't we go into town on Saturday? We can get a decent dinner and go to a cinema. I think it would be good for you to get away from here."

"I hate to spend the money. We might need it for a train ticket."

"Fannie, there is more to life than money."

"I'm aware of that, but it isn't going to be pleasure and good deeds that get us back to Virginia."

He took her into his arms. "Enjoy the present. We never know what tomorrow will bring."

Jess left to take care of Grace leaving Fannie standing by the sink. She took two pieces of chicken from the icebox and the only frying pan to use over the open fire outdoors. Fannie cooked up the meat and vegetables in the same pan and cut up fresh vegetables for a salad. It seemed the only variety in their supper was the meat. Sometimes Fannie cooked beans all day or added cooked rice to the vegetables. How she would love to bake a loaf of bread or fry up some kigleys. She closed her eyes and could smell the baking bread. She could also see the cabin and her friend Addie. Would she ever see Lockwood farm again?

Chapter 35

Fannie owed Addie a letter. If Maria was upset with her it would be better to stay out of Maria's garden today. She took her pencil and paper to the patio where she could sit and write.

July 12, 1919
Dear Addie,

I am sitting on the patio on a clear, warm day. Almost every day here is clear and warm. The local people say the rains come mostly during the winter months. I would relish a rain shower and the smell of green grass.

Which brings to mind that Jess hasn't had time to fix an outdoor shower for me.

Last Saturday we went to the ranch of Gabriel Flores for dinner. Yes, he does own a large ranch. He raises sheep and cattle and was very interested in hearing about the breed Alex raises.

Gabriel was a cordial host. I do not believe he has a wife or children. If he does there was no mention nor any sign of either in our presence. He said his land has been in his family for years. Some has been sold off and he leases quarries of gravel and sandstone for added income.

Of course you realize the prospect of leasing piqued Jess's interest to search out land. This area is booming. The motion picture studios have shot up around Hollywood bringing in hopefuls as well as some unsavory characters. I fear the real estate prices will escalate along with the influx.

Gabriel gave Jess a gray horse to use while we are here. We call her Grace. I have become fond of her and will conquer my fear of riding one day. You know the saying never look a gift horse in the mouth? Her teeth are fine, but along with the gift came expenses of food, shed and corral. Now Jess is going to buy a cart to bring the feed home from the farm store in town. Riding Grace saves his hike to and from work so I guess the added expense is worth it.

I have a feeling our landlady is miffed at me. I prodded her as to why she and Gabriel are at odds. I found out that she has a daughter who ran off with one of Gabriel's ranch hands. I do not understand if Gabriel had a part in that or if it is only because he hired the man she ran away with.

Jess told me to keep my nose out of it. I'm trying, but I feel Gabriel would like to be back in his mother's good graces. As for Doncia, the daughter, I know nothing but her name.

Jess says we need to go into town for dinner and a cinema. Now that we have the horse, it sounds like an easier trip, especially if he comes home with a cart. I do hate to spend the money. I keep hinting that August is drawing near and I promised Jess two months to find what he wants. The time seems to pass too quickly and I may have to renege on that promise. We have yet to see the ocean or visit the northern part with the giant redwood trees. I never told anyone they were my reason for agreeing to come. Now you know, but please don't tell anyone.

175

How is our dear Lottie? Tell her she is often in my thoughts and always in my prayers. Are you still taking care of baby Francis? I also think of Caleb and the strain he must be under.

I do wish we had put this trip off, but that is pure wishful thinking. I am here and I had better make the most of it.

I have been attending Mass on Sundays and taking part in the meal the villagers prepare afterward. Jess said I should learn some of the skills of the women. Once a month the young men of the village go into town and sell the wares of their neighbors. Maybe I will learn how to make baskets or throw pottery. Wouldn't that be a hoot if I sold some?

One day this week I plan to go into town with Jess when he leaves for work. I haven't been there just to spend the day and look at what's new in all the stores or sit in a park and people watch. Who knows? I may run into Douglas Fairbanks or Mary Pickford. Wouldn't that be something?

Well, Addie. I have gone on long enough. I hope this letter reaches you and you are well and happy.

My fondest regards,
Fannie

Fannie reread the letter before she put it in an envelope. Perhaps tomorrow would be the day to go into town with Jess.

She stood to take the letter into the house and glanced over at Maria's garden. Maria wasn't there. That was unusual. The old woman was always there first thing in the morning. Fannie decided that if the woman was not there within the next hour she should check on her whether Maria was unhappy with her or not.

An hour later she was knocking on Maria's door. When there was no answer, she tried the handle of the door and it opened.

"Mrs. Flores," she called. There was no answer.

Fannie went inside and called again, "Mrs. Flores. It's Fannie. Are you all right?"

After Fannie had no answer she waited no longer. She had never been in Maria's part of the house but knew it couldn't be too much bigger than the apartment she and Jess rented. Fannie opened a door and found a neat bedroom that looked as though it hadn't been disturbed in a long time. She tried the door next to it and there saw Maria lying in bed still as a fence post.

Fannie rushed to her side. "Mrs. Flores! Maria!"

The woman was breathing but unresponsive. Fannie felt her forehead. The woman was burning with fever. Fannie left the room to find towels and a pail of cold water. She was alone with no way to get help so she did what she thought was best.

Maria was bundled up like a mummy. Fannie set to work unbundling the layers of clothing leaving the old woman in a slip. She doused the towels in the tepid water and laid them on Maria's arms and legs and placed one on her forehead.

After half an hour of rinsing and reapplying the towels, Maria began to stir. She opened her eyes and was frightened when she saw Fannie leaning over her.

"You're sick," said Fannie. "Is there a doctor in the village?"

"Roberto."

"Roberto? Is he a doctor?"

"Get Roberto."

Fannie wasn't going to argue. "Is Roberto in the village?"

Maria closed her eyes with a nod of her head.

"You need water."

Fannie went around to her part of the house and took two aspirins and a cup of water back to Maria.

She held the ailing woman's head while she took the medicine. Maria was too sick to refuse, although she tried to grit her teeth when Fannie showed her the white aspirin tablets. So, Fannie crushed them with a spoon and mashed an avocado to help them go down easier. Maria swallowed the avocado mix down followed by sips of water.

Fannie gently lay Maria's head back on the pillow. She removed the wet towels and put a light sheet over the old woman. "I'm going to get Roberto," she said in Maria's ear.

Not sparing another moment, Fannie left the house and sprinted off to the village. Even hurrying like she did it took almost a half hour to get there, and she was fagged out as a wilting flower when she arrived. She grabbed the arm of the first person she saw. "Roberto?"

The man looked at her as though she were loco. He shook his head.

"I need Roberto." How could she get across she needed help for Maria?

Fannie shouted, "Roberto, doctor, Maria Flores." Then she put her hand to her head as though she would faint and pointed to the way she had come.

Her frantic speech and movement worked.

The man nodded he understood. "Si, Roberto." He motioned her to follow.

In one of the adobe huts was an old man with a kind smile. The man who brought Fannie spoke to him in Spanish. All Fannie understood was Maria, sounding much prettier tripping off his lips than when she said the name.

The man left and Roberto said to Fannie, "You have a worry about Maria Flores?"

Thank God he spoke English.

"She is very sick. She asked me to come and get you."

"I will come," said Roberto as he began to gather up bottles of liquid and dry herbs as he spoke.

"We have to hurry," Fannie said.

He smiled and took his time putting whatever he thought he needed in a basket.

Fannie's mind was racing. Why doesn't he hurry? Maria might be dead by the time we get back.

Behind the hut was a horse and cart. Roberto shouted a name and a young boy came and hitched up the horse. Fannie was relieved she didn't have to walk back. Roberto put his basket in the back of the cart, climbed onto the driver's seat, and motioned Fannie to sit beside him. He said something in Spanish to the horse and it took off in a lurch causing Fannie to grab onto the side of the seat. The horse seemed in his stride and skimmed over the road that led back to Maria.

Roberto looked over at Fannie. "Do not be sad. Maria is strong. It will take much for her to give up her life."

"I don't think Maria is a happy woman," said Fannie.

"She mourns for her dead daughter."

"Doncia is dead?"

"No, she is much alive. Because she ran away with a man, she is dead to Maria."

Fannie's mind was working overtime. "That is sad. She has pushed both her daughter and her son out of her life because of an elopement?"

"Marriage to us is important. It is a big time for celebration. Doncia should have been married in the church. To Maria it is shameful what her daughter did."

"I can understand that. Why has Maria shunned Gabriel?"

"He helped by giving them money."

"How old was Doncia?" asked Fannie.

Roberto laughed. "Too old. Twenty-nine. Senor Flores died when Doncia was little and Gabriel took his father's place. I think Maria was jealous that Doncia looked to Gabriel for advice, so she sent Gabriel off to be schooled by the Jesuits."

At last some answers, thought Fannie. "Then I guess Gabriel saw his sister's chance for happiness and did what he thought was right."

"That's true, I am telling you this for you to learn," said the healer as they pulled up in front of the house.

"So maybe I can understand Maria?"

He nodded. "Maria needs help even if she tries to push it away. Now, if you will please show me the way to Maria's sickbed."

Roberto answered a lot of questions Fannie hadn't asked. Could it be Providence stepping in?

Chapter 36

Jess bought a cart and harness at a farm store in Hollywood and hitched up Grace. He had only a few more days of work before the mansion was completed. He hadn't told Fannie this because he wanted to have another job before he gave her that news.

The cart, harness, and feed cost almost two weeks wages. If Fannie had balked at the cost of dinner and a cinema, how was she going to react about this outlay of cash? Jess didn't want to think about it.

He was later than usual getting home only to be surprised Fannie wasn't there and supper wasn't started. Everything looked in order. He checked the bedroom. Nothing was missing. A thought struck him that she may have gone to the village. Why? She had never gone during the week. What if she had decided to go to the village and something happened? What if she's hurt? Just before panic set in, Fannie came around the house.

He grabbed her up in his strong arms. "Where have you been? I've had all sorts of thoughts running through my head."

"If you'll stop squeezing the breath out of me, I'll tell you."

Jess relaxed his grip but didn't let her go.

"Maria is sick. I went to the village and got a man who is known to be a healer."

"A doctor?"

"Close to it. He mixed up some goopy, smelly stuff and rubbed it on her chest and arms. She is more awake."

Jess kissed her and released his hold. "What's the matter with her?"

"I don't know, and I'm not sure he does either. She was burning up with fever when I went to check on her. I noticed she wasn't in the garden."

Jess searched her face. "I'm proud of you," he said. "I'd probably think she decided to forget gardening for one day. I wouldn't have thought to check in on her. Do you think I should ride to tell Gabriel?"

Fannie shook her head. "If I know the people in the village, the word will reach him. I'll be spending the night at Maria's side. The fever took a lot out of her and Roberto left medicine for me to give to her."

"Who's Roberto?"

"He's the one close to a doctor."

"How old is he?"

Fannie let out a belly laugh. "Old enough to be my great-grandfather. Jealous?"

Jess shrugged a shoulder. "I was just curious."

"I needed a good laugh after the day I've put in." She kissed his cheek. "I haven't even thought about supper."

"I can start the fire outside," he suggested.

"I've got leftover chicken in the ice box. I thought I'd make some rice and grind a bit of chicken for a soup for Maria. Then I can throw together some peppers, onions and tomatoes to mix with rice and the rest of the chicken for us."

"Anything is welcome. I'm starved."

Fannie looked at him and smiled. "Don't you have something to tell me? I heard you come home."

Oh, oh. The time had come.

He cleared his throat. "I bought a cart and feed for the horse."

"And?"

"And, I had to buy a used harness to hitch her up."

"And, how much did that set us back?"

"I got a good deal on the cart and harness."

Fannie stood tapping her foot. "And it took all of the money you earned this week, didn't it?"

He nodded and felt relieved he didn't have to tell her the full price.

"Jess how are we ever going to get back to Virginia if we have to keep spending money on that horse? I was growing fond of her, but I'm quickly losing my admiration."

Jess put his arms around her. "We're going to do fine, my love."

Fannie wished she could believe it.

Chapter 37

Fannie spent two days and nights taking care of Maria. It was good the old woman was too weak to push her away.

When Gabriel arrived on the morning of the third day, Fannie wasn't surprised. She went out to meet him when she heard the sound of the horse's clip-clop. Gabriel looked as sharp as he usually did.

"Hello, Gabriel. I expected you might come yesterday."

"Hello, Fannie. I received word that my mother was sick but she had help and was in no danger of passing away."

"I wasn't sure of that when I found her. She has been very sick, but she is better."

He took Fannie's hand. "Thank you. How did this happen?"

Fannie removed her hand from his warm grasp. "She wasn't in her garden, which concerned me, so I went to look for her. I found her lying like a rag on her bed. After I was able to rouse her she told me to get Roberto."

His smile always lit up his face. "Ah, Roberto. How fortunate my mother is to have you here, and I am also."

"Come in, Gabriel. She has been sleeping much of the time, but she is awake now."

The sick room smelled of a mixture of antiseptic and herbs.

"I've been cleaning everything with alcohol. I figured that would kill most germs if whatever she has is catching," she explained.

He removed his hat, went to his mother's side, and took her hand. "Mama," he said and touched his lips to her forehead.

Maria opened her eyes and looked at him.

He spoke to his mother in Spanish and Fannie left the room. She did not understand what he was saying, but she felt it was between Gabriel and his mother, whether Fannie understood or not.

She went to her side of the house and sat on the patio assuming Gabriel would come after he finished his visit. It would be good to offer him cold tea after his long ride, so Fannie went into the house and prepared tea with chips of ice.

It was twenty minutes later when Gabriel came to where she sat. She offered him the tea and he accepted it with a gracious smile before he sat in the chair across from her. He put his hat on a stool beside him and wiped his forehead with his bandanna.

He looked at her for a moment before he said, "Fannie, I cannot repay you for taking care of my mother. She said you have been good to her."

"I only did what anyone else would have done in this situation."

Gabriel shook his head. "I don't think so. You have been with her day and night giving her the care she needed. She is still weak but strong enough to tell me how much she is thankful. There must be something I can do for you."

This was as good a time as any. "Gabriel, Roberto told me why there is a problem between you and your mother. I don't fully understand her reaction, but I can see she has been hurt."

He nodded and shrugged a shoulder. "Perhaps I was wrong to help Doncia. I don't know. All I know is that my sister had no future living under my mother's rule. She and Carlos were very much in love, and I wanted her to be happy. When she told my mother that she wanted to get married, my mother absolutely forbid it. Carlos wasn't good enough for her."

"You couldn't make your mother see otherwise?"

He sighed. "I tried. When Doncia came to me in tears, I did what I thought was right and gave them money to start a life together. They live near the ocean and own a small café."

"I've never seen the ocean," Fannie admitted.

Gabriel's mood brightened. He clapped his hands together. "Then that is how I can repay you. I will take you and Jess to the ocean. My sister has rooms above the café. I haven't seen her in a while. It will be good for me too."

Fannie grinned. "That sounds heavenly. I'll ask Jess when he gets home."

"How is the horse working out for him?"

"He is pleased." Fannie didn't need to tell him her chagrin at the added expense involved.

"Gabriel, are you married?"

He laughed and shook his head. "I am too busy keeping my affairs in order. Maybe one of these days before I'm old and gray. Why do you ask?"

Fannie was not one to hold back. "Because you are probably nearing forty and most men are married by the time they're twenty."

He smiled. "But not all men."

Fannie thought about it and nodded. "That's true. My friend, Addie, married Alex who is about your age."

"Is he the one who raises the special cattle?"

"That's Alex. I guess he was too busy building his career as a lawyer to get serious about a woman."

"Then your friend must be special."

A wistful look grazed her face. "She is, and I miss having her close."

Gabriel got to his feet. "Talk with Jess about a trip to the ocean. We will go once my mother is back working in her garden."

Fannie stood to say goodbye. "I think Jess will be more than happy to accept your offer."

"I hope so." Gabriel didn't offer his hand. He bowed with a nod of his head. "Thank you again."

Fannie watched as the sunlight caught the polished silver on the man and the horse. Gabriel Flores was definitely the grandest man she had ever met.

Fannie took the empty tea cups into the house before she went to see Maria. The old woman lay quietly with her eyes closed. Fannie looked closely. Was that a hint of a smile on the old woman's face?

She leaned toward the silent woman and said, "Gabriel has gone. He was happy to see that you are better."

Maria never opened her eyes nor acknowledged that she had heard.

Chapter 38

Fannie had kept the garden up all week as well as taking care of Maria. The woman was better but still not strong enough to tend the garden.

Fannie walked Maria outdoors and led her to a chair under the shade of a tree. Maria watched while Fannie worked in the garden. The old woman may still have been weak, but she was strong enough to give orders with her gesturing hands.

The ordering by gesturing irked Fannie. However, she was beginning to understand this complicated old Spanish woman. The one who was grateful for the care Fannie had given, yet too stubborn to let it show.

"The men will come for the crops tomorrow," Fannie called. "Do you want me to pick all that are ready?"

Maria nodded.

Fannie was grateful for the wide straw hat Maria had given her because it was afternoon and the sun was beating down. The crops needed picking and stacking and she was the only one to do it or let them rot in the garden.

After two hours there were still onions to pull and tomatoes to pick. Fannie stood, rubbed her back and went to Maria. "I'll take you in. You need to lie down."

Maria shook her head and pointed to the tomatoes.

That was too much for Fannie. She stood with hands on hips and shook her finger at Maria. "Look, Senora. You will go into the house, and I'll come back and pick those blasted tomatoes."

For the second time since Fannie had come, she heard Maria laugh aloud. Then the old woman waved her finger back and forth and shook her head at the red-faced Fannie who stood before her.

The thought of how she acted caused Fannie to laugh also. "I'm sorry. I guess I'm tired."

She helped Maria to her feet and guided her back into the adobe house where she removed the hat, shoes and heavy blouse Maria wore before she helped her onto the bed.

"I'll bring you a glass of water. You need to drink," Fannie said. She went to the kitchen. When she returned, Maria dutifully drank the full glass and lay back on the pillow. Fannie pulled up a light sheet over her. When she did, Maria grabbed her hand and kissed it. "Gracias."

This simple show of gratitude brought a lump to Fannie's throat. She patted the old woman's shoulder and left the room before Maria could see the tears.

The tears didn't stop even as Fannie went back to work in the garden. She pulled a handkerchief from the pocket of her apron and tried to wipe them away, but they continued. Perhaps they were tears of release after the anxious week she had put in. Maybe they were tears of homesickness. Or was it sheer frustration?

It was August and there was no sign that Jess had made any headway in satisfying the reason they had come. She was resigned to the fact that they weren't going to leave until Jess was ready. True, she could leave and go back to Lockwood by herself. Jess could come when he decided to. But Fannie didn't want to live her life without Jess at her side. She wiped the tears away and blew her nose.

Fannie looked at the baskets of tomatoes, the other crops she had piled around and felt satisfied with her efforts. Lottie would be proud of her.

Sometimes the days were long before Jess came home from work. Fannie understood why Maria spent so much time in the garden. It not only passed the time, but it was satisfying and profitable in the end.

Jess had agreed to Gabriel's offer of a trip to the ocean. He understood Gabriel wanted to repay Fannie for taking care of Maria. He did mull it around in his brain for a time because he didn't want to be beholding to Gabriel. The man had already lent him the use of his horse, albeit there was expense involved.

Jess placated any objections to the trip by deciding he could help at Gabriel's ranch. A trip to the ocean for a few days may just be what all three needed.

The construction work on the mansion had finished. Jess was now working at one of the movie lots building sets for picture shows. The pay was better, and Fannie liked the extra money. He was allowed to take any scrap lumber or materials he wanted.

Jess had an idea that he could build a chicken coop. Fannie could sell the eggs and the chickens. Would that be enough to make her agree to stay longer? Was he being fair? Two months sounded like a reasonable time for him to find his fortune or his future. However, time's almost up and, so far, he hasn't even come close.

Chapter 39

Fannie thought Maria would be able to be on her own in another week, and she figured it was time for Gabriel to pay another visit to check on his mother's welfare. The thought of a trip to the ocean sounded better every day.

When Jess came home that evening, he brought a letter from Addie. Fannie greeted him with a kiss and tore the envelope out of his hand.

July 31, 1919

Dear Fannie,

I cannot express how happy I was to receive your last letter. It seems you are getting settled into your new surroundings. It did bring a smile to my face that Gabriel, whoever he is, does indeed own a ranch. Did Jess apologize for doubting?

Your letter arrived at a time when it seemed everything was going wrong. I had made a costly error in my bookkeeping, which did not please Alex. It is interesting what an extra zero or a misplaced decimal can do. I did get the books straightened out before calamity hit.

We are still caring for Lottie's baby. If Lottie has gained any strength, it isn't noticeable. She insists on trying to help Crystal. I don't think she realizes that if she would just go to bed for two weeks and let people wait on her, she would be back on her feet. I have tried to tell her to no avail. I'd bet my prettiest dress that she would listen to you if you were here.

The baby has been colicky. I have even been up walking the floor with him all night doing whatever I thought would calm his poor crampy stomach. Peg has been giving him oat mush, and I think that is the problem. I told her to stop and only continue with the goat's milk that he tolerates well. Because Peg is older she thinks she knows better.

That same week, Caleb stuck his foot with a pitchfork. Luckily he wears those tough cowboy boots, but still the tine punctured through and Alex had to drive him down to Dr. Hawthorne. His foot was so swollen he couldn't work for four days. You can imagine what it is like if Caleb can't be working.

Alex tried to pick up the slack, but he isn't used to the daily drudge. Along with the office work and the baby, I had to work in time to try to ease Alex's aches and pains.

The final straw was that three calves were stillborn. Alex is now trying to track down the reason for that. His calves are worth money.

All of that bad news happened within a week and I almost bit my nails to the nub. There. Now I have poured out all my troubles, which I could say I didn't mean to do, but I did. Who else would listen to my lamentations?

Now you can smile because everything is improving. You know how I say something good comes out of something bad? Alex is giving Caleb a raise. I don't believe he fully appreciated what a gem he had in Caleb Dunn until Caleb was out of the picture.

You write that you want to see the Pacific Ocean and the giant redwoods. I have never seen either. When you finally get there you can appreciate them for both of us.

Goodness, how I have rambled on. This is not the most upbeat letter. Have you spent the day in town or run into any of those cinema stars? You may never return to Virginia if you get caught up in the glamor of Hollywood. At least that is what they call the place in magazines.

I went into Berryville a couple of days ago. Guess who I ran into? You're right. Lavinia Talley. She asked how that red-haired Irish girl was doing out in California.

I looked straight at her and said, "You must mean Fannie Edwards. I had a letter from her. She and her husband are doing very well." Then she asked me about Lottie and the baby and how were things at the farm. You understand how it is with her, the fewer words said the better. She was on her way to Coyner's, probably to tell Nettie a tidbit of gossip she'd heard from Irene Butler.

This is the longest letter I have ever written, but it does bring you up to date.

Keep our Lottie in your prayers.

I look forward to your next letter. I'm sure it will be full of news.

> *Your forever friend,*
> *Addie*

Fannie sat with letter in hand. "I do miss her, Jess. We certainly could have helped them out. Especially when Caleb got hurt. You could have been there easing the burden of worry."

"Don't let it gnaw at you," Jess told her. "That was only Addie feeling sorry for herself. Everything worked out. They have to learn to get along without us."

Fannie's jaw dropped. "That sounds final, Jess. We are going back, aren't we?"

He smiled at her. "We have some things to do here."

"What kind of an answer is that?"

He playfully touched her nose with his finger. "You want to see the ocean, I have to take care of the horse, and I'm ready for supper."

Fannie sent him a wry look before she got to her feet to prepare their meal. Jess had evaded her question. Were they never going to return to Lockwood?

After she had taken supper to Maria, they were surprised to see Gabriel driving up in a spiffy red car.

"Wow!" exclaimed Jess. "Will you look at that?"

The chrome on the fenders, grill and door handles was as shiny as the silver Gabriel always wore.

He jumped out of the topless car with a smile a mile wide.

"Where's your horse?" called Fannie.

197

Gabriel fairly danced to where they stood. She noticed he wasn't wearing any spurs on his fancy cowboy boots.

He shook Jess's hand and bowed to Fannie. "I thought since we are going to take a trip to the ocean, we should ride in style."

"It's stylish all right. I will say that," agreed Fannie.

"That must have set you back a few pesos," said Jess.

"I have leased another piece of my land. It's an easier trip than with my horses."

Jess laughed. "The horses are under the hood."

"Come take a look," Gabriel invited.

"Hold it," said Fannie. "You need to go in and see your mother. I am about to put supper on. Will you stay and eat with us?"

"Of course. Jess you can check out the new car while I go see my mother."

"When you are both finished, we'll eat," ordered Fannie.

She was busy cutting up vegetables when the sound of a horn made her jump. She looked toward the car and found Jess inspecting a horn on the driver's side. He squeezed a rubber bulb and the oogah that resulted caused her to jump again.

Jess trotted over to where Fannie was cooking over the outdoor fire. "What a great automobile!" he exclaimed.

Fannie stirred the chicken and vegetables. "Don't you think it's a bit flamboyant?"

He laughed. "I guess that's one way to describe it. I think it suits Gabriel. Picture us, my love, riding in that classy car all the way to the ocean and it won't cost us a thing."

"I don't care to have people gawking at us everywhere we go. Do you think he knows how to drive it well enough?"

"He will by the time we leave. The roads to his ranch will give him plenty of practice."

Gabriel came to join them as Fannie finished setting the small table. "My mother is much improved. Thank you, Fannie. She says she is going back to the garden on Monday. I told her we were going to the ocean for a few days so she would be on her own unless she wanted to come with us."

Fannie was pouring tea. "Did you tell her we were going to see Doncia?"

"Yes. She won't come. She says Doncia is dead to her."

"What a stubborn old woman she is," remarked Fannie. "Has she forgiven you?"

Gabriel shrugged. "I don't know."

Fannie dished out their meal. She served tortillas with the mixture and wished she was eating a piece of her own baked bread instead.

By the time they finished eating, the trip to the ocean was settled. Doncia lived at a small inn set in a wide cove. Gabriel knew the way.

Tomorrow Jess would tell the boss at work that he would be out for three days the next week.

Gabriel would be able to put a man in charge of his ranch while he was gone, and Fannie said it was enough time for her to prepare, which meant she would have to go into Hollywood and buy a bathing suit. She had never owned one. Perhaps she would buy a pretty new blouse and skirt. That meant talking herself into spending the money.

Chapter 40

On Sunday, Fannie decided to walk to the chapel rather than ride with Rosetta and Maria. She had thinking to do. The day was sunny as almost every day was. She needed a new pair of walking shoes because the soles were wearing thin on the only pair she owned. Her hope was that there would be a cobbler who could re-sole them while she waited. That was one more item for her trip to town and another expense.

Fannie wondered if there was any way she could get Maria to embrace her children. She decided to talk to Father Jose about it. Of course, it appeared he hadn't been successful if he had tried to help them mend fences. Is it possible Maria is so embittered she cannot see another side to her deep hurt?

Fannie didn't think so. The woman had kissed her hand and thanked her for taking care of her, so there was kindness in the old girl. If Fannie could find a way for Maria to loosen her closed mind, she was determined to try.

Father Jose arrived for Mass around noon. Fannie was glad she could attend one more time before they went to the ocean. She'd say a special prayer that Gabriel knew how to drive that flashy car of his. She planned to leave and return in one piece.

Today Fannie had brought a bouquet of wild poppies to brighten the crude banquet table. Her eye caught the priest as he was walking by. She hurried over to him and tugged at his sleeve. "I need to talk to you, Father."

His smile was always welcoming. "I'm on my way to talk with Roberto. Join me when it's time to eat."

She nodded.

They sat together on a small bench. Father Jose's ample form took up more than half.

"What is troubling you, Fannie?"

"I want Maria to accept her children. It isn't right that she's pushed them away."

He took a bite of food, chewed it, swallowed, and then answered. "That's your concern?"

"Yes. I'm not sure it should be. I thought you could tell me. I'm sure Gabriel would be pleased. We are going to meet his sister next week."

He looked at her. "We?"

"Yes. Gabriel, Jess and I. I want to see the ocean and Gabriel has offered to drive us out to where his sister lives. Maria refuses to go."

"I'm not surprised," he answered. "I have tried to help. Until the reunion becomes Maria's idea, I'm afraid she won't bend."

Fannie sighed. "I suppose. At least she didn't kick Gabriel out when he came to see her."

The padre laughed. "She was probably too weak. My advice is to go about your business. I do know Maria was grateful for your help while she was ailing."

"She was very sick. But, I have seen kindness, so I think there must be a way to break down that wall."

Father Jose finished his meal. "You may try to dangle a carrot in front of her nose, but you may get hurt in the process."

Fannie had already finished her plate so she took his empty plate with hers and rose from the bench. "Thank you for listening. I'd better go over to the group where I usually sit or they'll think I'm conspiring."

The priest laughed again. "No. They'll think you have a big trouble to confess."

Fannie smiled too. "I'll keep them guessing."

When it was time to leave, Fannie climbed onto Rosetta's cart. Today she decided to ask the younger woman some questions. The ride home was always too quiet.

"Are you married, Rosetta."

Her faint smile was pensive. "I was. My man is no more."

"I'm sorry," said Fannie.

"He died," Rosetta clarified.

"I shouldn't have asked. I am sorry."

Rosetta shook her head and shrugged a shoulder. "It is all right. He suffered much. It is better. No babies."

"Do you work?"

She nodded. "I take care of a big house."

"That's hard work," remarked Fannie. "I used to clean a big, big house."

Rosetta smiled at her. "So you know. I am happy. Are you happy?" Rosetta surprised Fannie with the question.

Fannie had to think about that. She did miss Virginia. Then she nodded. "I think we have to make our own happiness."

Rosetta sighed a deep sigh. "Or we sour."

When they got home, Fannie helped Maria from the cart. The woman never looked at her nor said a word to Rosetta. She went to her door and went inside.

"Maria is not happy," said Rosetta. She tapped her pony with the reins and waved to Fannie as she left.

Jess was out spreading hay for the horse.

Fannie walked to where he worked. "I talked with Father Jose today about helping Maria reconcile with her children."

"What did he say?"

"There is no harm in trying."

Jess set the hayfork aside and wiped his brow. "Why is it you feel the need to solve everyone's problems?"

"I don't."

"Yes you do. You're not pleased that we aren't at Lockwood helping Lottie and Addie. You had to take Ota under your wing on the train. Now you feel it's your duty to bring Maria and her children together."

Fannie stood her ground. "I guess I'm a take-care-of kind of person. You have to admit it worked out to Ota's benefit. And, both Addie and Lottie could use the extra help. And, I feel sorry for Maria."

"It's her own doing, Fannie."

"I know, but I can try."

He shook his head. "You might get hurt in the process."

"The priest said the same thing. I'm sure the old woman can be spiteful. I promise I won't come crying to you."

Jess put his arm around her while they walked to the patio. "Who else can you go crying to? You know I'll be here to kiss your tears away."

Fannie stopped and put her arms around her big, strong husband's neck. "How did I rate such a considerate man? I do love you, Jess Edwards."

He swept her up off her feet, kissed her soundly, and carried her the rest of the way. "Fannie, my love, we were born for each other."

Chapter 41

Hollywood was bursting with energy before seven o'clock in the morning when Fannie rode into the town with Jess. He would meet her at the main trolley stop after he finished work, which he planned to do two hours early. Fannie had the whole day to roam about as she pleased.

Jess let her off at a small café. She went inside. The cash register sat at the front as she entered and a smiling busy waitress told her to sit wherever she could find a spot. Fannie sat at a small table with two chairs.

She ordered coffee, scrambled eggs and toast. The café was pleasant. An eating bar sat across the back wall. Fannie had worked in a café so she sat and watched the patrons come and go. Some were regulars, she could tell by the casual way they sat at the bar or searched out their favorite table. Some were newcomers. The bold ones took their time oblivious to the stares of those seated while the timid tried to slide in without being noticed. Fannie loved to people watch. She and Addie had done a lot of it when they lived in Washington.

She was eating her eggs and toast when a gentleman in casual attire stopped by her table.

"It's crowded this morning. Do you mind if I sit at your table?"

She looked up and smiled. "That's fine."

"Will you consider me rude if I read the paper?"

"Not at all."

Fannie continued to eat while the man unfolded the paper. He wasn't tall, nor was there anything outstanding about him. Rather plain with a build destined to be rather portly as he aged, she thought. What caught her eye was the revolver he carried at his hip.

He scanned the first page, peered around the paper, and asked, "Are you from around here?"

"No, I'm from Virginia."

"Come out for the moving pictures?"

"No."

"Unusual," he said. "They flock in by the car-loads with stars in their eyes."

He went back to the paper where a section seemed to catch his eye.

Fannie drank her coffee and the waitress came by to fill it up again as she brought the man's breakfast.

"Will there be anything else, sir?" the waitress asked.

Fannie looked up as he shook his head.

He tucked the paper away and devoured his breakfast in earnest. In between bites, he said, "I apologize for not being an eager conversationalist after you've been good enough to allow me to sit here. I have a busy schedule ahead of me for the day. And the days to come," he added.

His smile was pleasant. He hurried through his breakfast and nodded at Fannie as he rose to leave. "Thank you again."

Fannie looked after him in dismay as he paid his bill and left the café.

The waitress came by to clear away the soiled dishes.

"Do you know that gentleman who joined me at this table?" Fannie asked.

"That's Mr. DeMille. He comes in every morning."

Fannie gulped. "Do you mean the DeMille who makes silent moving pictures?"

"The same. He lives up in the hills and every morning rides his horse down here."

"Does he always carry a pistol?"

"He's not the only one. The way this place is growing a person can't be too careful. He's a kindly man. He paid for your breakfast."

Surprise caught Fannie. "He is more than kind."

She finished her coffee and left the café with a lighter step. Wait until I tell Addie about this, thought Fannie.

She walked around the streets wasting time until the department and clothing stores opened. At a grocer's, she stood and watched as the owner filled the bins in front of the store with assorted fresh fruits and vegetables.

Fannie wandered inside to see what was new on the shelves. She walked by the dill pickle barrel and cracker bins to find the penny candy in glass display cases on the counter. She bought two peppermint sticks only because she felt guilty after spending a half hour cruising the store. After all, she hadn't had to pay for her breakfast.

There were many more people on the streets when she left the grocer's. She turned and walked up Vine Street. There were a few tall buildings.

She passed a Dodge dealership. A car was not anything they could afford so she walked right by without even stopping to see the models displayed at the front of the lot.

A few doors down was a dress shop and in the window she saw a bathing suit on a dress form. A red bathing cap was placed over the neck of the form. The bathing cap had a flower on the side. Fannie decided to go in to see if there was the same cap in a different color. If she bought a bathing suit to venture into the ocean, she would most likely need a cap.

"Good morning," greeted the saleslady upon Fannie's entrance.

"Good morning. I noticed the bathing cap in the window. Do you carry them in a different color?"

"That we do." She led Fannie to a counter where there were bathing caps of every color imaginable. "What color is your bathing suit?"

"I don't have one," Fannie confessed. "My husband and I are going to the ocean."

"Well, my goodness." The saleslady's eyes opened wide. "You will definitely need a suit. We have a new shipment of Jansen. They've come out with more solid colors, stripes and plaids. They are also more daring. They scrimped on material during the war; and I think women like the less cumbersome styles."

"And, the companies are making more money with less material," surmised Fannie.

The lady smiled at her. "They catch us one way or another, don't they. Follow me. We'll find a suit and then you can pick out a cap."

There was a varied selection of bathing suits and Fannie wanted one that would cover as much of her body as possible because of the sun. There weren't many. She finally settled on a one-piece teal wool with a short skirt and mid-thigh legs that peeked under the skirt. The shoulders were about two inches wide with two white buttons sewn on the right shoulder. The skirt was trimmed with white stripes around the bottom and a white cloth belt was attached to the empire waist. Fannie laughed when she looked in the mirror and said to herself, "I believe a chemise covers more territory."

The saleslady waited outside the booth. "Did you say something?"

Fannie raised her voice to be heard. "I was talking to myself."

The lady chuckled. "I thought I was the only one who did that."

Fannie changed into her street clothes and opened the half door of the dressing area. "I'll take this one."

"That will look very nice with your coloring. We do have a matching cap."

"I had hoped this suit would cover better. I have to be careful of the sun."

"If you'd like to look, we have some lovely cover-ups for that purpose."

Why was Fannie not surprised? Her groan was inward, more money. "I'd like to see them."

By the time she left the store she had a rubber bathing cap, wool bathing suit, white organdy sun cover and a white parasol to match. The parasol was free if you bought the protective sun garment. The total came to $13.10.

Fannie did her best not to gasp when told the price. She forgot about a new blouse. Gabriel Flores was costing them money. A table of yard goods caught her eye as she was leaving with pretty light and bright materials greeting her. Is it possible she could hand sew a blouse? She bought a pattern, thread, needle, and material of delicately flowered light blue cotton. For forty-five cents she was determined to try. Lottie would have the blouse cut and sewn in an hour. But, Lottie wasn't here.

Fannie also bought elastic for the top and waist. The pattern was for a peasant blouse because buttons and buttonholes were too labor intensive. One more stop at the cobbler's shop for new soles and she would be through. How were they ever going to save up to go back to Virginia if they kept frittering their money away?

Chapter 42

Maria Flores was back in her garden so Fannie didn't feel guilty about leaving her for three days.

Gabriel arrived in his spiffy red car with no top. Jess was excited and Fannie was doing her best to match his enthusiasm.

Fannie decided to wear her long-sleeved white blouse and navy skirt. The outfit would take her anywhere. She packed a sheet in her tote bag just in case. In case of what she wasn't sure, but it seemed a wise idea.

Gabriel was as flashy as his car. He wore a flowered shirt and cream-colored trousers that matched his wide-brimmed hat. His silver jewelry glinted in the sunlight.

Jess wore his cowboy hat, cream shirt and black pants. To Fannie he was as dapper as Gabriel without the jazz.

"We can all three ride in the front seat," Gabriel said as he came to meet them.

"How would it be if you two men sat in the front and I sat in the back?" suggested Fannie. "It would give more room. You said we have a long trip ahead of us."

"Are you sure you want to ride in the back, Fannie?" asked Jess.

"I do."

Gabriel packed their suitcases in the trunk of the car while Jess helped Fannie into the back seat. She kept her tote bag with her. It was close to nine o'clock when they left the adobe house. If Maria was watching, she was nowhere in sight.

The sky was blue with a few wispy clouds, the sun was shining, the white leather seat was comfortable, and Fannie was finally ready for this adventure.

Jess and Gabriel chatted away like old friends. She couldn't understand their words in the back seat of the open car. It wasn't long before Fannie took off her straw hat that she had been holding on with one hand because of the wind of the moving car. She pulled a ribbon from her tote and tied her flying hair. Then she pulled out a silk scarf, replaced her hat, and tied the scarf around her hat and under her chin before it went sailing in the wind. She had never ridden in an open car. The sun was beating down. There was no use in using an umbrella or parasol because they would be whipped away.

After an hour she felt like the sun was burning through her clothes and wished she had worn that big hat Maria had given her. The last thing she needed was a sunburn. Fannie pulled the bed sheet out of her tote and wrapped herself up like a mummy. It wasn't easy fighting the billowing air, but she was determined.

"How are you doing back there, my love?" questioned Jess without turning around.

He didn't see her grimace. "Just fine."

They rode on the hard-packed dirt roads, up hills, down hills, around sharp corners, and along flat surfaces with scenery of scrub trees, scrub bushes, sandy brown soil and palm trees. It seemed any greenery in California was where men's hands made water available.

"A few more minutes," Gabriel called.

Good. Fannie unwrapped the sheet and rolled it into a ball then struggled to jam it back into the tote.

When she straightened up, beyond her she saw the beautiful blue water of the Pacific. The scene took her breath away. The blue went on forever. Fannie leaned into the front seat and touched her husband's shoulder. "Oh, Jess. Isn't it glorious?"

He patted her hand. "I knew you wouldn't be disappointed."

Gabriel turned the car to the left. "Doncia's place is down this way."

The road was narrow. They passed small shops along the way. Most were one-story and many carried Spanish architecture: white stucco, red-tiled roofs, garden courtyards, and lots of flowering vines.

Gabriel pointed to a white stone arch with the words La Vista painted across the archway. He pulled the car into a space across the street.

"Here we are. The rooms are upstairs and the café is down. I'll find my sister and tell her we've arrived."

"What does La Vista mean?" asked Fannie.

Gabriel's smile spread wide, "The view."

Jess helped Fannie from the back seat. They stood surveying this place where they were going to spend the next three days. Land sloped to the beach below. They could see people out in the water and others lounging on the sandy beach. Gabriel said it was a quieter beach. From what Fannie saw it was busy enough for her.

There was high ground on each side of the beach. "Is this a cove, Jess?"

"I would call it that. What do you think? Are you glad we came?"

"I would be disappointed if we hadn't come. Gabriel has been good to us."

"You were good to his mother," he said and kissed her cheek.

Gabriel came up the outside stairs that led down to the café. Behind him was a short plain woman who looked much like the women in the village near Maria's. If this was Gabriel's sister there was little resemblance except for their coloring. Then she smiled and there was no mistaking she was Gabriel's sister.

Gabriel put his arm around her as he introduced Doncia to Jess and Fannie.

"Welcome to LaVista. We are happy to have you here." Although she spoke with an accent her English was clear.

"We are pleased to be here," answered Fannie. "Doubly pleased that you speak English."

Doncia nodded. "Gabriel insisted. Come I will show you the rooms."

They entered and walked down a hallway with a window at the end where they could see the ocean as they walked. It was like looking at a painting. There were six rooms, three on each side.

Doncia gave Gabriel a key to his room and opened the door for Jess and Fannie before she handed them the key.

"I'll be across the hall," said Gabriel as he turned the key in the lock.

"The café is open from seven in the morning to eight o'clock in the evening. These are our best rooms. Each has its own bathroom. We have electric lights and there is a one burner electric stove if you want to make coffee. The coffee and cups are in the cupboard above it. If there is anything you need, we are downstairs."

"Gracias, Senora Doncia," said Jess.

A smile came to her face. "You speak Spanish?"

"Only enough to show off once in a while."

Doncia laughed aloud. "I think we are going to be very happy to have you here."

After she left the room, Jess pulled Fannie into his arms and smacked a big delicious kiss on her lips. "That bed looks inviting," he whispered in her ear.

She twirled his hair with her fingers and teased him with a seductive smile. "It's one o'clock in the afternoon. Aren't you tired from that long ride?"

"I'm never too tired," he replied before he swooped her up in his arms. "This is the honeymoon we never had."

"I believe you said that of the Palmer House in Chicago."

"That I did, Fannie, my love. This will be our second."

Chapter 43

Fannie luxuriated in the tub. How long had it been since she'd had a tub bath? The outdoor shower Jess had rigged up was a big help, but there is nothing like a tub, especially one this size where she could stretch her legs out in front of her.

She dressed back into the navy skirt. Instead of the white blouse, she put on the flowered peasant one she had hand sewn. She combed her hair back and tied it with a ribbon. Her face held a pink glow. I guess that's what people call sun-kissed, thought Fannie. It was enough kissing from the sun. She would be extra careful for the next couple of days.

Jess was lying on the bed when she came out of the bathroom. "You look lovely and refreshed."

"Thank you. I feel lovely and refreshed. When are we going to eat? I'm starved."

"So am I. We haven't had lunch. Shall we venture out and find a sandwich?"

"I'm sure they serve them in the café," remarked Fannie.

"We're having supper in the cafe with Gabriel at seven o'clock."

"When did you decide this?"

"While you were dreaming in your bath."

"I wasn't dreaming. When you went to see Gabriel, you didn't leave me in the tub with an unlocked door, I hope."

Jess smiled. "I didn't have to. He came to the door on his way to the beach."

Fannie looked out the window in the room that had a gorgeous view of the beach and ocean. "I can see why they call this place La Vista." She turned to Jess and laughed. "Gabriel isn't hard to spot. He's got on a red and white striped bathing suit."

"How do you know that's Gabriel?"

"Because all the women are watching him. Maybe I should have bought a man's bathing suit. It covers better. The legs stop above the knees, the neck is higher and the straps wider."

"I don't think women buy men's bathing suits. What's your opinion?"

"Of women buying men's bathing suits?"

A sly look came over his face. "I mean of Gabriel."

Fannie turned from the window. "I think he looks terrific!" She ran and jumped on the bed and gave her husband a kiss. "But not as terrific as you!"

Jess snickered. "Careful. We may not get out of this room."

She hoped off the bed. "Not likely. Let's go find some vittles."

They walked out through the archway. After looking right and left they decided to turn right. There were a couple of hotels at the end of the town that stood out because they were taller than the shops. They weren't grand hotels but they looked inviting.

Fannie was curious. "How many rooms do you think they hold?"

"I don't know. They probably have eating places and shops on the main floor. That leaves three floors for rooms. Why do you ask?"

"If this is a quieter and smaller beach, think how crowded the big ones are."

"That would never occur to me, Fannie. Do you want to walk down there?"

"No. Let's stop in here."

Jess looked up at the sign: Specialty Hot Dogs. "I wonder what's so special about a hotdog?"

"Let's go find out."

The shop was small. There were two people ahead of them so they waited in line. The owner stood behind a display counter and took orders. Behind and above him on the wall was a menu. All they sold were hotdogs, sodas, and packages of potato chips.

The hotdogs were German, juicy inside and thick skinned outside. They came with either: sauerkraut, chili, cheese, sweet pickle relish, onions, chutney, spicy mustard, sweet mustard or plain mustard. You could choose any or all. The owner made his own rolls because the hotdogs were two inches longer than packaged ones.

Jess asked for one with sauerkraut, onions, spicy mustard and cheese. Fannie settled for one with sweet mustard. Jess bought two colas and a package of chips. The man set the hot dogs in heavy paper trays. There were chairs and tables outside. Fannie picked up a couple of paper napkins from the counter before they took seats at a small table for two.

Jess spied a bottle top opener hanging from a string on a post. He popped the tops off the sodas and handed a bottle to Fannie. She took the hotdog trays out of the bag and opened the potato chips. There was a gentle breeze coming off the ocean.

"I understand why people go on vacation," said Fannie. "Any of life's problems seem to disappear."

Jess was busily looking at the loaded hotdog trying to figure out how he was going to attack it. "What life's problems' do you have, wife of mine."

Fannie smiled at him as she bit into a potato chip. "I don't know. I am concerned about Lottie. I wish there was a way to get Maria to accept her children. They're nice people so she must have been a good mother. And the way we've been spending money, I'm worried we may never get back to Virginia. Don't you miss the green grass, the tall trees, the Blue Ridge, our cozy cabin?"

"As I've said before, Lottie is not our problem, and if Maria is to get back with her children that is up to her. Nate and Crystal have taken over the cabin. That wasn't meant to be our home. That was a starting place. We have options to check out here, Fannie."

She swallowed a bite of hotdog. "So you don't miss Lockwood?"

He shook his head. "Not yet."

Those were not words Fannie wanted to hear, but she wasn't going to ruin this idyllic setting by pushing any further. Although the Palmer House in Chicago was a luxury, this ocean trip was turning out to be the true honeymoon they never had. She wasn't going to spoil it.

"I can see why he only sells hotdogs," said Jess after they finished. "Mine was good enough to come back for more. I'll bet the weekends are busy here with people coming out to escape Los Angeles."

Fannie nodded. "I might if I lived here. I get tired of a big city. Let's wander in and out of some shops now that my hunger is satisfied."

Jess took the soda bottles back into the eating place before they resumed strolling along the wooden sidewalk.

"Look, Jess," Fannie pointed to a hat on display in a store window. "That's a perfect hat for the beach. Do you mind if I go in and try it on?"

"Let's go," he said as he opened the door.

A clerk came to help them.

"I'd like to try on the hat that's on display in the window."

"That's our last beach hat. I expect a new shipment on Friday." She went to the front of the store and lifted the hat off the display. "It's a popular style. There's a mirror over here."

Fannie and Jess followed. The saleslady handed the hat to Fannie. "You have pretty hair, miss. Just enough red, thickness and wave to set the hat off."

Fannie placed the hat on her head, looked in the mirror, and agreed the clerk's compliment was deserved. She did look becoming.

221

The clerk continued with her sales pitch. "The wavy wide brim keeps the sun away and flutters in the breeze. It seems there is always a breeze from the ocean."

"I like the way the band comes through the holes on the sides and ties under the chin."

"The ladies even wear them out to wade in the water if they prefer not to swim. The reeds in this hat have been dyed to give it the rich color of our golden sand."

The multicolored cotton band circled the crown before the tails dropped through to be tied. The colors would go well with her bathing suit.

"How much is it?" asked Fannie.

"It's a quality hat. The price is six dollars."

Fannie was about to hand it back to the lady when Jess stepped up. "She'll take it," he said.

"But…"

His stern look stopped her before she said another word.

The clerk brought a hat box in which Fannie placed her own straw hat. She decided to wear the new one.

As soon as they left the shop, she turned her face up to look at Jess. "I have never spent six dollars on a hat."

"It's time you did. You look like a million bucks. I'm a lucky man."

She placed her arm through his as they walked back to La Vista.

Chapter 44

Jess and Fannie were having breakfast on the balcony at the café. They sat at the same table they had shared with Gabriel the evening before.

Fannie wore her new floppy hat because the sun was out. Wasn't it always?

"The ocean goes on forever, doesn't it, Jess?"

"I guess until it hits a land mass. Do you think we are in paradise?"

She smiled at him across the table. "Probably as close as we'll ever be."

He was devouring his breakfast at a fast pace. "I was hungry this morning. Last night's feast should have held me over. Would you like to live here?"

The remark, casual as it was, caused Fannie to look straight at him. "I hope you're not thinking about it. The answer is no."

He shrugged a shoulder.

"Jess, I gave you two months and I've extended it. I won't extend it indefinitely."

Doncia came to refill their coffee cups. "You have the perfect hat for the sun, Fannie. Did you sleep well?"

"We were both dead to the world. Gabriel said you are expecting a baby. Is that supposed to be a secret?"

She blushed. "No but I haven't shouted it out. I am shy because I am not young."

"You're not much older than me. I'll be twenty-two next month."

Doncia's smile was wide. "You can add a dozen years."

The figure was a surprise. "That's wonderful. I am very happy for you and Carlos. May I tell your mother when I return?

A sad look replaced the beaming smile. "She will not care. I am sorry for my mother. If it wasn't for Gabriel, I would still be wasting away in the old ways. Gabriel, Carlos and I are family and soon we will have a baby to add."

Fannie took the opportunity. "I thought Gabriel would be married with a family."

Doncia shook her head. "Not my brother. He has been too busy making money. I am praying someone will come along. Gabriel is four years older than me." She finished refilling their cups. "If there isn't anything else, you will have to excuse me or Carlos will be shooing me away. He always tells me not to talk too long with the guests because most are here to get away from people."

"Tell Carlos I enjoy talking with Gabriel's sister."

Doncia blushed again. "Your breakfast is paid for. You have the rest of the day to enjoy."

"We intend to pay for breakfast," Jess joined in.

Doncia shook her head. "Gabriel says you are his guests. He would not be pleased if you paid for your meals. It is his way of not feeling indebted for you caring for our mother, and he is glad you are living at her house. It takes worries off his shoulders."

"One more thing," said Fannie as Doncia turned to leave. "Where is the best gift shop here?"

"That is an easy answer. Lucia's is across the street and three shops down on the left." She whispered in Fannie's ear, "The rents are cheaper on that side so the prices are better."

Fannie grinned. "Thank you."

They wiped their hands with cloth napkins and left the café. Jess was eager to go swimming. They went back to the room and changed into bathing suits. He gave a low whistle when Fannie emerged from the bathroom in her new teal suit.

"I feel half-dressed," she said.

His suit was all black. The top was round necked with wide shoulder straps. The pants were knee-length.

"Where did you get that bathing suit?" she asked.

"In Washington. When I came to court you, I stayed at the YMCA, if you'll remember. They had a swimming pool."

"It fits you good so my cooking must not be adding any weight," Fannie teased.

"You look fetching," he replied and grabbed her around the waist. "Having a good honeymoon?"

"I am."

Fannie put on the white cover-up and floppy hat. She put a fashion magazine, the sheet she'd brought, the bathing cap and the parasol into her tote. They walked barefoot down the outside stairs onto the beach.

"Ouch, that sand is hot!" Fannie declared.

Jess carried wooden folding chairs, a curtesy for the guests of La Vista. He set them up to the right side. The sand wasn't as hot because it was shaded from the higher land to the side where the sun had not yet penetrated. They were as protected from the other beachgoers as they could be.

"Fannie, I never asked if you could swim."

She laughed. "Not a stroke."

"Then I guess we'll have to wade."

"I'll go wading. Then I'll sit and read my magazine while you swim."

"It's a deal."

Fannie put her cover-up and tote on a chair. She put on the rubber bathing cap and decided she was ready for the venture into the Pacific Ocean.

They walked to the edge and watched the frothy gentle waves as they lapped against the shore. Farther out were the rolling, high waves that sent sprays of water into the air. Her mind could only imagine the force of that body of water during a storm.

Fannie stuck her foot in the water and pulled it right back. "Egads! That's cold."

"You'll get used to it," encouraged Jess.

He took her hand and they slowly made their way along the shore with the sand squishing between their toes. Fannie was fascinated by the stones and shells. They waded out to knee deep water.

"This is far enough for me, Jess."

"Doesn't it feel good?" He sat down and let the water come up to his neck. "This is one big bathtub."

Fannie shivered. "It's too cold for me! I'm going back where it's shallower and maybe warmer."

He smiled at her. "If you feel comfortable, I'll go for a swim."

"Go ahead, but be careful."

Jess stood up, kissed her cheek and went out farther while Fannie made her way back to where she could comfortably sit with water up to her waist. She was surprised it was difficult to sit flat with the water trying to keep her afloat and sending her off balance. It was better just to wade. As she started to get up a forceful wave caught her off guard and knocked her down. The salty water stung her nose and she gulped a mouthful of the ocean water before she could spit it out. She struggled to her knees as another wave plunged her down while she was working hard to stand.

Once more Fannie was pushed over until a pair of strong hands caught her. She spluttered and wiped her face with her hands. Grinning at her was Gabriel. "You have to get used to the rhythm of the ocean."

"Thank you. I'll stick to the land."

"Where is Jess?"

Fannie pointed. "I headed back to the shore and he went for a swim." She pulled off the bathing cap. "A lot of good this thing does, my hair is soaked and my ears are full of water."

227

"I'll walk you back," he offered.

Fannie shook her head. "No. I won't be foolish enough to try to sit."

"If you won't allow me the honor to accompany such a charming young lady, then I shall go join her husband for a swim."

Fannie chuckled. "Gabriel Flores, I do believe flattery is your strong suit. Did you learn the skill in that Jesuit school?"

Her words brought a hearty laugh. "Believe me, there was no one there to flatter. I only speak the truth."

Gabriel went to find Jess and Fannie waded back to shore. She was more than uncomfortable. The sun seemed to be baking the salty water to her skin and her suit felt like it was filled with sand grating as she walked. By the time she reached the chairs she had made a decision. Putting on the cool cover-up, she picked up her tote and went back to their room.

She filled the tub, peeled off the irritating bathing suit and climbed into the clean soothing water. When she felt clean she washed her hair. After toweling dry, she pulled the plug and watched the water drain out leaving a trail of sand behind in the bottom of the tub.

Fannie dressed in a silk chemise and put the white cover-up over it. No one had to know she wasn't wearing a bathing suit under the opaque material.

Fannie went to Doncia, borrowed a broom and dustpan and swept up all the gritty sand left on the floor and in the tub. She hung the rinsed out bathing suit over the tub faucet to dry. Feeling much more comfortable, Fannie tied her long red hair back and placed the floppy hat on her head. She left the room, walked down the stairs, strolled out onto the balcony, took out the magazine she carried, and waited for the swimmers. So much for the sand, the sun, and the sea, thought Fannie.

**

It was mid-afternoon when Jess and Gabriel decided to leave the beach. Fannie had abandoned the hot spot a couple hours before and sat on the balcony of La Vista enjoying cold tea.

Jess came to her after he changed into street clothes. "I thought you were going to sit on the beach and read."

"So did I until I felt like I was burning up. I did my best to cover myself from the sun, but I'll bet I got more than I planned. Let's go find Lucia's and a place to buy witch hazel. Maybe that will ward off a burn."

"It'll help take away the sting, anyway."

She scrunched up her face. "That's encouraging."

Lucia's was a pleasant walk with the gentle breeze blowing from the sea. The shop was small and filled with all kinds of goods from jewelry to jam.

Fannie took her time looking for the exact gifts she wanted: for Lottie, a jar of boysenberry jam, for Addie, a moonstone necklace, for Peg a

229

folding hand fan with the picture of an ocean scene, and for Maria, a candle with a picture of the Virgin Mary holding baby Jesus.

Jess had wandered about the store and came to her with a bottle of witch hazel, a deck of cards, and a box of Fannie Farmer chocolates.

Fannie smiled at him. "Chocolates?"

"It's got your name on the box."

"They'll probably melt."

He grinned. "It's a small box."

Jess paid for the merchandise and Lucia packaged it with care.

They were going to have dinner with Gabriel at a different restaurant than the café. Gabriel said it was a favorite of his when he came to the beach. It meant taking the car.

At six o'clock they met Gabriel as he was coming out of his room. Jess was clean shaven and dressed in his cream shirt and black pants.

Fannie wore a light and breezy yellow blouse she'd admired in Lucia's store. The blouse was elbow length, elastic in the sleeves with small white bows on each sleeve. It had a peplum waist and a panel of white lace down the front. The blouse looked smart with the tan skirt she had packed. As they were going in the car, Fannie chose the floppy hat that tied under her chin.

She had gotten too much sun which had reddened her face. Powder would never cover the burn. She rubbed Pond's cold cream to soothe the tingling feeling and put Vaseline on her parched lips.

Gabriel was his usual dashing self, dressed in a red shirt and cream trousers. The silver cross was at his throat and silver cuff bracelet that matched the turquoise ring.

"We'll be back around eight before the sun sets. I don't care to drive the road after dark. The restaurant is only fifteen minutes away."

They walked across the street to the car where Jess helped Fannie onto the running board and into the back seat. "We can all three sit in front," he offered.

"No. I like the extra room." She liked the extra room but not the wind from the moving car.

Fannie understood why Gabriel wanted to be back before dark. The road was narrow with sheer drop-offs into the Pacific below. If a car went off the road on one of the sharp curves, it would smash on the huge boulders where big waves slammed into them. The sight made Fannie's stomach queasy. She wanted to close her eyes but watched the road instead, gripping the shawl she carried with white knuckles.

They arrived at the restaurant with her knees feeling wobbly as she climbed from the back seat. Jess had a firm grip on her arm. "That was like a carnival ride," he whispered. "Are you all right?"

"I will be once my knees stop knocking."

He laughed as he bent and kissed her cheek.

The restaurant was deceiving. They walked in on flat ground but before them the room ahead jutted out over the water. The waiter showed them to their table, which sat with wide windows in front so they had a commanding view of the Pacific. They watched the coming and going of the crashing ocean surf as it splashed on the rocks and sent spouts of water into the air before their eyes. It didn't feel real.

Fannie looked over at Jess. "Are we still on earth?"

Gabriel chuckled. "Do you see why I like to come here?"

"We would like to treat you to dinner," said Jess.

Gabriel shook his head. "No, friend. I promised a trip to the ocean. I would not be happy with myself if you paid."

"Gabriel, you have provided the transportation, the room at La Vista, and have paid for our meals. Caring for your mother didn't cost me a thing," said Fannie.

"She could have died if you hadn't been there. Bringing you here to my sister's place has allowed me time away from the cares of my ranch. That can't be counted up in money."

"Are you saying that if it weren't for us, you wouldn't be here?" asked Jess.

"I am saying that I have trouble making time for myself. I am saying thanks to you my mother is back in her garden. Thanks to you living there I do not have to worry and wonder about her all the time, and best of all because we have come I find I am going to be an uncle. It has been a good time, has it not?"

The waiter came by. "We shall have champagne," Gabriel said to him.

The waiter smiled. "Prohibition hasn't caught up with us yet, sir. I will bring a bottle of our best." He left them with menus.

When Jess saw the prices of the epicurean meals, he was more than happy Gabriel was picking up the tab.

They toasted to their friendship with the first glass of champagne. Then they spent an hour and a half tasting all kinds of fish and meat dishes cooked in exotic spices and sauces.

Gabriel and Jess each chose a decadent dessert but Fannie was too full. "I couldn't possibly eat another bite," she said.

"It's all that swimming we did," informed Jess. "Gabriel and I had to push against the waves."

"I watched," said Fannie. "You two were having entirely too much fun."

"I'll teach you to swim," offered Jess.

She shook her head. "No thanks. I'll sit in the shade and watch."

She excused herself to go to the ladies' room. One look in the mirror and she could see her face looked like a cooked lobster. She patted her face with a powder puff just to feel the gentleness of the soft cotton before she went back to the table.

The sun would be setting soon. Gabriel paid the bill and Fannie took one last look out the picture windows at the vast sea. She may never see it again and she wanted the memory.

On the way back to La Vista she sat on the opposite side of the seat so she didn't have to see the perilous precipice with the sea and boulders below. They had finished the bottle of champagne. Gabriel seemed to be steady on his feet, but still Fannie gave a silent prayer they would make it back without incident.

Chapter 45

Jess and Fannie were eating a late breakfast while Gabriel took his last swim before they left. They were the only customers on the balcony.

"It is so peaceful here," said Fannie as she looked out at the ocean. The waves were calm and few people were on the beach.

Doncia came to refill their coffee cups.

"Sit with us before we have to leave," Fannie invited.

Jess stood and pulled out a chair so Doncia could sit. She shot a glance into where Carlos was busy. He nodded.

"It feels good to get off my feet," she said as she sat in the chair Jess offered. "You are leaving at the right time. Tomorrow the people come in from the city for the weekend. The rooms are all rented, so we will spend tomorrow stocking the kitchen and cleaning the place spotless. This is our third year here."

"What are you going to do when the baby comes?" asked Fannie.

Doncia gave a quizzical look. "The same as I do now."

"I guess what I mean is will you have time to rest up?"

"The baby is coming before Christmas. It is not as busy here."

Gabriel came hustling onto the balcony and waved at Carlos before he came to their table. "The swim was what I needed." He kissed Doncia on the cheek. "As soon as my sister brings my favorite breakfast, I will eat the delicious food, and we can be on our way."

The inn keeper rose from her chair. "I will miss all of you." Turning to her brother, she said, "I will bring your breakfast, Gabriel. I'm sure Carlos has it prepared."

"Carlos works too hard. He needs to get out of the kitchen and come out here to sit with us for a few minutes," said Gabriel.

Doncia gave him a playful tap on the shoulder. "Works too hard? He learned it from you, my brother."

Gabriel cocked his head to the side. "Probably so."

They packed their belongings in the car. Once again the men sat in the front seat. Fannie took the bed sheet she had brought and wrapped up like a monk pulling the hood part far forward over her head to shield her face. She had used witch hazel which did help to soothe the stinging of the sunburn, and she slathered Vaseline on her lips to help heal the tiny blisters that had formed.

Gabriel stopped at a gas station to fill the gas tank. It was clear the young attendant admired Gabriel's nifty car. He looked long and hard at the huddled, bundled, white mass in the back seat. "Looks like your passenger doesn't enjoy the open air," he remarked as he washed the short windshield.

"She's a nun," kidded Jess. "We just picked her up from Santa Barbara where she was visiting the missions."

The attendant stepped back from the auto after finishing his job and directed his voice to the back seat. "I'm sorry, Sister. I didn't mean to stare," he apologized.

"That's quite all right," she replied in a soft voice. "The hilarious man up front is my husband."

Gabriel guffawed and they were off leaving the confused young man scratching his head.

It was late afternoon when they arrived at Maria's adobe house. Gabriel opened the trunk and helped remove their suitcases and the boxes of articles they had bought.

Fannie gave him a friendly hug and Jess shook his hand. "You have given us a wonderful honeymoon. We didn't have one when we married."

"Then I am twice happy," said Gabriel. "Someday maybe I will have a honeymoon at Doncia's."

On a serious note, Fannie said. "Gabriel, your sister says it is all right to tell your mother about the baby coming. Do you mind if I tell her?"

He leaned against the car. "I am not sure how she will accept the news. Such a stubborn unforgiving woman."

"Gabriel, she is your mother and she must have been a good mother to raise two such considerate children." It was an unusual mild chastisement from Fannie.

"You are right," he agreed. "She wasn't always hard-hearted. It was after my father died that she sent me away to school and clung to Doncia." He gave a deep sigh. " Now, I must be on my way before evening settles in. As you know the roads to my ranch are not the easiest."

He opened the front door and sat in the driver's seat. "It was a good three days."

"They couldn't have been better," replied Jess. "If you ever need help, you can count on me."

Gabriel nodded and headed away.

Jess and Fannie Edwards stood together and waved as they watched him leave.

"Do you think Providence has guided us to this spot, Jess?"

"That's a good question Fannie."

Chapter 46

Maria was out in her garden the next morning. Fannie was preparing to do laundry in the big tubs near the patio. Jess had filled the tubs with water from the well before he left. By noontime the water would be lukewarm. Fannie walked to the garden to see Maria.

"I am going to wash clothes. Do you have anything you want me to wash?"

Maria looked up at her and nodded. She left the garden, went to the house, and brought underclothes, a long black skirt and black top.

Fannie knew from the time she had taken care of the woman that Maria had two black skirts and two black tops that she alternated wearing. Fannie wished she had bought the woman a white blouse from Lucia's store. But, in truth, she knew Maria wouldn't wear it if she did.

Fannie took the pile of clothes and put them with her laundry. She knew Maria would let her wash the clothes together because Maria didn't want to waste water. She had balked when Jess put up the outdoor shower until he told her it saved water in the long run.

By the time Fannie had finished the wash and hung it on the line, Maria had left the garden. Fannie fixed a glass of cold tea and went to sit while the clothes dried. They didn't take long to dry in the sun and dry breeze. While she sat she closed her eyes and visualized the ocean scene and smiled at the recollection. It truly had been a wonderful time.

The clothes were dry. Fannie folded them and went around to Maria's side of the house to give her the clean clothes. She knocked on the door and Maria came to answer it.

"I've brought your clothes and I have a present for you. May I come inside?"

The old woman stepped back from the door. Fannie put the clothes on a chair and handed a bag to Maria.

She opened it and brought out the candle Fannie had bought. A faint smile came to her weathered face.

"Mrs. Flores, we met Doncia this weekend. She is going to have a baby. I thought you could light this candle every day until the baby comes."

Maria took the candle in her hand. Fannie couldn't tell if she was pleased with the news because she showed no emotion. But she did raise the candle to her lips and kissed the likeness of the infant.

Fannie went back to sort her laundry and put the clothes away. She folded the teal bathing suit and cap and put them in the bottom drawer of the dresser, doubting she would ever wear them again.

When she went back outside Maria came to the patio. In her hand was a saucer of mushy looking green paste. She motioned Fannie to stay seated. Then Maria put her knobby fingers into the mess and began dabbing it on Fannie's sunburned face and tender lips. She shook her head as if Fannie should have known better.

"I tried to be careful."

Maria touched the skin on Fannie's arm and pointed to the sun. She shook her head again.

"I know. My color is not good for California. We will go back home one of these days."

Fannie's face felt cooler. "Where did you get this stuff?"

Maria pointed to the garden and pretended to cut with a knife and mix with her hands.

Gesturing again. "Mrs. Flores, I wish you would talk to me. I know you understand and can speak enough English. Couldn't you say the garden or my plants or something?"

Maria's smile was faint as she shrugged her shoulders. Just as though she was keeping a big secret to herself. She handed the saucer to Fannie, turned and left.

At least Fannie had gotten some reaction.

When Jess came home he took one look at her and laughed aloud. "What's that green goo on your face?"

"Maria put it on for my sunburn. I'll wash it off before we eat. My face feels better."

"Maria? Did you tell her about Doncia?"

Fannie nodded. "I don't know how she accepted it. I could tell she liked the candle I gave to her."

"How old do you think she is?" questioned Jess.

241

"I don't know. If Gabriel is almost forty she's probably around sixty. Why do you ask?"

Jess took a seat on the patio. "Maybe she's not as old as I thought she was. I was afraid she might drop dead on us one day."

"Jess Edwards! That's a morbid thought. She's still independent and strong enough. I think that's why she won't go to live at Gabriel's ranch."

Jess sighed. "It could be and it could be she is making it as difficult for Gabriel as she can. She knows he worries about her. I feel sorry for him."

"You feel sorry for Gabriel? He has the world by its tail."

Jess pulled her onto his lap. "He doesn't have a pretty wife who cooks his meals, does his laundry, takes care of his every need, and greets him with green goo on her face."

Fannie wiped her face with a finger and spread the soft mush on Jess's cheek. "A wife who shares everything," she said and kissed him with her gooey lips.

"Ugh, that stuff tastes awful." He wiped his lips with the back of his hand.

Fannie left his lap. "A little something to drive home the fact California doesn't agree with me."

"Guess what," he changed the subject.

"I couldn't."

"We finished building that set today and the director of the movie the set's built for came by to check it out. He saw me saddling up Grace and asked if I was good at riding. We got to talking and he said he needs men who know how to ride and handle cattle for the picture he's making."

"And, you said?"

"I was interested. I'm going to meet him tomorrow morning."

"Is that wise?"

"He said it would be like extra money. It wouldn't be every day. They make out a calendar and let me know what days I would work. I can work it around another job and use the movie money to buy land."

"Here or in Virginia?"

"Gabriel does well leasing his quarries."

Fannie didn't answer right away. After sorting her thoughts she said, "All right. Perhaps that's why we came. Gabriel can help you find a piece of land. Once you sign a lease, we are heading home."

He hopped up from the chair and put his arms around her. "That is agreeable. Gabriel asked me to work for him at the ranch. I can work there and come into town when the movie guy needs me."

She shook her head. "The ranch is too far away."

"He's got a place there where we can live."

"That would leave Maria alone."

"She was alone when we arrived."

"If we move to Gabriel's ranch that would be one more reason for Maria to resent him."

"That's a problem between Gabriel and his mother."

"Do you have an answer for everything, Jess? I guess you're set on taking up his offer."

He kissed her forehead. "The pay is better, the movie work is extra, and we'll get back home sooner."

This is the first time he had said back home. She sighed. "I hope you're right."

Chapter 47

Jess returned from town after he met with the movie director and signed a contract.

Fannie wasn't happy with the news. "When will the movie be finished?"

"He said maybe the first of October."

"Maybe! You shouldn't have signed that contract!"

"Fannie, I want to buy a piece of land. If the movie money is the answer, it meant signing the contract."

"That doesn't please me one bit! I'm going to help Maria in the garden!" She stalked off the patio.

Jess wasn't happy that he had displeased her, but he was going to make this trip to California worthwhile.

As he stood and watched her go, he heard the sound of galloping hoof beats coming toward the house. It was Antonio from Gabriel's ranch.

"Senor Gabriel say you come?"

"Come? To the ranch?"

"Si, you come, now!"

Fannie heard the commotion and started from the garden. "What's going on?" she called as she hurried to meet Jess.

"Antonio says Gabriel wants me to go to the ranch right away."

"Whatever for?"

"I don't know but from Antonio's insistence, it seems important. Look, he's saddling Grace before I even said I would go."

"You'd better. Gabriel wouldn't send someone on a whim."

Jess kissed her. "I'll be back tomorrow."

Maria was watching from the garden, but bent down to work when she saw Fannie coming back.

"Gabriel has sent for Jess. I think something is wrong at the ranch."

Maria showed no emotion and kept working. Fannie couldn't tell if the frustrating woman was evading her words or not. Perhaps it didn't make any difference. Tomorrow Jess would be back with news of what the problem was, if there was one.

Fannie left the garden and went back in the house. She needed to write a letter to Addie. From the cupboard in the kitchen, she took out stationery and pencil. The lead on the end of the pencil was broken so she pulled out a paring knife and shaved it back to a decent lead point. She poured a cup of tea and put chips of ice in it before she left the kitchen.

Settled on the patio she began her letter.

September 2, 1919
Dear Addie,

A lot has happened since I last wrote to you. The most wonderful news is that Jess and I went to the Pacific Ocean with Gabriel for three days. It took us over two hours to get there but it was worth it.

Gabriel drove us in his red car, which is as flashy as he is. The car has lots of shiny chrome, a short windshield and no top. I understand why they call it a windshield as it was some protection from the wind for the men in the front seat. I chose to ride in the back seat by myself to have more room. The wind from the moving car whipped around and the sun beat down unmercifully. I got smart before we left for home and wrapped up in a bed sheet I had brought.

Jess told an attendant at a gas station I was a nun. He does get his jollies.

Still, even with my diligence, my face and lips are sunburned. Maria, our landlady, mixed up some herbs from her garden to slather on my face. I have to say whatever her concoction, it has helped and I am now only a pinkish glow. I even had blistered lips. You can see this California does not agree with me.

Anyway, Jess called our trip the honeymoon we never had. I recommend it for you and Alex as he was too busy for a honeymoon when you got married.

Gabriel's sister and her husband own a small inn and café on the ocean side. When I saw that great body of water it took my breath away. Addie, the blue of the ocean is just as you see it in pictures. It seems to go on forever.

The beach is smaller than at other beaches here so we are told, but it was perfect for us. I bought a bathing suit, which I truly believe I will never wear again. I wore it wading one time. When I got into deeper water and tried to sit like in a bathtub, I was knocked over by the force of the waves, not once but three times as I tried to right myself. That was enough for me. The bathing cap did not keep out water and the sand from the roaring waves filled my bathing suit with sand from the ocean bottom. I was miserable. Then the sand on the beach was so hot on my bare feet I thought they would blister.

This sounds like I am complaining, which I am. I took a nice bath, put witch hazel on the parts of my body that looked like a cooked lobster and sat on the balcony under the shade of an umbrella.

Doncia, that's Gabriel's sister, brought me a cold glass of tea and I read a fashion magazine while Jess and Gabriel were swimming and cavorting in the high waves. Sitting on the balcony and watching the ocean and those on the beach coming and going was pure heaven.

We had our breakfasts on the balcony and shopped in the small shops that cater to visitors. I have presents for you, Peg, and Lottie that I will have Jess mail when he goes into town.

I bought a fashionable floppy hat which is perfect protection from the sun. I have found in California that the people wear brighter colors and more daring fashions than those back in the East. I guess that must be from the warmer climate. But, it could be from their more carefree ways.

Oh, yes, before I forget, the inn has electricity and indoor plumbing, two luxuries I don't have here at the place we are renting. Of course, we didn't have those luxuries in the cabin at your place, either, but I could take a bath in your tub when I wanted to.

The next news I guess is that Jess finished his job of building a set for a moving picture and has signed a contract to work on the movie. The director said he needed men who know how to ride and take care of cattle. I don't know if Jess's face will ever be shown, but he likes the idea of extra money to buy a piece of land.

No. We are not staying here if that was your thought when you read the last sentence. We will be returning once this is all settled. The movie is going to extend our stay at least into October. I was not pleased when Jess said he had to sign or forget it. It ties us here.

Today he had an urgent request from Gabriel to come out to his ranch. I can't imagine what the problem is. Jess will return tomorrow so I will only have to worry for the night.

Are you still taking care of Lottie's baby or is she back on her feet? How is Caleb? I hope he healed fully after the accident with the pitchfork. And their sweet children? I think that if Lottie could come out here she would be back feeling as good as new.

The trains are getting faster and more convenient. Wouldn't it be a hoot if you and Lottie could come out here for a visit? Speaking of hoot that's the name of the actor who is supposed to be the star in the movie Jess has signed for. Hoot Gibson. He must be new; one of the many people who are piling into Hollywood because of the moving picture business.

Addie, I can't remember what I wrote in my last letter so if I have repeated myself you will have to forgive me. And, look, here I have used up two solid sheets of paper.

I will close and look forward to your answering letter. You must tell me everything that is going on at the farm and around the county. September is always such a pretty time in Virginia. I count the days until we are on the train heading home.

Please give our best to Alex, Peg and the Dunn family.

Your friend,
Fannie

Fannie reread the letter before she put it into an envelope and sealed it shut. Stamps had gone up to three cents since her last letter, but Addie was worth it. She didn't want to think how much it would cost to mail the presents she had bought.

The young men from the village would be by tomorrow on their way into town. Fannie planned to have them mail the letter for her.

As Jess wasn't coming back until the next day there was no need to start a fire. She fixed a salad and bowl of fruit for supper.

To her surprise while she sat on the patio, Maria came around the corner of the house with a bowl of corn, beans and rice and handed it to Fannie.

"Mrs. Flores, thank you. I didn't cook because Jess won't be home tonight."

Certainly Maria thought of that, but she didn't say a word before she turned and went back to her part of the house.

The food tasted good to Fannie. When she was finished eating she rinsed out the pottery bowl and took it to Maria. She knocked on the door, which was opened half way.

"I'm retuning your bowl. Thank you again. The meal was perfect."

Maria took the bowl and when she let go of the door it opened enough that Fannie spied the candle she had given to the old woman. It was aglow with a lighted wick.

Fannie turned away with a smile on her face as Maria closed the door. Aha! Perhaps the woman is pleased about a new baby coming. Fannie could only guess that was the reason.

Chapter 48

It wasn't Jess who arrived the next morning. The young men from the village had already left and had taken Fannie's letter to mail along with what Maria had to sell from her garden. That was an hour before a young hand from the ranch rode his horse to where Fannie stood in the yard. He handed her a folded piece of paper without getting off his horse or saying a word as he turned and galloped back in the direction he'd come.

Fannie's first reaction was puzzlement until she saw her name in Jess's handwriting. The note read:

Fannie,

Gabriel was in severe pain, throwing up and had a high fever when I got here. I drove him to the hospital in his car. He is under the care of a doctor named Gordon. The doctor said Gabriel had a ruptured appendix and he did surgery. The rupture has caused abdominal infection. Gabriel's in bad shape. I'm at the ranch. Will get word to you later. Love,

Jess

Ruptured appendix! Fannie was shocked at the news. She wasn't sure what to do. Should she tell Maria? What if Gabriel dies? She had heard of people dying from a ruptured appendix.

As the frightening thoughts stopped bombarding her senses, she calmed and thought rationally. It wasn't doing anyone any good to sit here and worry. Fannie put on her floppy hat and walking shoes and left for the village to find Roberto.

Forty minutes later she was hot and tired but relieved she found him in his adobe.

"Ah, Senora Fannie. Come in."

"I need your advice," she told him.

"You have had too much sun."

"Yes. We went to the ocean. It's better now with something Maria prepared."

Roberto fumbled around with bottles on a shelf. He took one down. "This will be best. He poured some into an empty vial. Take this and put it on before you go to bed."

"That isn't why I came. It's Gabriel, Maria's son. He is in the hospital. My husband said he has a ruptured appendix that has spread infection. I haven't told Maria. I wanted to talk to you first."

The old man sat absorbing the information before he spoke. "We must take her to see him."

"I don't have a way. Jess has the horse."

Roberto went to the door and called, "Rafael". A teenaged boy came to the adobe. Roberto talked to him in Spanish and the boy hurried away. Roberto went back to his stock of medicines. He put something into a canvas bag, turned to Fannie and declared he was ready.

A two-seated roofed carriage was pulled up to the adobe with the young boy driving the horse.

"Come, Fannie. We will get Maria and go to the hospital."

"What if she refuses?"

253

He shook his head. "She will not."

Fannie was glad he was confident because she wasn't.

Maria was in the front yard trimming bushes. She looked up as the carriage came up the lane but made no move to stop what she was doing.

"Stay in your seat," Roberto said to Fannie. "I will get her."

That was fine with Fannie. She didn't want to have to try to convince the woman. She watched as Roberto talked and Maria shook her head. Roberto shook his head, took the shears out of her hands, and placed his hand under her elbow. Fannie could tell Maria wasn't a willing participant, but Roberto wasn't going to allow her to refuse as he gently took her arm and guided her to the waiting carriage.

He helped her into the back seat next to Fannie and took his seat in front with Rafael. The boy slapped the reins and they were off.

The hospital was on the outskirts of the town. Every time Fannie came here Hollywood seemed to change. It had been a silent ride in the back seat while Roberto conversed with the teen in Spanish in the front.

The boy pulled in front of a two-story building of Spanish architecture. They walked through a white stone archway, then up a set of four steps to double front doors. There were windows arched above the doors that allowed light into the hallway.

At the end of the hallway was a desk where a middle-aged lady sat looking important. Roberto went to talk with her while Fannie and Maria waited.

Fannie heard the conversation. "We are here to see Senor Gabriel Flores. His mother is with us and we are family."

Roberto lying? Fannie smiled to herself. Apparently, Roberto has been here before and knows how to navigate the hospital.

The woman gave him directions. They went down a corridor smelling of antiseptic to find Gabriel's room. Fannie wasn't sure what to expect and dreaded seeing what her mind had conjured up.

There was a curtained half door with a full door behind it. The full door was open. Roberto pulled the handle on the half door and stood in front of them barring the women's view.

He turned, took Maria's hand and led her into the room. Fannie followed. In the iron hospital bed lay a motionless Gabriel. His black hair and deeply tanned skin were in contrast with the stark white sheets. There was an iron pole with a bottle of fluid hanging. A long rubber tube was attached to a narrow glass tube on the bottle. The other end was attached to a needle inserted under the skin of Gabriel's forearm.

Fannie covered her mouth with her hand to stifle the sound of a gasp.

Maria moved to the bedside. She pushed the damp hair back from his face and placed a tender kiss on her son's forehead.

Gabriel's eyelids fluttered but his eyes didn't open. The room was deathly quiet except for a ticking clock on the wall.

Fannie stepped out of the room so the other two visitors didn't see the tears that ran down her cheeks. Two days ago Gabriel had been a lively carefree man laughing and running at full speed into the crashing waves of the Pacific Ocean. Now he lay as lifeless as a pebble on the beach.

She was wiping the tears from her cheeks when a nurse came by carrying a tray.

"Are you all right?" she asked in a quiet voice.

Fannie nodded her head. "I guess I thought I was prepared to see my friend, but I wasn't."

"I understand," replied the nurse. "He has one of our best doctors caring for him. I am taking in this glycerin to moisten his lips. When I come back would you care for a cup of tea?"

"Gabriel's mother and friend are with him now. I don't know how long they'll be."

"Do you want to go back into the room?"

Fannie shook her head.

"Then I will give you a cup of tea when I return. I'm sure they will want to sit with him for a while. He may wake enough to know they are here. I have found the Spanish are patient with their loved ones."

Fannie went to the end of the corridor where she could look out the window and sit at a small table.

It was only a few minutes when the nurse came with a tray holding a small teapot and two cups. She sat opposite Fannie.

"My name is Jeanette Cole. I just finished duty for the day. If you don't mind, I'll join you for tea."

Fannie smiled, glad to have the company. Fannie watched the young woman with brown hair and brown eyes while she poured their tea. "I'm Fannie Edwards. Gabriel is a friend of ours. We recently came back from a trip to the ocean with him."

Jeanette looked at her. "I see you are married. Is your husband the big man who brought Mr. Flores in?"

Fannie smiled at the thought. "That would be Jess."

"I was here when he arrived. Your husband was very concerned."

"I'm sure he was. It takes a lot to upset Jess. I haven't talked to him because he went back to Gabriel's ranch. I'm sure everyone out there is worried about their employer."

Jeanette appeared a few years older than Fannie. She had a wholesome look and a pleasing way about her. She wasn't pretty but the all-American–girl appearance was attractive. "You're not from around here," she said to Fannie.

"No," Fannie answered. "I'm from Virginia, born and raised in Washington, D.C."

"I'd love to see the capitol city one day," said Jeanette. "I'm from Nebraska and there isn't much there except a lot of flat farm land and animals. That's why I came out here."

Fannie laughed. "We came on a lark. My husband gets the itch to see something different and he thought California sounded like an opportunity."

"I think many people feel the same. It's nice to see you smiling. Perhaps you will be ready to go back to see Mr. Flores before the visitors are ready to leave," surmised the kind nurse.

"Thank you," Fannie said. "Thank you for the tea and for our conversation. I've recovered from my initial blow. I hope I will see you again."

Jeanette stood up and picked up the empty cups. "We are doing the best we can for your friend."

Fannie walked down the corridor with her until she came to Gabriel's room, where she was bolstered enough to see him. Jeanette continued down the hall.

Roberto looked up at her when she entered. "You are recovered?"

Fannie nodded. "Does he know you're here?"

"He feels his mother's touch," he replied.

Marie sat by the bedside holding Gabriel's hand.

Before they left, Roberto took a small pill from the canvas bag he carried. He gently pulled down Gabriel's lower jaw and placed the pill in the side of Gabriel's cheek.

Fannie's eyes widened. "Roberto," she whispered. "You can get in trouble."

The old man smiled at her. "Who is to know except you and Maria? We will give Gabriel his best chance."

Fannie didn't protest. She trusted Roberto. He certainly wasn't going to give Gabriel anything harmful, or was he? Was Gabriel in such a state Roberto didn't want him to suffer?

Chapter 49

When they returned from the hospital last evening, Fannie had fixed supper for both herself and Maria. The woman hadn't said a word the whole day except for her refusal to Roberto.

Fannie didn't know how Maria felt. She had been caring with Gabriel. Fannie hated to think it would take Gabriel hovering near death for Maria to finally accept him back into her life. Perhaps it was Providence at work. That thought brought up Father Jose. Gabriel had wandered from the church, but a visit from a man of the cloth wouldn't hurt.

Fannie had been so engrossed in Gabriel's misfortune and Jess not being here with her, she had forgotten today was Sunday. She pulled out her watch and saw it was almost one o'clock. She had missed the service, but if she hurried she might make the village before the priest left.

Fannie hurried to put on a skirt and blouse, her sun hat and walking shoes. If Father Jose had left the village, she might meet him on the road.

Looking in the mirror as she pinned her hat, she was pleased to see her face looking much improved. Only a faint glow remained. Her lips were back to normal and she rubbed Vaseline on them as a protection.

When she reached the village she saw Rosetta and Maria sitting with their usual group. Fannie had been so drained of energy after seeing

Gabriel that she had slept through the rattle of Rosetta's cart. Was it possible the old woman had more stamina than Fannie?

The food on the table was almost gone. She saw Father Jose on his favorite bench under a tree. Fannie tossed some food on a plate and went to sit with him.

"Good afternoon, Father," she said. "May I sit with you?"

"Hello, Senora Fannie. I didn't see you at Mass."

"I overslept. Has Maria talked to you?"

"No. Why are you wearing a frown?"

Fannie sat on the part of the bench his girth didn't cover.

"Her son, Gabriel, is very sick. He is in the hospital in town. It is questionable if he will recover."

The priest listened as she told him what had happened. He wasn't surprised.

"Roberto told me. I planned on going to the hospital when I get back."

Fannie offered a wry look. "If Roberto told you, why did you let me continue?"

"Because I wanted to see if your record of events was the same."

Fannie nibbled on a raw carrot. "I guess I didn't have to hurry over here."

"I'm glad you did. Roberto has given me a bottle of pills. He wants me to give one to Gabriel. He says he is too old to make the trip in to the hospital every day."

"Are you going to do it?"

"I'm wrestling with my conscience. Will you do it, Fannie?"

Fannie thought about it. "I trust Roberto. If the pills are to make Gabriel better, I will do it, but Jess has the horse. I'll have to walk."

"Where is your husband?"

"He's taking care of Gabriel's ranch. I don't know when I'm going to hear from him."

"Perhaps Rosetta can take you."

Fannie shook her head. "She works every day."

Roberto had spied them and came to where they sat. He tipped his hat to Fannie. "Is the good Father trying to talk you into giving Gabriel the pills I gave to him?"

Fannie laughed. "How did you know?"

"Because Father Jose was not comfortable with my request."

Father Jose nodded. "You are too wise, Roberto."

Fannie spoke up. "I watched as you gave Gabriel a pill yesterday. I wasn't sure if was to help him heal."

"Of course it was to heal. If a life is taken, it is up to the Lord, not we mortals here on earth."

"Roberto, I can't get to the hospital today. It's after two now, and I don't have a way except with my own two feet."

"I will have Rafael take you. I don't have to tell you Gabriel is gravely ill. They are using what English medicine they know, and we will add our methods. We must give him the best chance to survive."

Fannie was still unsure. "What will happen if I get caught?"

"You will have to take that chance. Once the pill is in his mouth it will dissolve."

Roberto didn't wait for her to agree, he called to Rafael and the boy was there with a buggy.

Fannie put the bottle of pills in her skirt pocket and climbed onto the seat next to Rafael. No one watched them as they left, but Fannie knew Maria's eyes were on her.

Rafael spoke only Spanish making it a quiet ride into Hollywood. He was adept at avoiding the various traffic on the streets. The noise of the autos seemed to make the horse nervous even with eye blinders. Rafael held tight to the reins and talked to the horse in a soothing voice whenever the horse shied at the sound of a horn.

Fannie walked into the hospital and past the desk at the end of the hall. The important lady wasn't there. She walked with a quick pace to Gabriel's room only to be startled when she saw Jess standing next to the bed.

He didn't say a word. He walked to her, and put his arms around her. He whispered, "Let's go out in the hall."

They walked to where the table and two chairs sat.

"What are you doing here?" he asked.

She told him about being there yesterday with Maria and Roberto and about her conversation with the priest a short time ago.

"I'm sorry I didn't get Grace back to you so you have a way of getting around. I want you to come stay at the ranch. I'm trying to keep it going while Gabriel is laid up, but I'm having a devil of a time getting over the language barrier."

"Has Gabriel stirred enough to talk to you?" asked Fannie.

"I got here a few minutes before you. I guess you didn't get my note today."

She shook her head. "No. It's probably waiting for me. I came from the village. Jess, I'm afraid to give the pills to Gabriel."

"It can't be as hard as delivering Lottie's baby."

Fannie smiled at the thought. "That's for sure. Do you think I should give him the medicine?"

He nodded. "Roberto wouldn't give it unless he thinks it will help." They rose from the table and went back to the sick room. Fannie said a silent prayer that she was doing right before she opened the bottle, removed a pill, and opened Gabriel's mouth as she had watched Roberto do yesterday.

Jess stood at the half door watching to see if anyone was coming.

Gabriel groaned. Jess looked back at the bed. "That's the first encouraging sound I've heard since they opened him up," said Jess as he walked to Fannie's side.

Fannie kept her voice low. "I believe it's called surgery, Jess. Why do I feel like a criminal?"

"Because you are, but a good one."

Gabriel stirred in the bed and moaned. He opened his eyes to slits.

Fannie touched his hand. "Can you see us?"

His eyes closed again and he was back into silence.

While they were standing at the bedside, Jeanette Cole came into the room. "Hello again," she said to Fannie.

"You've met my husband, Jess."

"Not formally. My name is Jeanette Cole. It's nice to meet you, Mr. Edwards."

"Jess," he said. "Is there any news about Gabriel's condition?"

"We are doing what we can," was her answer. "I came in to make him more comfortable. His fever is down so that is an improvement."

"Thank you for taking care of him," said Jess. "We have to be on our way. We'll drop by tomorrow."

Jeanette smiled. "He is lucky to have such good friends."

They left the room and walked to the front door of the hospital.

"Jess, I forgot to ask you how you knew enough to drive Gabriel's car. Is that something else I didn't know about you?"

"I watched Gabriel. The car has a steering wheel, gear shift, clutch, brake and gas pedal. Just like that tractor Alex bought."

"Did you bring that nifty auto today?"

"No. The car belongs to Gabriel and it won't move until I come to bring him home. I rode Grace."

Jess walked her to where the buggy waited. Rafael was talking to a young girl who wasn't shy about batting her eyelashes at him. He was embarrassed when he saw Jess and Fannie approach and hurried to the buggy to take his seat.

"Fannie, I'll send someone to pick you up tomorrow. Don't worry about Maria."

"Do you think I should bring her with me?"

"She could help as an interpreter if you can get her to come. The kitchen girl, Elana, can be the go between, but she's young so the workers don't listen to her."

Jess kissed Fannie goodbye and she hated to leave him. There was no question that she would join him at the ranch, whether Maria came with her or not.

Chapter 50

Fannie's suitcase was packed. Maria, never one to show her emotions, had been her usual non-committal self when Fannie told her about the visit to see Gabriel. When she explained to Maria that Jess needed her help at the ranch, Maria nodded her head. Fannie assumed the nod to be agreement to go to Gabriel's ranch.

Fannie went to Maria's door when she heard a cart coming. To her delight Maria was waiting. Fannie gave a quick glance to see if the candle she had given Maria was in sight. It was gone.

Antonio was the driver. He helped the older woman up to sit next to him and Fannie hopped into the back. On the way, Maria and Antonio conversed on and off in their native language. Fannie didn't care what they said. She was pleased to be going to her husband.

They rode up and down hills. On one of the highest hills Fannie saw citrus groves and barley fields in the distance. The Juniper and Joshua trees weren't tall enough to block her view. She would rather be looking at the Blue Ridge Mountains and heading up the oak lined drive to the big stucco house on the hill. She closed her eyes and envisioned Addie standing on the wide columned porch waiting for her. There were times when Fannie ached to see her friends at Lockwood.

They rode down into the valley where the ranch sat. Antonio turned up the lane leaving a trail of dust behind him. Jess was waiting and hurried off the low porch to greet them. Antonio came around the cart to help Maria and Jess gave Fannie a hand from the back. Then he removed their belongings.

He hugged Fannie tight with a voice meant only for her ears. "You don't know how happy I am to see you. You must have given a convincing speech to the old woman."

"I guess I did."

Jess went to Maria and gave a bow of his head. "It is good you are here."

Then he turned to the older man. "Antonio, take Senora Flores and her bags to the house."

Maria went with Antonio.

"We're staying in the little adobe over there," he informed and pointed to a place apart from the ranch house. "Carlos and Doncia lived there before they moved. We'll be by ourselves."

At the mention of the name, Fannie came alive. "Doncia! Does she know? I have been so concerned about Gabriel I didn't think of her."

"I phoned her when I was in town. She says she is coming."

Fannie drew in her breath. "She shouldn't travel before the baby comes."

"That's what I suggested, but she insisted."

"What about their place at the beach? Who's going to take care of that?"

"That's a problem for Carlos and Doncia. Fannie, my love, why do you have to take on other people's problems? I'm just trying to keep this place going."

Fannie took his hand. "I know, Jess. I'll do what I can. When are we going in to see Gabriel? We should take Maria with us."

"It hasn't been an easy ride over here. The trip to town may be too much for her."

"We'll give her the choice," said Fannie.

Jess agreed. "I found a broken down buggy in the shed. I've fixed it up enough that we can take it in."

They were at the adobe and Jess opened the wooden door to let Fannie enter. He had to duck his head as he went inside. He set her suitcase on the colorful tiled floor. "I hope we won't have to be here too long."

Fannie looked through the place. "It's as big as Maria's and we have the whole place."

Then she espied a luxury. "Look, it's got an indoor pump."

"That's not all," said Jess as he slid aside a blanket and there sat a copper tub.

Fannie gasped. "My own bathtub!"

"Unpack your suitcase and I'll go to the house to see if Maria wants to come with us. We need to be on our way."

Fannie went to the sink with curtained shelves above it. She took out a tall pottery cup. Then she pumped the handle of the sink pump until water started to trickle out. After rinsing the cup, she filled it with cold well water and drank every drop. The ride had been dusty and dry.

Maria declined to go to the hospital. Jess assured her he would report on Gabriel's condition.

"Take Roberto's medicine," she'd ordered.

Fannie heard her. The woman actually spoke in English.

** **

Jess pulled the buggy into a parking spot and tied the reins to a hitching post under a tree. It would shade the horse while they were gone.

Inside the hospital, the important lady was back at her desk in the hall. Jess told her why they were there.

"Are you his family?"

Fannie stepped forward. "Yes. I was here with Mr. Flores's mother the other day."

The woman eyed them with a skeptical stare before she relented to let them pass.

Jess leaned over and whispered to Fannie, "Why did you tell her we were family?"

"Because Roberto did," she whispered back.

"I don't think she believed you."

"She let us pass, didn't she?"

Jess couldn't argue that point.

They were at Gabriel's room but the full door was closed.

"Go ahead and tap on it," said Fannie.

Jess was tentative, but he did as she asked.

They waited until the door opened to see Jeanette Cole was coming out of the room with an armful of soiled linens.

Jess held the half door open for her.

"You can go in," she said. "I just finished cleaning him up."

The room smelled putrid.

They stood looking down at him.

Gabriel moaned and groaned and slipped back to the quiet state.

Jeanette came back into the room. "I apologize for the smell. I have put clean dressings on. The poison is draining from a rubber tube the doctor inserted, so the foul odor is a good sign the infection is clearing." She went to the window and opened it a crack to let either the fresh air in or the sickly smelling air out. With the full door open a draft was created between the half door and window.

"He is coming in and out of consciousness," Jeanette said. "He still carries a slight fever. Dr. Gordon says the next two days are critical."

"Has Gabriel said anything?" asked Fannie.

"His ramblings are incoherent."

"We aren't going to stay long," Jess said. "We'll be back tomorrow."

"We are keeping him comfortable, Mr. Edwards."

"We are friends of Gabriel's who will check in on him every day. We would feel more comfortable if you would call us Jess and Fannie."

Jeanette smiled. "I can do that as long as my supervisor doesn't hear me being too familiar."

"Good," said Jess. "When you talk to Gabriel use our first names. It might help."

"I talk to Mr. Flores all the time. We are never sure what our patients hear even though they are not responding to us." The nurse looked down at her silent patient. "I'm off duty now. I wanted to make one last check before I left for the day."

As soon as the nurse was gone, Fannie took the bottle of pills out of her pocketbook and placed one in Gabriel's mouth as she had done the day before. A silent prayer went up; please, Lord, help me do what is right.

They went back to the buggy with its ragged leather seats and headed for home.

"Jess, once this ordeal is over, I'll need to go to confession."

"For what?"

"Because I don't like to be dishonest. For one thing, I lied to the woman at the desk, for another, I'm giving unauthorized medicine, and I'm deceiving Jeanette Cole."

"Don't be so hard on yourself. Why are you doing it?"

She looked at him in puzzlement. "I think it's what's best for Gabriel."

"Then don't feel guilty. How do you know it isn't Providence guiding you?"

Those words coming from Jess? "I never saw it in that light," she said.

He gave a sideways glance. "Fannie, you are a good person. Otherwise, I wouldn't have married you."

She gave him a playful tap on his arm. "Aren't you the lucky one."

Chapter 51

The ranch was running smoothly. Between Maria and Antonio, Jess was able to get his instructions across. Maria went right to the men and ordered them about. Fannie was surprised at how forceful the little woman could be. There was no hesitation by the rancheros. They listened, nodded, bowed, and went about their work.

Fannie and Jess took their meals at the ranch house. Maria preferred to take her meals in her room.

At breakfast, Elana came to refill their cups.

"I will start at the high school next week," she said.

"That's good news," replied Fannie. "How will you get there?"

"Antonio will drive me in. I will have to stay with my Tia Elana and her family. Antonio will bring me home on the weekends and holidays."

"You are named for your aunt?"

Elana nodded. "She is my mother's sister."

"It's good you are going to school," said Jess. "School is important."

"I think so. So does Senor Flores. Mama says I should learn to be a housewife and not waste my time on books."

"You have plenty of time to be a housewife. The way California is changing you're going to

273

need what school teaches," said Fannie. "Your mother can teach you how to keep a house."

"How is Senor Gabriel?" inquired Elana. "We are going to the hospital to see him today. He is still very sick."

"We all miss him here. The ranch would not survive without him. He takes good care of us."

"I know he does," said an empathetic Fannie. "We have to remain hoping and praying."

"Senora Flores lights a candle every night. Is that for him?"

Fannie's eyebrows raised at this revelation. "What does the candle look like?"

"It is in a glass and has a picture of the Madonna holding the baby Jesus."

Fannie smiled to herself. "Perhaps she lights the candle for Gabriel and others."

After breakfast, Jess went out to check on the ranch hands and Fannie went to change into a blouse and skirt. She chose the blouse she had sewn and her copper-colored skirt. September's temperatures were less intense and the shorter-sleeved blouse would be comfortable.

They left the ranch before noon. Doncia was to arrive on the one o'clock trolley.

Jess went to the post office to see if he had a letter from the movie director. They should have a schedule for him by now, he thought, and he had to work around overseeing the ranch, although Maria was doing a fine job of it.

Fannie waited in the buggy. She had draped a striped woven blanket over the tattered leather

274

seat. It not only looked better, the dry curl of the leather wasn't poking into her. She saw Jess coming out of the post office with a big grin on his deeply tanned face.

He climbed onto the seat beside her. "They won't need me for another week."

"That's good news," said Fannie.

"And, here is a letter for you."

Fannie snatched the letter from his hand. "It's from Addie!"

"Who else would it be from?"

"Do I have time to read it before the trolley gets here?"

"It's best to wait until we get back to the ranch."

"You know I'm dying to open it."

"Fannie, tuck it into your pocketbook. I don't want Doncia to wait, and we have to go to the hospital. The news in the letter isn't going to change."

"I guess it's better to read it when there are no distractions."

Jess smiled at her. "I didn't want to give the letter to you yet, but I didn't have any place to keep it."

"It gives me something pleasurable to look forward to."

The trolley was five minutes late. Jess left the buggy parked and went to meet Gabriel's sister as soon as the trolley stopped.

He called, "Doncia, come with me. Fannie is waiting."

Doncia hugged him. "I am so grateful for you and Fannie. How is my brother?"

Jess took the bag she carried. "We're going straight to the hospital so you can see for yourself."

Jess helped Doncia onto the step and onto the seat next to Fannie, tossed the bag into the back, and took the driver's place. He tapped the reins.

Fannie took Doncia's hand. "We are glad you are here, but we thought it might be too much of a trip before the baby comes."

"It would have been worse for me to sit and worry about Gabriel."

"How is Carlos?" asked Fannie.

Doncia smiled. "He is fine. He said I am not to worry because he has hired a young couple to help. They can stay in one of the rooms."

"Your mother is at the ranch," said Jess. "I needed her to interpret for me. She has no problem keeping the men in line."

"That is no surprise. Does she know I am coming?"

"No," Fannie replied. "We decided it was best not to tell her."

Doncia nodded. "She knows about the baby?"

"I told her. I can't tell you how she feels about it because Maria is not one to show her emotions. She has been to see Gabriel once. Do you remember Roberto?"

"Yes. He is the old man the Mexicans in the village use for a doctor."

Fannie looked over at her. "He talked your mother into going to the hospital." Fannie thought a moment before she decided to tell. "Roberto gave Gabriel medicine of his own. No one at the hospital knows it. Roberto ordered me to give Gabriel one pill every day, which I have done. I think your mother is satisfied Roberto's medicine is going to work and that's why she hasn't gone back to the hospital again."

"I know my mother and she wouldn't trust only the English medicine."

Jess parked the buggy where he had parked it the day before. He came to help the women to the ground. Jess was strong and Gabriel's sister was no light weight.

They walked through the arch and up the few steps to the door of the hospital.

Fannie leaned near Doncia. "I told the lady at the desk we are relatives. At least you look the part and Jess is close in coloring."

Doncia shrugged. "There is no question with me."

They stopped at the desk where they received a long look. "All relatives of Mr. Flores?"

All three nodded.

Miss Importance offered a wry smile. "You may go to his room."

Doncia took in a deep breath when she saw Gabriel. Without hesitation she hurried to the bedside and put her arms around him. She murmured something in Spanish and kissed his cheek.

His eyes fluttered open for a split second and a weak voice said, "Doncia?"

She held his hand to her cheek. Then put it down gently as the tears rolled from her eyes.

Fannie put her arm around her friend and led her to a chair.

Jess went to the bedside. "Gabriel. Can you hear me?"

The answer was incoherent mumbling as Gabriel drifted back into a dream state.

The ever caring nurse, Jeanette Cole, came into the room. She wiped Gabriel's face with a cool cloth and moistened his lips. "The fever is gone," she whispered, and motioned them into the hall.

"Dr. Gordon was in earlier. He said he is leaving the drain until he is sure the infection is gone. The doctor is surprised Mr. Flores is doing as well as he is."

"Has he talked at all?" asked Jess.

She shook her head. "Nothing that makes sense. The best change is that the needle feeding fluid into his arm has been discontinued. He takes sips of water and tea. It may be a subconscious act but he draws in on the straw and has kept it down."

"Jeanette, this is Gabriel's sister," said Fannie.

"He said my name," Doncia told her.

Jeanette smiled. "Perhaps you are the best medicine."

Doncia went back into the room to see her brother before they left for the ranch.

When they arrived, Maria was sitting in a rocker on the porch. Antonio came to take care of the horse and buggy. His smile was wide as he helped Doncia off the buggy and kissed her with obvious pleasure. She addressed him in Spanish and kissed him back.

Fannie knew Maria was watching from the porch, but she didn't leave her chair or change her expression.

Doncia hesitated to meet her mother. She stood on the porch step and said, "Hola, Mama."

Maria motioned to her to come and kiss her cheek. It was like Doncia was a guilt-ridden five-year-old trying to get back into her mother's good graces.

"Elana will show where you'll be staying," Fannie told her.

Doncia followed the young girl.

The meeting between mother and daughter had been too much for Fannie as her temper flared. She walked right to where Maria sat and shook an accusing finger.

"Maria Flores, you are a selfish, selfish woman! Your daughter has found happiness and she wants to share it with you. The same with Gabriel. I know you care for your children. I see it in your eyes along with the pain that is of your own doing. Forgive them and yourself!" Fannie turned on her heel and stalked away.

There was no regret when she got back to the adobe and threw her pocketbook on the table. It was then she remembered Addie's letter. She poured a tall cup of water and went outside to read it.

September, 1919
Dear Fannie,

It was so good to receive your last letter. It was full of news. I read it to Peg and Lottie and they were especially impressed to learn that Jess will be in a moving picture.

Lottie says maybe that's why Jess wanted to go. He liked those Western cinemas we had seen at the theater in Berryville.

Lottie is somewhat improved. She now has the baby at home while Crystal is still there taking care of the house and the two little ones. I don't know for how long that arrangement will last because Crystal and Nate are expecting a baby. I will take one day at a time with that situation. Why doesn't life flow at a steady pace of calm?

The trip to the Pacific Ocean sounds heavenly. We are looking forward to the gifts you are sending us.

Oh my goodness, thought Fannie. I forgot about mailing them!

I would like to meet your friend, Gabriel. I can almost see you riding in the back seat of his flashy car and he and Jess having a gay old chat in the front oblivious to your discomfort. You are right. You do not have the complexion for the sun.

You asked about Caleb's foot. He healed well. I don't know what Alex would do without him. With both he and Lottie under the weather, the Dunn house was not a happy place to visit.

Last week I packed a lunch and took Lottie to the Shenandoah for a picnic. She did enjoy the outing. We took fishing gear with us and fished for two hours. Of course, we didn't catch anything worth keeping, but it was good to get away from the house. I think Lottie's color is better, although she is still pale and too thin.

Dr. Burke told her that sometimes women's systems get out of whack after a baby is born. He thinks that has been a part of Lottie's problem, especially with such a difficult birth. Lottie confided in me that at first she was afraid she was going to die, and then she didn't care if she did. Don't ever tell anyone about this.

I didn't realize she was in such a state, and I don't have to tell you I am relieved to see she has turned the corner. It will take time.

Next week I am taking her into Berryville for the day. We'll go to Coyner's to see what is new and lunch at the Battletown Inn.

Alex and I are going to a lawn party in a couple of weeks. Therefore, I want a new outfit, which means a stop at Irene Butler's dress shop. I am hoping we don't run into Lavinia, but it's difficult to go into town and avoid her. I know she and Irene will be shocked at Lottie's appearance, but I hope they are tactful enough not to act that way. One is never sure with the two tactless gossips in the town.

Lavinia will ask about "that Irish girl" and I'll only tell her that I received a letter that you are doing well.

There is nothing new around Lockwood. Alex brings home the Washington Post newspaper from the news stand. I hate to read it. There is much

*upheaval in this country. Things were supposed to
be better after the war, but unions are striking, even
the Boston police threaten to. What is unsettling is
that there have been letter bombs being sent. Then
I read about racial riots in Chicago.*

*I do wonder how effective President Wilson
is after being partially paralyzed from his apoplexic
shock (I believe I spelled that right). I once read
that's what Lord Fairfax died of.*

*Enough of that discouraging information.
I'm sure you have read it also.*

*I so wish you were here. I am not pleased
that Jess's contract is extending your stay.*

> *Your forever friend,*
> *Addie*

Fannie sat with the letter in her hand. She
was not up to date on what was happening in the
country because Jess didn't spend money on a
newspaper. There was enough going on in her life
that she didn't need to take on any more troubles.
Besides, the problems Addie spoke of weren't
happening in California. At least not that Fannie
knew of. Let the politicians in Washington deal
with the unrest.

Jess came in before dinner and Fannie read
the letter to him.

"I'm glad Lottie's better. As for all the
political garbage, I can't be concerned right now."

"If they have riots in Chicago, do you think
that will affect us on our way back to Virginia?"

"Our return is over a month away, if then.
Let's forget about what doesn't affect us. You

know Addie. She'll find something to be bothered about."

Fannie put the letter back into the envelope with a sigh. "I guess we need to concentrate on getting Gabriel back here."

He touched the tip of her nose with his finger. "That would be top on my list. I'm starved. Let's go see what Meriam has cooked up for us."

Chapter 52

Doncia joined them for breakfast. Her round face was smiling.

"Good morning," Jess greeted her, "You look bright and chipper."

"I am. Fannie, I don't know what you said to my mother, but she came to me and said she was sorry for the way she has acted. She is happy about the baby coming."

Jess sent a cautious look to his wife. "What did you say?"

Fannie didn't look at him. "I told her she was a selfish, selfish woman."

"What else?"

Fannie's defenses were at the fore as she looked at her husband. "I told her she is causing herself pain, and she should forgive her children and herself."

"That wasn't your place. You overstepped your bounds," was his admonishment.

"I'm not sorry for the outburst. It appears it was effective!"

Jess cocked his head to one side. "Still, I've witnessed you in action. I hope Maria hasn't been hurt."

Doncia looked from Jess to Fannie and Fannie to Jess.

"Have I caused bad feelings?"

Fannie laughed. "No. My husband thinks I overreact sometimes."

Doncia laughed also. "I think that is the way with many husbands."

Jess rolled his eyes.

Doncia asked, "When do we leave for the hospital?"

"I need to check on the workers. We'll leave after that." Jess pulled out his pocket watch. "I figure we'll be ready in an hour."

They finished breakfast. Jess walked out to where horses were penned while the women sat talking as women have a tendency to do.

At the hospital Miss Importance was at her desk. She looked up, peered over her glasses, uttered not a word, and waved them by.

The full solid door was closed so they waited in the hall until a nurse propped the door open and came out into the hall. The nurse was older than Jeanette Cole, heavy and homely, but she offered a kind smile.

"He might wake up for you. I've finished cleaning him up for the day."

"We expected to see Miss Cole," said Fannie.

"This is her day off," the nurse replied. "You can go on in."

The three entered the quiet room and stood looking at the silent Gabriel. Doncia went to the bedside, leaned over and kissed his forehead.

His eyes opened. It took time for him to focus before his low hoarse voice said, "Doncia."

She took his hand and kissed his fingers. "Yes, brother. I am here. You are awake now?"

"I think so."

"Jess and Fannie are here with me."

They came to stand beside her.

"Jess," Gabriel said and tried to raise his other hand. "I hurt all over."

Jess touched his hand. "I'm sure you do. You've been here in the hospital for close to a week."

"You brought me?"

"I did. Don't try to talk."

"Mama is at the ranch," Doncia told him. "She said she has forgiven us."

A pained smile came across Gabriel's face. "Good." Then he drifted back to his quiet state.

The half door opened and in walked Jeanette Cole in street clothes. She offered a shy smile. "Today is my day off, but I wanted to see how Mr. Flores is doing."

"He has talked to us," said Fannie.

"He was beginning to come around when I left yesterday. The pain medicine makes him come and go. I decided to come and get fluids down him. If he does well he can start taking broth tomorrow."

"Is there any news from the doctor?" asked Jess.

"He plans to take the drain out tomorrow. Then we need to start our patient moving so he doesn't contract pneumonia."

"So he is past the danger point," surmised Jess.

Jeanette gave a nod of her head. "At this time."

"Do you think we should stay?" Fannie asked.

"Certainly you are welcome to. I plan to be here for the rest of the day. All the available beds on this floor are filled without extra help for the nursing staff. They can't give the personal care he needs."

"Then we will leave him in your good hands," said Jess.

"I will remind him that you were here, and assure him you are taking care of his ranch. Isn't that what you told me?"

Jess nodded. "Thanks. We probably won't be here tomorrow."

"You have been diligent visitors. I hope, when you do return, he will be more awake."

They left with an upbeat feeling.

"You didn't give him a pill, Fannie," observed Doncia.

"Roberto gave me five pills. Yesterday was the last. I wonder if Roberto's medicine helped."

Jess took her hand as they walked back to the buggy. "We'll never know."

"Mama will say yes when I tell her how well he is doing," Doncia chimed in. "This has been a wonderful day. I will be glad to rest up tomorrow."

"Why aren't we coming tomorrow, Jess?"

"Fannie, my love, you need to send those presents, and I need to become a movie star."

"You're going to work on the movie tomorrow?" she asked.

"My first day on that schedule he gave me. We'll go back to Maria's place tonight."

She looked at him in question. "What about the ranch?"

"I'll leave orders. Sargent Maria can handle it for one day."

Chapter 53

In early morning Jess drove Fannie in the buggy to Maria's adobe. Fannie went into their area of the house with a box she had found at the ranch. She wrapped the package for Lockwood with care before tying it securely with stout string.

Jess had gone to the garden. It appeared all the produce had been picked. Did the young men from the village pick the crop or was it stolen by someone knowing Maria wasn't home? It didn't matter to Jess either way. The food wasn't rotting. He would tell Maria when they returned to the ranch this evening.

He wondered what was in store with this moving picture stint. Was he being fair to Fannie? She had bent to his wishes so far, even to the fact that he wanted to buy a piece of land. Gabriel was the key to that because he knew this area. Land around Hollywood was destined to increase in value with the way the whole place was growing. Hollywood was a part of Los Angeles and would keep spreading out and out. He had seen it in the eastern states, which was one of the reasons he had left New York. The other reason was because he had that foot that wanted to be on the go.

Fannie came out of the house as he was leaving the garden.

"The crops have been picked," he said as he neared.

"The men from the village may have picked them," she replied. "It's like the villagers have a secret code the way they know everything that's going on with their people."

"I figure Maria will be pleased," he said. "You haven't seen her since you chewed her out. How do you think she's going to act toward you?"

His words did not set well. "I didn't 'chew her out' as you put it. I said what needed to be said."

He shrugged. "Probably so. Sorry."

"I accept your apology. Let's get going before I change my mind."

Jess howled with laughter and kissed her cheek. "Fannie, wife of mine, you make me smile."

The day was pleasant as they took the road into town. Jess knew the way to the Paramount Pictures lot because that's where he had helped build the set for the picture.

Fannie was taken aback by the size of the place.

"Twenty-three acres," informed Jess. "I need to find the office."

They were in luck because there was a man at the entrance who directed them.

The office wasn't much. There was a young and pretty receptionist at a desk, and there were a few empty chairs along one wall.

Jess told her why they were there.

"Mr. Sandstone is on the set," she reported. "He told me to direct extras there. It's…"

Jess interrupted, "Thank you. I know where the set is located."

She offered a demure smile and fluttered her eyes. "That makes my work easier. It's nice to meet you, Mr. Edwards."

Was she flirting with Jess? Almost twenty-three, Fannie felt old next to the coy teenager.

Jess and Fannie got back into the buggy and drove to the spot.

"You'll get to see what a good carpenter your husband is."

"I'm glad I came. Do you think they are going to allow me to watch them film the movie?"

He shrugged a shoulder. "I don't know. I'm not sure what to expect for myself. The girl at the desk would have stopped you if you weren't allowed."

There was a lot of activity when they arrived. A man with a clipboard in his hand came to meet Jess. "Your name?"

"Jess Edwards."

"Go over there with that group standing next to the horses." The man turned to Fannie. "Your name."

Fannie smiled. "I'm his wife. I came to watch."

The man pointed to a group of chairs. "Go over there and sit. Don't move from the chair until I tell you to."

Fannie wouldn't think of it. She and Jess parted. After she took a chair she was struck by the scene in front of here. The set was like a small town.

Women in bonnets and long dresses stood around in small groups carrying baskets as though they were ready to shop. That was the scene in front. Behind the façade was nothing, but support beams to hold up the would-be buildings.

She sat next to an older man who didn't raise his eyes from the papers he was reading.

Fannie watched as a couple more men went to the group standing with Jess.

The man giving the orders, placed the bonneted women in various places before he came to where she sat, and addressed the man with the papers. "We're ready, Mr. Sandstone."

Mr. Sandstone, the director, was tall and lanky and dressed in western garb. Fannie watched him walk to Jess's group. She could hear every word.

"This film is called, *Wagon Tracks*. You men are going to hold up the stage. Does everyone know how to ride?"

They all nodded.

"Pick a horse over there. They're all saddled. You can ride around back of the set to get the feel of the horse under you. When I give the signal there will be a stage barreling down that road." He pointed in the opposite direction.

He walked to the men and looked them up and down then came back in front to address the group. "I want you, the big man in the black hat, as the head of the gang. You ride out to slow the stage horses just outside of town. The rest of you men are to surround the stage. You'll all wear bandannas covering the lower half of your face. Only your eyes will show under your hats. We'll practice a few times before we shoot. Any questions?"

"Do we ride as a bunch?" one man asked.

"No," said the director. "I think it will be better if you ride two abreast then part to circle the stage once it has slowed down. That is except for you. What's your name, son?" he called.

"Jess."

"Jess, a good name. Now Jess, you are to ride out as the leader. Once the stage has stopped, you draw your gun and go back to open the door of the stage. All you other men will have your guns drawn. Everyone got that?"

"I got it, but I don't have a gun," replied Jess.

"That's an oversight," said the disgruntled director. "Where's the props man?" he hollered.

Out from a side door hurried a short man with a big box and promptly outfitted every man robbing the stage with a belt and six-gun.

"The guns aren't loaded because the audience will only hear the piano music. Now take five minutes to acclimate to the horses and we'll be ready."

While the director was giving orders some-one had placed three chairs closer to the action. He turned from the group and came to sit in the chair that had *Director* written on the back.

Fannie sat on the edge of her chair. The whole scene before her caused her nerves to tingle. It was like being at a real life cinema.

The director shouted through a megaphone. "Okay, Harry, get that stage rolling. When it gets to that sagebrush send in the robbers." The director's men in charge of the stage and robbers each waved a handkerchief to show they were ready.

"Get rolling," shouted the director, and Fannie gasped as the stage came at top speed with real dust flying. Then in rode Jess with the men behind. With guns drawn and masked faces they could all pass for outlaws.

By the time they practiced the robbery of the stage six times, Fannie was ready to leave. The seventh time was a charm and the director was satisfied with the filming, which was done by a man riding in a wagon parallel to the stage.

"You people are through for the day," Mr. Sandstone announced. "I'll watch this film tonight. If I'm not satisfied we'll have to stage it again tomorrow."

"Tomorrow isn't on my schedule," said Jess.

The director looked at the group. "Do you want to stay and finish this right now?"

They all shook their heads. "Drop by the studio at seven tomorrow morning. You'll know whether we have to shoot again. Edwards, I'd like to have a word with you."

There was grumbling among the men but there was no choice. They had signed a contract.

It was a tiring trip back to the ranch, which they reached as the sun was going down. Antonio came to take care of the horse and buggy and Elana came out of the house. "Mama saved supper for you."

"Wonderful," said Jess. "We'll be right in."

Doncia came to the dining room to sit with them. "How was this big movie making?"

"Tiring," answered Jess.

"I agree with that," said Fannie. "They do the same thing over and over until the director is satisfied."

"Did you get to see Gabriel?"

"Not today," said Jess. "I have to be back in Hollywood at seven in the morning. I should get to see him in the afternoon."

"Will you go Fannie?"

"No, Doncia. I am not going to spend another day sitting around and waiting. At first it was exciting. Then I felt bored."

She didn't realize Jess let out a quiet sigh of relief. Fannie didn't know the director had offered Jess a part in the next picture he had in mind.

"I'll ride Grace tomorrow. You and Doncia can take the buggy."

Fannie was reluctant. "Jess, I haven't driven the buggy."

"You know how to drive the cart. The buggy is bigger but easier. You'll do fine. Antonio can get it ready."

"I would like to see how Gabriel is doing and so does Doncia. Perhaps Antonio can drive us in."

Jess smiled at her. "Don't doubt your abilities Fannie. You delivered Lottie's baby."

295

Again she smiled at the memory. "I had you to guide me."

Doncia giggled. "Maybe you will deliver my baby."

Fannie shook her head. "I hope to be back in Virginia long before your baby arrives."

Chapter 54

Jess was up and gone from the adobe at five o'clock in the morning. He'd told Fannie that Antonio would have the buggy hitched and ready to go around ten.

Fannie wore a plain cream-colored blouse and navy blue skirt. She chose the floppy hat she'd bought at the ocean and leather gloves. They would give her a more secure feel of the reins and avoid blisters.

Meriam had breakfast ready when she arrived at the ranch house at nine. She and Doncia were almost through the meal when Maria came to join them. The two younger women exchanged glances.

Fannie hadn't seen Maria since her blow-up. However, Maria showed no sign of displeasure as she said, "I will go to see Gabriel."

"He will be pleased," replied Fannie. "Antonio will bring the buggy in a few minutes."

Maria nodded her head and left.

Doncia kept her voice low. "I am so happy Mama is coming with us."

"I guess she isn't angry with me."

"No, Fannie. I think you opened her eyes."

"I will apologize to her." She pushed her empty plate aside and finished her coffee. "I hear the buggy coming. Are you set?"

Doncia nodded. "I'll get Mama."

However, she didn't have to because Maria was coming into the room. She carried a small satchel with her.

Antonio helped Maria and Doncia into the buggy while Fannie went to the driver's side. "Does this horse behave, Antonio? I don't want any surprises."

The older man smiled. "Si, Senora."

Fannie tapped the reins and the three women were off to visit Gabriel.

Fannie had no problem driving the buggy. She parked it in the same place where Jess had parked when he drove. Fannie hopped off the seat and secured the reins to a post before she went to help the other ladies. Maria was already off the buggy and Doncia was being careful to place her foot on the step. In her maternal condition she wasn't as balanced. Fannie stood ready to help if there was a misstep.

They went into the hospital where Miss Important waved them by. Only the half door to Gabriel's room was closed. Fannie opened it gingerly and saw Jeanette Cole in her calf-length white uniform, apron and white cap standing by the bedside where Gabriel sat on the side of the bed.

"Ah, you have visitors Mr. Flores. Come in."

Gabriel looked up with a pained expression. He tried to smile.

"Tomorrow he will be up in a chair," announced the nurse.

The three women came into the room.

Jeanette held a glass of water with a glass straw. "A couple more swallows and you can lie back down."

Gabriel complied. The nurse put one arm under his knees and the other around his waist as he rolled back onto the bed. A few adjustments, a couple groans and he was on his back.

Jeanette smiled at the women. "I don't think I've exhausted him. Let me know if you need anything." She picked up an empty tray and left the room.

Doncia rushed to his side. She put her arms around him and kissed his forehead. "Mama has come with us. You are looking so much better."

"I feel like I have been trampled by a herd of horses."

He raised his hand and Maria came forward to grasp it. She spoke to him in Spanish and he smiled and kissed her hand. Then she opened the small satchel she carried and wound Rosary beads around the short iron bedpost. She reached in again and brought out a small bag of dried leaves. The bag looked like the kind that held tobacco, but the sweet smell of the dried material didn't smell like tobacco.

Fannie whispered to Doncia, "What is she giving him?"

"Something to make him feel better. It is her own mixture. She used to give it to us when we were sick."

Fannie shrugged. She wasn't completely trusting of this Mexican medicine.

Maria took out a pinch and put it in Gabriel's mouth. It wasn't long before his beautiful smile was back. He had lost weight and a few facial lines had appeared from his ordeal, yet he was still a handsome magnetic man.

He looked at Fannie. "How is Jess? Jeanette told me he was taking care of the ranch."

Gabriel had trouble pronouncing Jeanette but the name sounded musical coming off his lips.

Fannie moved to the bed. "He plans on coming by today, if he doesn't get tied up in that movie making foolishness."

He smiled. "You have been good friends. I cannot repay you."

"But you can," countered Fannie. "When you are healthy, you can find Jess a good piece of land to buy so we can go home."

He nodded. "I can do that. You don't wish to stay in California?"

Fannie shook her head. "No, Gabriel. I would like to come and visit."

"My ranch is always open to you."

The nurse returned. "Mr. Flores, I have medicine for you."

A sly smile came to his face. "I call you Jeanette, why do you not call me Gabriel?"

Surprisingly, Fannie could see the confident nurse was flustered. "We do not call patients by their first names."

"But I am a special patient."

If Jeanette Cole's face got any redder it would burst into flames. She cleared her throat.

300

"Mr. Flores has asked me to be his nurse at the ranch until he is back on his feet."

Doncia looked over at Fannie with a slight raise of the eyebrows.

"That's wonderful," exclaimed Fannie. "Has the doctor said anything about when you will be going home?"

Jeanette answered. "Dr. Gordon said in a few days if Mr. Flores tolerates being out of bed and shows no signs of a cold."

All the women were pleased with that news. Doncia could return to the inn, Maria could return to her adobe, and Fannie and Jess only had to stay until his part in the movie was finished. Or would he be finished? What had the director called him aside for yesterday? When Fannie had asked, Jess said it was nothing important.

There was the matter of buying land. That didn't bother Fannie because the way Gabriel had talked before he got sick, he was on the cusp of buying some for himself. The research was done.

After they left the hospital Doncia announced she was hungry. Fannie remembered they had passed a small café on the way. She drove the buggy to that spot where she parked it a few yards away. The three women went into the eating place. It was a pleasing spot with small iron tables and chairs reminding Fannie of an ice cream parlor, especially with ceiling fans moving the air.

A young waitress came to wait on them. Fannie was intent on the menu before she looked up. "Ota!"

"Miss Fannie!" exclaimed the startled teen.

"What are you doing here? I thought you and Greta were working in Los Angeles."

Ota nodded. "We were. Her aunt and uncle bought this place and sent us out here. Greta's in the kitchen."

"Tell her I said hello. Are you happy?"

"Oh, Miss Fannie, I am. I love it out here. I believe you saved my life."

"I am pleased you are doing well. Now, I will have a cup of tea and an egg salad sandwich."

Doncia and Maria paid no attention to the conversation between Ota and Fannie. Doncia ordered for her mother and herself.

Fannie took this time to apologize to Maria. "I'm sorry for being upset the other day, Mrs. Flores. That was unkind of me."

The old woman actually smiled at Fannie. "No. Now I smile."

There was no need to elaborate and Fannie felt vindicated.

It was nearing three o'clock when they started for the ranch. Greta wouldn't let them pay for lunch, and Ota wanted to be sure Fannie told Mr. Jess how she was doing.

Fannie was glad to get away from the traffic. The horse had startled a few times but Fannie held tight on the reins. It was the time of day of highest heat and Fannie felt perspiration running down her forehead. She pulled a handkerchief from her pocket and wiped it away. Her whole person felt moist.

They were thirty minutes out of town when she heard a cracking noise. Fannie stopped the buggy, got down from the seat, checked what was visible and found nothing wrong. They rode on further until there was a big cracking noise throwing the buggy down on one side and throwing Maria from the seat.

Doncia screamed. The horse startled and Fannie held back with as much force as she could muster so the frightened animal didn't bolt.

Doncia was thrown into Fannie's shoulder but managed to stay in the lop-sided seat.

Fannie ordered, "Doncia, hold the reins and I'll check on your mother."

Tears were streaming down Doncia's face but she held tight to the reins.

Maria was on her hands and knees when Fannie approached. She helped the old woman to her feet.

"Are you all right?"

Maria nodded.

Fannie led her over under a Joshua tree before she went to see about Doncia.

Fannie patted the horse and talked in a calm voice. "I'll take care of you in a minute," she whispered as if the horse understood. She called, "Doncia, can you climb down?"

Doncia wiped her face with her skirt. "What about the horse?"

"I've got a hold of his bridle. I don't think he's going anywhere. Loosen your hold on the reins then let them down carefully and go sit by your mother."

The still shaken Doncia did as Fannie asked.

Fannie's thoughts were a jumble. What was she going to do now? Her first thought was the expectant mother. Had anything happened to the baby? Doncia appeared to be in good shape except for the fright, and Maria said she was not hurt. But, Fannie knew they were not up to walking to the ranch. She could go, which meant leaving the two women behind, and it was getting late.

She set about unhooking the horse from the broken-down buggy and walked him out of the bulky harness. Holding onto the side of the bridle and reins, she led him to a half-grown tree and secured the reins on a strong branch. Then she went to check on the two passengers huddled together under the tree.

"The only thing I know to do is to walk to the ranch for help," she told them.

"Mama can't walk. She's hurt her ankle."

Fannie bent down to examine the bruised ankle. She didn't think it was broken but it was swelling at a fast rate. It was good Maria wore the heavy skirt and blouse because they softened the blow. Still, as Fannie checked further, Maria had bruises and scrapes on her arms, her face and her leg.

Maria hadn't uttered a word. Fannie knew she had to do something and soon. She vowed she would have Jess teach her how to ride a horse. It should be easy enough. She'd watched people ride and she had ridden in the saddle that one time with

Jess. The problem was she didn't know anything about this horse. Was he one to be ridden?

While she was mulling over their dilemma, Doncia called. "Fannie, look! Way down the road there's a rider coming. Maybe he can help us."

Fannie squinted her eyes and at a distance could make out a lone person on horseback. She hoped the stranger was friendly. Fannie went to sit with the two women. There was safety in numbers, but she picked up a baseball sized rock before she sat to watch and wait.

The rider came at an easy pace leaving a trail of dust until he spotted the buggy and then he sprinted into a gallop to the group under the tree.

"Jess!" Fannie hollered. "Thank God it's you!" She ran straight into his strong arms when he jumped off the horse.

"What happened?"

"I think the axle broke."

"Is anyone hurt?"

"Maria. She was thrown from the seat. I think her injuries are minor."

Jess walked to the two women who hadn't moved. "Fannie said you're hurt, Maria."

"No much. We go."

He shook his head. "The buggy's no good. I'm going to ride to the ranch and bring a wagon back for you. We'll have to hurry, it'll be dark soon."

He took Fannie aside. "I'll take both horses and get back here as soon as I can. Keep this." He secretly handed her a revolver.

305

"What am I supposed to do with that?"

"I forgot to leave it on the set. It hasn't got any bullets in it but it'll scare somebody off."

"I don't even like the feel of it."

"Don't let the others see it. Put it in your pocket."

"All right. I think it's foolish. I haven't seen another soul on this godforsaken road."

After a quick kiss Jess was off with both horses. Fannie went back to sit under the Joshua tree. She wondered what she would be doing if she were back at Lockwood. Probably sitting by the stream and listening to the sounds of the country. Fannie could still dream.

Jess returned over an hour later driving Gabriel's fancy car. He jumped out of the driver's seat. "I decided this is faster than hitching up a horse and wagon."

Maria protested but Jess ignored her as he carried her to the car and sat her in the front seat. Fannie and Doncia were already seated in the back.

"I don't think Mama has ever ridden in a car," Doncia confided in Fannie.

Fannie laughed. "There's a first time for everything." She tied the strings of her hat under her chin.

They were back at the ranch in a half hour. Maria protested again but Jess carried her right to her bedroom. Meriam and Elana watched with big eyes.

"I'll take care of her," said Doncia. "We are all tired and hungry."

"Mama has supper ready. I will set the table and you can eat after you wash up."

Fannie and Jess washed hands and face at the outdoor well.

The meal was roast beef and potatoes with fried apples, corn bread and rice pudding for dessert. Elana took Maria's meal to her room while the other three weary travelers ate with gusto.

"Jess, we stopped at a café and I got one of the surprises of my life. Ota and Greta are working there. It seems Greta's relatives are doing well so they bought the place and sent the girls to run it. And, by the way, Gabriel may be coming home in a few days."

"That is good to hear. I was tied up all day so I didn't get to the hospital. You can't say you haven't had an adventurous day, Mrs. Edwards."

"I don't care to repeat it," said Fannie. "Do you have to go into town tomorrow?"

"No," he answered.

"Good," Fannie replied. "Let's sleep 'til noon."

Chapter 55

Three days later Jess drove Gabriel's car into Hollywood.

Gabriel was in a wheelchair with Jeanette Cole wheeling him to the waiting car at the back door of the hospital.

Jess took his arm and helped him to the passenger's seat.

"I'll take this wheelchair back inside and be right back," said Jeanette. "My bag is packed. I'll bring it out."

"I can help with that," offered Jess.

"Thank you, but no. Make sure Mr. Flores is comfortable."

When she returned Gabriel held up a halting hand. "You must call me Gabriel before you get into my slick car."

Jeanette hesitated. "What if I don't?"

He dazzled her with a smile. "You would pass up taking care of your special patient?"

She looked at him, back at the hospital, back at him. Would she pass up this opportunity to leave the hectic drudge of the hospital?

"You win, Gabriel."

Jess helped her into the back seat of the open car.

The men in front chatted back and forth all the way to the ranch. When the car turned up the dirt lane there were Gabriel's workers along the way taking off their hats and waving him back home.

Antonio waited for the car to stop. He addressed Gabriel in Spanish and received a firm handshake.

Waiting on the porch were: Maria, Doncia, Fannie, Elana, and Meriam. An audible gasp was heard from both Elana and Meriam when they saw the weakened Gabriel being assisted by Jess and his private nurse. Where was the man who was so robust and full of life not long ago?

They all clapped as the trio neared the porch.

"It's good to be home," Gabriel said.

Jess handed Jeanette's bag to Elana who took it to the room where she would be staying next to Gabriel's.

Fannie felt an unusual calm. It was good that Gabriel was back and that he had Jeanette Cole to help him get back to the Gabriel who brightened the lives of everyone whose life he touched.

Meriam had prepared all the favorite foods of her employer. Fannie and Jess knew they were in for a feast, and so did the rancheros because they all lined up at the door of the kitchen where Elana and Meriam filled their plates with food.

Jess, Fannie and Doncia ate together in the dining room. Maria took her meal in her room because her ankle was too painful and swollen to walk.

Jeanette took on the responsibility of caring for Maria, also, for which Doncia was delighted. She could return to Carlos and not have to worry about either her mother or her brother.

"I'll drive you into town for the trolley when you're ready to leave," Jess offered.

"I would like that," said Doncia. "I will take three days to rest up and to give Mama and Gabriel more time before I go. I can call Carlos once I leave the trolley and get a train ticket back so he can meet me."

"Then we won't have to be concerned about you, either," said Fannie. And continued, "If all is well, I'll ride into town when you leave. Jess and I can go back to your mother's place. I don't think it's good to leave it unoccupied."

"I don't worry about that," said Doncia. "My mother is well thought of in the village. They will watch over it."

"Do you think your mother will come here to live as Gabriel would like?" asked Jess.

She shook her head. "Not until she is unable to care for herself, or something changes in her way of life. Los Angeles keeps growing and spreading and one day it will swallow up the little people. Gabriel is wise to hold onto this ranch and keep buying what land he can."

"Was it Gabriel's idea to buy the inn?"

"Yes. He said it was a good start for us even though it was not in good shape. Carlos and I did a lot of work and we still work hard, but we will leave something good for our child, thanks to my generous brother."

Elana came into the dining room. "Senora Doncia, your mama asks that you stop to see her before you retire."

"Thank you, Elana."

Jess pulled out his pocket watch. "It is getting close to bedtime. It's been a long day."

"A good day," said Doncia. "My brother will not forget your kindness for him and his family. I'll go to see what my mother wants and then I will drop off to a pleasant sleep."

Jess and Fannie rose from their chairs as Doncia left the room.

"I think she has the right idea," remarked Fannie.

They said good night to Elana and Meriam and walked to the adobe. The moon was up and the night air was comfortable, which carried the music of guitars and Spanish voices singing. Sounds of happiness that Senor Gabriel is back.

"What has the director said about the movie? Is your part almost finished?"

"Mr. Sandstone is a detailed man. We repeat a scene until he's satisfied, if he ever is. Now he has me robbing a bank with my gang of outlaws. I'm hoping the sheriff shoots me dead when I come out of the bank."

Fannie laughed aloud. "That should put an end to it. You don't know what to expect?"

"Fannie, Mr. Sandstone asked me to be in his next picture. He said I'm perfect for the Westerns. He said I have the makings of a star."

Fannie stopped in her tracks and felt her heart stop with her. "What did you tell him?"

"There's good money in it, my love."

She looked straight at him. "What did you tell him?"

He leaned over and kissed her cheek. "Although I was sorely tempted, I told him no."

She let out a big sigh. "Jess I almost died right here. So you don't know what tomorrow will bring?"

"Not until I get there. Fannie, one thing I've learned."

"What's that?"

"I've watched and seen a lot. Hollywood life is superficial. I am not cut out to be a movie star."

Chapter 56

Jess went to the Paramount lot the next day with hopes it would be his last day. He was tired of this movie making business. The carrot dangling before him was the money he was earning to buy land.

Jess had owned that mine in Colorado with Caleb, then walked away from it. He didn't begrudge that decision or did he? At the time he was a single man with no thought for tomorrow. Now, he was a married man with responsibilities to his wife. He couldn't afford to make snap decisions, pick up and leave at the drop of a hat as he had before. He wondered if the Leadville mine might be worth something one day. He didn't dwell on it. His best friend, Caleb, could certainly use some good luck.

Jess had ridden Grace and hitched her up next to the horses they used in the movie. Mr. Sandstone was already giving directions to his assistants as to what he wanted.

Jess walked to where his band of outlaw actors were standing in a group. "Have I missed anything?" he asked one of the men.

The man shook his head. "No. He just finished ordering his crew. I hope this is our last day; he's a hard man to please."

"He is that," Jess agreed.

The director and his assistant came to where they stood.

"Jess. As yesterday, you lead into the bank, then Joe here will send in the rest of the gang. There'll be gunplay when you leave and I've decided you'll be shot dead. That way the gang won't have a leader and they'll scatter in different directions. If you get it right, we'll wrap this thing up."

That was good news to the men waiting to carry out his wishes.

"Your paychecks will be ready at five o'clock."

That was even better news.

It took four takes until Sandstone was satisfied, and Jess had hit the ground four times each time a little harder. By then it was three o'clock. Jess decided to find that café Fannie told him about. Ota could use a tip.

Before Jess left, the director came to him and asked if he'd changed his mind. He was passing up a prosperous position, according to Mr. Sandstone. Jess thanked him for the offer, but the movie making business was not for him.

When he walked into the cafe, Ota was taking a tray of food to a customer. She recognized him immediately and radiated a wide smile. Ota's cheeks were rosy and she had put on some weight. She was no longer the skinny waifish girl Fannie had saved from the bawdy house.

He took a seat on a padded iron chair, a chair that wasn't made for a man of his size.

Ota came hurrying over. "Mr. Jess. I am so happy to see you. Miss Fannie said you are making a movie."

"I was. We finished today. You'll never recognize me because I have a bandanna over my face all the time. The movie is called *Wagon Tracks.* "Once it comes out if you go to see it, I'm the leader of the gang of robbers and I get shot dead."

Ota was excited that she knew someone in the movies. "I surely will go to see it. Me and Greta so we can tell our friends."

After Jess had eaten, he told Ota that he and Fannie would be going back to Virginia, and he was glad to see her doing so well.

"Thanks, Mr. Jess. I'm doing right fine. You and Miss Fannie stay safe."

Jess picked up his movie check at five o'clock and smiled at the amount of two hundred and fifty-five dollars and twenty-five cents. The movies paid well. The banks were closed so Jess tucked his hard-earned check carefully into a saddle bag. Then set Grace at a quick pace to the ranch.

Fannie was at the adobe when he returned as dusk set in. She came out to meet him as he rode the horse to the corral.

She watched as he closed the gate. "What's the news?" she asked. "I heard you whistling."

He grabbed her up in a bear hug. "I'm a free man! We finished the movie and I got my pay. Once Gabriel gets back on his feet we can deal on the land, and then, Fannie, my love, I'll take you home."

315

Fannie didn't expect her reaction. Without any warning tears began to flow. "Oh, Jess. I can't believe it. I was so worried we wouldn't go home. I don't mean to cry."

He kissed her forehead and released her from his strong hold. "Tears of happiness, I expect."

Fannie used her apron to wipe her face and walked beside him to the outdoor well, where he could wash up.

"Meriam said she would hold dinner until you returned."

"I'm famished," he said.

Gabriel, Doncia and Jeanette were already seated in the dining room.

"Ah, my friends," said Gabriel. "I would get up but it's too slow and painful. It's good to be home."

"It's good to see you out of bed," said Jess.

Meriam put the food on the table because Elana had gone back to school.

"Gabriel, will you please tell Meriam that she is a great cook?" asked Jess.

The ranch owner was quick to comply. Meriam's answer was a nod and embarrassed smile.

"Have you decided when you will be leaving?" Fannie asked Doncia.

"I would like to go tomorrow. My brother is doing well with Jeanette's help and Mama is also. Carlos will not have concerns once I'm back at the inn."

Jess had piled his plate and was enjoying the food with one ear open to the conversation. He swallowed and took a drink of tea. "Doncia, we can take you into town for the trolley unless you want us to take you into Los Angeles to the train station."

"To the trolley is enough."

"Have they fixed that buggy?" asked Jess.

Gabriel nodded. "Antonio says it is ready."

"That settles it. After we see Doncia off, Fannie and I will go to Maria's house for the night."

That sounded satisfactory to those involved.

Gabriel looked at Jess. "When you return I'll go over the deed for land you wanted,"

Jess's eyebrows flew up. "Will you be up to it? Do you already have a spot picked out?"

Gabriel's dashing smile appeared. "It's only a matter of looking over some papers with you. We'll discuss it when you get back."

After dinner, Jess almost danced back to the adobe.

"I've never seen you so excited," said Fannie.

"This is it, my love. The reason we were meant to come to California."

"You don't know anything about this land," she cautioned.

"I've got that good feeling. Gabriel is not the type to steer me wrong."

This day had been too good. Maybe it had been too good.

Chapter 57

Doncia was antsy to get on the way the next morning when Jess and Fannie pulled up to the ranch house in the buggy. Maria sat in a rocking chair on the porch. Gabriel sat next to her in another.

Doncia kissed her brother. "When the baby arrives, you will be well enough to bring Mama to the inn." Then she whispered in his ear, "She won't tell you but she likes riding in your flashy car."

She went to her mother and kissed her. Maria took her hand, placed it to her cheek and spoke to her daughter in Spanish. Doncia nodded and kissed her again.

Fannie watched the scene with a catch in her throat. She had done her best to help without getting emotionally attached. Life didn't work that way. Fannie thought of the others: the people in the village, Father Jose, Roberto, Rosetta, Antonio. They had all made a spot in her heart. It was a happy trio that left the ranch in the once ill-fated buggy. They rode the dirt lane to the hard-packed road that led into town.

The trolley was on time. Jess retrieved Doncia's bag and helped the expectant mother off the buggy. "Are you sure you will have no problem getting to the train?"

She smiled at him. "I know the way." She looked up at Fannie. "Thank you for bringing my family back together." Then to Jess she said, "And, thanks to you my brother is still alive. One day when you feel the need for a change, you must come to the inn. Carlos and I will have one of the best rooms for you."

"We want to know when that beautiful baby arrives," called Fannie.

Doncia waved as she walked to the trolley stop.

Jess went into the bank and cashed the moving picture check. He put the money in a canvas bag, two hundred and fifty-five dollars. The twenty-five cents he put in his pocket to buy sandwiches for him and Fannie to eat on the way to Maria's adobe.

He wasn't sure how much the piece of land would cost, but he did have money coming for working at Gabriel's ranch. That should be enough for their tickets back home. He didn't discuss the finances with Fannie because he didn't want her to have any concerns on the way back East.

Maria's house looked just as they had left it almost three weeks ago. It was October, six weeks past the time Fannie had given Jess to find whatever he was looking for.

The purchase of land. Was that the answer? Or could it have been the unseen hand of Providence sending them to save Ota, bringing the Flores family together, and saving Gabriel's life?

The next morning Fannie was getting ready for Sunday Mass when Jess said, "I'll go with you this morning. I'll hitch up the buggy and make an easier trip."

Jess coming to church? The New York minister's son who had strayed from the fold? And, who was Fannie to notice? She hadn't set foot in a church for a year before she came to California.

"I'd like that," she answered.

Father Jose was on time. After the service he shook Jess's hand. "It was good to have you join us. The people in the village gave me all the news about Maria and her family."

"How did they know?" Jess asked.

The priest smiled. "They have their ways. I understand you will be leaving and going back home."

"That's the plan," replied Jess. "I have a couple of things to tie up."

Father Jose turned to Fannie. "You're ready to leave?"

Fannie laughed. "I have been ready since we arrived."

His laugh was hearty. "Let's eat. They have prepared a feast."

Jess sat with Father Jose and Fannie sat with Rosetta's group.

When they were ready to leave, Rosetta gave Fannie a hand-made basket filled with herbs the women had prepared and medicines from Roberto. He had labeled each one to use for different ailments. Fannie was going to miss these kind people.

Back at the adobe, Jess told her to pack up because they wouldn't be back. Maria's place was safe until she returned or decided to move to the ranch.

That evening they both walked through the garden, past the outdoor shower and the stable where Grace, the loyal borrowed horse, had rested.

Jess put his arm around her waist as they walked back to their side of the house. "We found a good spot."

"Yes we did. Little did we know what was in store for us when we read the advertisement in the paper."

Chapter 58

The next day they were at the ranch. Fannie chatted with Jeanette while Jess went to talk with Gabriel.

The piece of land Gabriel had set aside on his land for Jess contained a quarry. Jess would receive a monthly check for the lease.

Jess was honest. "I only have two hundred and fifty-five dollars. I'm sure that isn't going to cover the quarry."

"You are right, so I am putting in some of the money you have earned from the ranch work."

"That's fair," said Jess. "Gabriel I will have to work a few days to earn money for my trip back to Virginia."

Gabriel offered that genuine and irresistible smile as he handed Jess an envelope. "My friend, there is enough money left over for you to take Fannie back to where her heart desires to go."

Jess knew better than to act humble and protest. He needed whatever money was in the envelope.

"Stay with us one more night," said Gabriel. "Meriam will prepare a banquet to celebrate."

Chapter 59

When Jess and Fannie left the next morning, after saying their goodbyes, Fannie noticed Jeanette Cole had her hand on Gabriel's shoulder and Gabriel's hand covered hers. Perhaps Senor Gabriel Flores was, indeed, a special patient. Had Fannie missed something?

When they reached Hollywood, they said goodbye to the dependable Antonio who had driven them in. Jess checked the post office box one more time before he handed in the key. There was a letter. He held onto it until they had boarded the Union Pacific train in Los Angeles headed back to the East.

Gabriel had rewarded them well because they were riding in a private Pullman car with their own sleepers and service from the dining car.

After they were settled, and Fannie had recovered from the shock of riding in a private railcar, he handed her the letter.

September 21, 1919

My dear Fannie,

It will soon be October and I haven't heard a word from you as to when you will be coming home.

Nate and Crystal have gone back to Pennsylvania. She wants to be near her family when the baby comes.

Alex is beside himself trying to find a suitable replacement because Caleb cannot handle the farm by himself. Alex tries to help, but he has never been cut out to be a farm worker only a farm owner.

Lottie is some better. Much of my spare time left from running the office is spent helping her. Peg helps too but she has her hands full with this big house.

You can probably discern from this writing that I am in a quandary. How I wish you were here to help me through this unsettling time.

Alex says I am making too much of it, but you know how I like organization.

The cabin is clean and ready for you whenever Jess is ready to return. I am still working hard at forgiving him for dragging you three thousand miles away.

I am sorry to write such a short and burdensome letter, but I had to.

Your forever friend,
Addie

Fannie read the letter to Jess and he laughed. "That's Addie for you. She'll forgive me once I get you back and give Caleb a hand."

"When we get to the next stop, we'll send her a Western Union telegram. I want her to know we're on our way."

Jess nodded. "You know, Fannie, with the money we'll get from that leased land, we can buy our own place, which I've always wanted."

As the train chugged along the rails a red flag flew up in Fannie's mind. "Where will that be?"

"No more roaming. We'll find a place in your beloved Clarke County. Whenever I get an itchy foot, we'll take a vacation."

Fannie Edwards took a pencil and paper from her tote and handed them to Jess. "I want those words in writing."

Other Books by Millie Curtis

Beyond the Red Gate

The Milliner

The Newcomer

Window of Hope

Of Course She Knew!

Never a Sure Thing

Roseville's Blooming Lilly

English Lessons

Available at Amazon and Barnes &Noble